Praise For
LOON LAKE

"A fascinating, tantalizing novel...It's so rich....The experience of reading it was exhilarating."

The New York Times Book Review

"One dazzling solo performance after another ...Anatomizes America with insight, passion and inventiveness."

The Washington Post Book World

"A genuine thriller...A marvelous exploration of the complexities, even contradictions of the American Dream...Not under any circumstances would we reveal the truly shattering climax."

Dallas Morning News

"Compelling...Brilliantly done."

St. Louis Post-Dispatch

A Novel by
E. L. Doctorow

LOON LAKE

FAWCETT CREST • NEW YORK

Library of Congress Catalog Card Number: 79-5526

ISBN 0-449-21603-9

This edition published by arrangement with Random House, Inc.

Printed in Canada

First Ballantine Books Edition: September 1988
Second Printing: February 1989

To Helen Henslee

LOON LAKE

THEY WERE HATEFUL PRESENCES IN ME. LIKE A LIT- tle old couple in the woods, all alone for each other, the son only a whim of fate. It was their lousy little house, they never let me forget that. They lived on a linoleum terrain and sat in the evenings by their radio. What were they expecting to hear? If I came in early I distracted them, if I came in late I enraged them, it was my life they resented, the juicy fullness of being they couldn't abide. They were all dried up. They were slightly smoking sticks. They were crumbling into ash. What, after all, was the tragedy in their lives implicit in the profoundly reproachful looks they sent my way? That things hadn't worked out for them? How did that make them different from anyone else on Mechanic Street, even the houses were the same, two by two, the same asphalt palace over and over, streetcars rang the bell on the whole fucking neighborhood. Only the maniacs were alive, the men and women who lived on the street, there was one we called Saint Garbage who went from ash can to ash can collecting what poor people had no use for—can you imagine?—and whatever he found he put on his cart or on his back, he wore several hats several jackets coats pairs of pants, socks over shoes over slippers, you couldn't look at his face, it was bearded and red and raw and one of his eyes ran with some yellow excrescence oh Saint Garbage. And three blocks away was the mill where everybody in Paterson made the wages to keep up their wonderful life, including my father including my mother they went there together and came home together and ate their meals and went to the same bed together. Where was I in all of this, they only paid attention to me if I got sick. For a while there I got sick all the time, coughing and running fevers and wheezing, threatening them with scarlet fever or whooping cough or diphtheria, my only power was in suggesting to them the terrible consequence of one mindless moment of their lust. They clung to their miserable lives, held to their meager rituals on Sundays going to Mass with the other suckers as if some monumental plan was working out that might be personally painful to them but made Sense because God had to make Sense even if the poor dumb hollow-eyed hunkies didn't know what it was. And I despised that. I grew up in a dervish spin of health and sickness and by the time I was fifteen everything was fine, I knew my life and I made it work, I raced down alleys and jumped fences a few seconds before the cops, I stole what I needed and went after girls like prey, I went looking for trouble and was keen for it, I was keen for life, I ran down the street to follow the

airships sailing by, I climbed firescapes and watched
old women struggle into their corsets, I joined a gang
and carried a penknife I had sharpened like an Arab,
like a Dago, I stuck it in the vegetable peddler's horse,
I stuck it in a feeb with a watermelon head, I slit awn-
ings with it, I played peg with it, I robbed little kids
with it, I took a girl on the roof with it and got her to
take off her clothes with it. I only wanted to be
famous!

And the coal trucks releasing their fearsome
anthracite down the sliding chutes to the dark base-
ments, and Ricco the Sweet Potato man putting into
your hand a hot orange potato in a half sheet of the
Daily News for three cents, the filthy black snow lying
banked in the streets, the wind smelling of soot and
machine oil blowing down Mechanic Street and you
are holding your hands on the sweet heat, cupping it
holding it up to your red face. The taking humbly, almost unconsciously of goodness by little kids who took
it all, the rage of parents, the madness of old women in
the dank stairwells, murder, robbery, threat in the sky,
the unendurable prison of schoolrooms. In the five-
and-ten was the cornucopia of small tin cars with
wind-up keys made in Japan and rubber cops on mo-
torcycles, and rubber chiefs in sidecars from Japan
there were tin autogyros and tin DC-3s! You went for
the small things, the molded metal car models that
would fit in your palm, you watched the lady in her
green smock and the eyeglasses looping from a black
string around her neck, and when she turned, out
came the white hand like a frog's tongue, like a
cobra's, and down the aisles you went, another toy of
goodness, bright-painted toy of gladness in your
pocket.

But I was alone in this, I was alone in it all, alone at night in the spread of warmth waking to the warm pool of undeniable satisfaction pissed from my infant cock into the flat world of the sheet and only when it turned cold and chafed my thighs did I admit to being awake, mama, oh mama, the sense of real catastrophe, he wet the bed again—alone in that, alone for years in all of that. I don't remember anyone's name, I don't remember who the gang members were, I don't remember the names of my schoolteachers, I was alone in all of it, there was some faculty of being alone I was born with, in the noise of life and clatter of tenement war, my brain was alone in the silence of observation and perception and understanding, that true silence of waiting for conclusions, of waiting for everything to add up to a judgment, a decision, that silence worse than the silence of the deaf and dumb.

And then one day I am caught breaking the lock on the poorbox, the fat priest in his skirts grabbing my neck with a hand like pincers, not the first time slapping my head with his flat hand and giving me the bum's rush back to the sacristy behind the stone Christs and Marys and the votive candles flickering like a distant jungle encampment and I conceive of what a great vaulting stone penitence this is, with its dark light quite deliberate and its hard stone floors and its cathedral carved space intimating the inside of the cross of man the glory of God, the sin of existence, my sin of existence, born with it stuck with it enraging them all with it God the Father the Son and That Other One really pissing them off with my existence I twist turn kick the Father has balls they don't cut off their own balls they don't go that far the son of a bitch —spungo! I aim truly and he's no priest going down now with eyes about to pop out of his head, red apoplectic face I know the feeling Father but you're no father of mine he is on his hands and knees on the stone he is gasping for breath You want your money I scream take your fucking money and rearing back throw it to heaven run under it as it rains down pennies from heaven on the stone floor ringing like chaos loosed on the good stern Father. I run through the money coming down like slants of rain from the black vaults of heaven.

I LIVED IN NEW YORK FOR A COUPLE OF MONTHS. IT seemed to me at first an incredibly clean place with well-dressed people and washed cars and bright-painted red-and-yellow streetcars and white buildings. It was a stone city then, and in midtown the skyscrapers were white stone and the sanitation men went around pushing big cans on two-wheeled carts and they'd stop here and there and sweep the gutters, that seems incredible to me now, they wore white jackets and white pants and military style caps of khaki. And in Central Park, which I thought of as the country, the park men came along with broomsticks with a nail on the end of them and impaled cigarette wrappers and ice cream wrappers on these sticks and then wiped the sticks off in these burlap bags they carried over their shoulders. The park was glorious and green. The city hummed with enterprise. It was a wonderful city! I thought, a place where things happened and where everyone was important even streetsweepers just from being there not like Paterson where nothing mattered because it was Paterson where nothing important could happen where even death was unimportant. It had size it had magnitude, it gave life magnitude it was one of the great cities of the world. And it went on, it was colossal, miles of streets of grand famous stores and miles of streetcar tracks, great ships bassoing in the harbor and gulls gliding lazily over the docks. I rode the clattering elevated trains that rocked and careened around the corners and when the weather was cold I stayed aboard making complete circles around the city keeping warm on the rush seats set over the heaters. I got to know the city. It calmed me down. Off on its edges you could always get a place to flop, there were still shanties on the hillsides below Riverside Drive, there were mission houses where you could get a bed down at the Bowery and be fumigated and there was a whole network of welfare places where you could get soup and bread if you weren't proud. But I looked for work, I tried to stay clean and present myself at employment agencies crowds of pushing shoving men staring at jobs described in chalk on blackboards at employment agencies it was very difficult to persuade yourself you and not any of a hundred others were the man for the job.

One day I got wise. I saw a fat kid delivering groceries. He was wearing an apron over his clothes and pushing a cart, one of those wooden carts with giant steel-banded wheels. The name and address of the grocery was painted on the slats. His arms full, he went down the steps to the trade entrance of a brownstone, rang the bell and disappeared inside. The cobra strikes! I raced down the street clattering the cart over the cobblestones, I tore around the corner, I went down a side street made dark by the gridwork shadows

of industrial firescapes and dark green iron fronts, I
felt like Charlie Chaplin, turning one way, braking,
doing an about face, scooting off another way, I think I
was laughing, imagining a squad of Keystone Kops pil-
ing up behind me, I thought of the fat kid's face, even
if he knew where to look he couldn't catch me. I sat
down for a while in an alley and caught my breath.
Eventually, like the most conscientious grocery boy in
the world, I trundled my cart back the way I had come
and delivered every last one of the orders. Each bag
and box had a bill stuck inside with the name and address of the customer. I took tips and cash receipts. I
was polite. I pushed my cart back to Graeber's Groceries Fancy Fruits and Vegetables and found Graeber
himself loading up another cart grumbling and saying
things in German and making life hell for his clerks.
No fat kid among them. Graeber was angry, suspicious, skeptical. He didn't believe I found the cart
abandoned at a tilt in an alley. And then I turned over
into his hands the cash receipts. To the penny.

And that's how I came to be a grocery delivery boy
in the rich precincts of Murray Hill. I wore the long
white apron and pushed the wooden cart and I earned
three dollars a week and tips.

At one home in Gramercy Park I made the acquaintance of a maid she had an eye for me she liked my
innocent face. She was an older woman, some kind of
Scandinavian wore her hair in braids. She was no great
shakes but she had her own room and late one night I
was admitted and led up all the flights of this mansion
and brought to a small bathroom top floor at the back.
She sat me in a claw-foot tub and gave me a bath, this
hefty hot steaming red-faced woman. I don't remember her name Hilda Bertha something like that,

and she knows herself well before we make love she pulls a pillow over her head to muffle the noise she makes and it is really interesting to go at this great chunky energetic big-bellied soft-assed flop-titted but headless woman, teasing it with a touch, watching it quiver, hearing its muffled squeaks, composing a fuck for it, the likes of which I like to imagine she has never known.

Come with me

Compose with me

Coming she is coming is she

She was very decent really and for my love gave me little presents, castoff sweaters and shoes, food sometimes. I tried to save as much of my wages as I could. My luxuries were cigarettes and movies. I liked to go to the movies and sit there you could see two features and a newsreel for a dime. I liked comedies and musicals and pictures with high style. I always went alone. In my mind was the quiet fellow trying to see himself, hear what he sounded like. He fitted himself out in movie stars he discarded them. I was interested in the way I instantly knew who the situation called for and became him. For Graeber, who wore a straw hat and a bow tie, a stubblehead German with an accent you better not laugh at, I was the honest young fellow who wanted to make something of himself. For Hilda the maid I was the boy who thought he was lucky to have her. When I went along after work with my tips in my pocket I was John D. Rockefeller. I came to make the distinction between the great busy glorious city of civilization on the one hand, and the meagerness or pretense of any one individual I looked at on the other. It was a matter of the distance you took, if you went to the top of the Empire State Building as I liked to do seeing it all was thrilling you had to admire the human race making its encampment like this I could hear the sound of traffic rising like some song to God and love His Genius for shining the sun on it. But down on the docks men slept in the open pulled up like babies on beds of newspapers, hands palm on palm for a pillow. Not their dereliction, that wasn't the point, but their meagerness, for I saw this too as I stood at the piers and watched the ocean liners sail. I watched the well-dressed men and women going up the gangways, turning to wave at their friends, I saw the stevedores taking aboard their steamer trunks and wicker hatboxes, I saw the women wrapping their fur collars tighter against the chill coming up off the water, the men in sporty caps and spats looking self-consciously important, I saw their exhaustion, their pretense, their terror, and in these too, the lucky ones, I understood the meagerness of the adult world. It was an important bit of knowledge and no shock at all for a Paterson mill kid. Adults were in one way or another the ones who were done, finished, living past their hope or their purpose. Even the gulls sitting on the tops of the pilings had more class. The gulls lifting in the wind and spreading their wings over the Hudson.

I distinguished myself from whomever I looked at when I felt the need to, which was often, I felt I could get by make my way whatever the circumstances. I would sell pencils on the sidewalk in front of department stores I would be a newsboy I would steal kill use all my cunning but never would I lose the look in my eye of the living spirit, or give up till that silent secret presence grew out to the edges of me and I was the same as he, imposed upon myself in full comple-

tion, the same man with all men, the one man in all
events—

I remember this roughneck boy more whole than he
knew. Going down the dark stairs of the mansion on
Gramercy Park one night trusted to let myself out by
the drowsy spent maid, I lifted a silver platter a silver
creamer and teapot and a pair of silver candlesticks
from the dining room. Even now I see the curved glass
cabinet doors in the streetlight coming through the
French windows. I hear my breathing. I catch sight of
my own face in the salver. Loot-laden I tiptoed over
the thick rug I half walked half ran through the streets
clutching my lumpy lumberjacket. I had a room on the
West Side in a rooming house fifty cents a night no
cooking. In the morning going to work from across the
wide cobblestone street the cars going past, the streetcars ringing their bells horns blowing trucks ratcheting
along with chain-wheel drive I see in Graeber's Groceries Fancy Fruits and Vegetables an officer of the law
in earnest conversation with my employer.

Come with me
Compute with me
Computerized she prints out me

Commingling with me she becomes me
Coming she is coming is she
Coming she is a comrade of mine

Sometimes around those fires by the river a man
would talk a war veteran usually who had a vision of
things, who could say more than how he felt or what
was so unfair or who he was going to get someday.
And invariably he was a socialist or a communist or an
anarchist and he'd call you brother or comrade this

fellow and he was always contemplative and didn't
seem to mind if anyone listened to him or not. Not
that he was wise or especially decent or kind or even
that he was sober but even if none of these in those
fitful flashes of lucidity like momentary flares of a
dying fire he'd say why things were as they were. I
liked that. It was a kind of music, I lingered by the
edges of the city with the hobos and at night that grand
and glorious civilization now had walls all around it we
were on the outside looking up at this immense looming presence, a fortress now it was a kind of music to
point to the walls and suggest why they would come
down. And if you didn't have a true friend, someone
in the world as close to you as you were to yourself,
this kind of music was interesting to hear. At night you
smelled the river in daylight you didn't, I smelled the
river scum and felt the mosquitoes and followed the
shadows of the great rats who butted right through
the tar-paper shacks and dove into the shitholes, and
some poor tramp on Sterno would suddenly present
with incredible grace an eloquent analysis of monopoly
capitalism. It would go on two three minutes he'd take
a swig eyes would roll up in his skull and he'd pass out
falling backward into the fire and he'd roast his brains
if we didn't pull him out his hair smoking his singed
burned hair. Wide awake again he'd tell us more.

But it was here I also learned about California. In
California you could eat the oranges off the trees,
along the seaside boulevards the avocados fell when
they were ripe and you found them everywhere and
peeled them and you ate them on the seaside boulevards. When you were sleepy you slept on the sand
and when you were hot you went wading in the warm
Pacific surf and the waves lit up at night off the shore

with their own light. And off beyond the waves was a gambling ship.

I decided to go to California.

Armed only with his unpronounceable last name, he went down to the freight yards to begin his journey. He confuses this now in his mind with the West Side slaughtering plant such atomized extract of organic essence, such a perfumery of disembowelment, that in the fetid blood spumed viscera mist about the yards helplessly flew flights of gulls schools of pigeons moths bats insect plagues all swirling round and round in a great squawking endlessly ejaculative anguish.

I found a door that slid open, got it wide enough to slip through, climbed in, pulled the door almost shut behind me stood in the darkness breathing triumph. The car lurches again, almost stops, begins to roll, I was thrown into something that moved. I look around my private car my eyes accustoming themselves to the darkness, soot and pungent cinder begins to flow through the boards, that railroad tang, my eyes see all around the perimeter of my private car a cargo of youths. We are the shipped manufacture of this nation there must have been thirty or forty of us in that car gradually my eyes made out fifty sixty sitting on the floor by the dawn in eastern Pennsylvania at a siding in the chill frosted morning a hundred of us jumped and ran when the bulls came shouting ahead from the engine. Later alone in the tall weeds of another crossing a toot and leisurely around the bend bell-clanging another stately red ball my chance I make for it all around me from the weeds a thousand like me leap I thought I was alone.

I let it go. All my gaunt brothers in my own rags

carrying my roped valise hopped the freight. I watched it go. I put up my collar pulled my cap down on my head stuck my hands in my pockets and headed north up the road.

Come with me
Compute with me
Computerized she prints out me

Commingling with me she becomes me
Coming she is coming is she
Coming she is a comrade of mine
Comrades come all over comrades
Communists come upon communists
Hi. Hi.

We are here to complete our fusion
We are here to create confusion
Do you confuse coming with confession?
Do you fuel for nuclear compression?
I'm for funicular ascension.

Decline all word temptation
Define all worldly tension

Deride all prayerful intervention
Computer nukes come pray with me
Before the war, the war, after the war
Before the war the war after the war the war before
    the war
Disestablishes human character.

Computer data composes World War One poet
Warren Penfield born Indianapolis Indiana
City of Indians in the Plains Wars after the peace
City of Indians going about their business
Indian poets in headbands walking on grid streets
Secure in their city of Indian architecture of cool con-
    crete
Bernard Cornfield Investors Overseas Securities

Data linkage escape this is not emergency
Before the war before the last war
A boy stood on the dirt street in Ludlow Colorado.
The wind of the plain blew the coat dust under his
    eyelids
The wind blew the black dust down the canyons of the
    Sangre de
Cristo. The clothesline stretching across the plain
The miner's cotton swung its arms and legs wildly in
    the wind.
A miner's wife stepped from a tent with an infant girl
suspended from her hands. She held the child beyond
the edge of the wood sidewalk over the dirt the dust
    blowing
back along the ground like hordes of microscopic crea-
    tures running.
The infant's girl's dress raised under her arms
she hung from her knees and underarms

so as to have her hairless child's fruit expressed
for the purpose indicated by the mother's sibilant
sound effects
punctuated with foreign words of encouragement.
The boy standing there happening to be there remained to watch
shamelessly and the beautiful little girl turned upon
him a face
of such outrage that he immediately recognized her
willing white neck companion of the old monk it's you
and with then saintly inability to withstand life she
closed
her eyes and allowed the thin stream of golden water
to cascade
into the dust where instantly formed minuscule tulips
he beheld the fruition of a small fertile universe.

WHEN THE NIGHTS WERE BAD, WHEN THE UN-
canny sounds in the woods kept him awake, when the
crack of a twig in the pine forest was inexplicable or
some distant whimpering creature sounded in his mind
like a child being fucked he swore it was still better
than going with the red ball. Whowhoo. Better to take
alone whatever came. Soft web of night threads across
the face. Something watching breathing in the dark a

few feet away. He had heard of people having a foot cut off for the dollar in their shoe. It was still better. It was still better to take alone whatever came. Better to die in the open. Whowhoo. Lying in a city mission flop in the great stink of mankind was worse. Arraigned in the ranks of the self-deluding in their bunkbeds was worse.

It was the bums of the commonest conversation who angered him the most, the casuists of misfortune who bragged about the labels inside their torn filthy coats, or swore there was some brand of alcohol they wouldn't be so low as to drink. Or the ones who claimed to be only temporarily down on their luck, en route to some glorious destination not where they had a job waiting or a family, but where they were *known*, where what they were did not have to be proved.

I didn't want these mockeries to my own kingship of consciousness, with all the conquests of my life still to come. How could I hope or scheme however idly in a flophouse with a hundred others, a thousand others, a hundred thousand others where the dreams rise on the breath and dissolve one another in a precipitate element not your own—and you are trapped in it, a dark underwater kingdom fed by springs of alcoholic piss and sweat, in which there live and swim the vilest phantoms of God.

And strangely enough each morning I woke up still alive. In the lake villages and the small towns of old mills, I was moved along by the constable but a shade more gently. I didn't feel like a tramp when I asked for work. I even had a certain distinction. We were like birds or insects, pestilential, when we buzzed or flocked in great numbers, but one sole specimen could be tolerated with a certain scientific interest. Sometimes I washed dishes for a meal. Sometimes I stole my food. Sometimes I found a day's work at some farm.

Then in one town, walking down the main street in a manner that suggested I had someplace to go, I saw coming out of the drugstore three midgets and a heavyset dwarf who huddled over them like their father. They took their quick little steps down the street, all talking at the same time, the muscular torso of the dwarf jolting from side to side with each step. I followed them. Even when they noticed me following them I followed them. They led me to the edge of town. In a grass lot between two stands of trees was the Hearn Bros. carnival, a traveling show of tattered brown tents, old trucks, kiddy rides and paint-peeled wagons. I heard the growl of a big cat.

Ah, what I felt standing there in the sun! A broken-down carnival—a few acts, a few rides and a contingent of freaks. But the sight of it made me a boy again. I was going backward. Those ridiculous bickering midgets had called up my love for tiny things, my great unslaked child's thirst for tiny things, as if I had never held enough toys that were small to my small hand. Holy shit a carnival! I knew it was for me as sure as I knew my own face in the mirror.

I hung around. I made myself useful. They were still putting it together. I helped lay the wooden track for the kiddy cars. I heaved-ho the tent ropes, I set the corral poles for the pony ride. There were three or four tired stiffs doing these things. I recognized them for what they were, every one of them had a pint of wine in his pocket, they were no problem at all. I thought the Hearn Bros. were lucky to have me.

But nothing happened. Nobody paid attention. At dusk the generator was cranked, and the power went on with a thump. The string lights glowed, the Victrola band music came out of the loudspeakers, the Wheel of Fortune went ratatat-tat, and I saw how money was made from the poor. They drifted in, appearing starved and sucked dry, but holding in their palms the nickels and dimes that would give them a view of Wolf Woman, Lizard Man, the Living Oyster, the Fingerling Family and in fact the whole Hearn Bros. bestiary of human virtue and excellence.

The clear favorite was Fanny the Fat Lady. She sat on a scale that was like a porch swing. Over her head a big red arrow attested to six hundred and eight pounds. Someone doubted that. She responded with an emphatic sigh and the arrow fluctuated wildly, going as high as nine hundred. This made people laugh. She was dressed in a short jumper with a big collar and a bow in her hair, just like Shirley Temple. Her dyed red hair was set in waves over her small skull. The other freaks did routines or sold souvenirs and pamphlets of their life stories. Not the Fat Lady. She only sat and suffered herself to be gazed on, her slathered legs crossed at the ankles. I couldn't stop looking at her. Finally I caught her attention, and her little painted mouth widened like the wings of a butterfly as if it were basking on some pulpy extragalactic flower. The folds of her chins rising in cups of delicate hue, her blue eyes setting like moons behind her cheeks, she smiled at me and unsmiled, smiled and unsmiled, sitting there with each arm resting on the base of a plump hand supported by a knee that was like the cap of an exotic giant white mushroom.

I realized she was slow-witted. Behind her and off to the side was a woman who was keeping an eye out, maybe a relative, a mother, an aunt. This woman looked at me with the alert eyes of the carney.

And as I went about I saw those eyes everywhere behind the show, alert carney eyes on the gaunt man with a white shirt and tie and sleeve garters, on the girl in the ticket booth, on the freaks themselves staring out from their enclosures. What were they looking for? Life! A threat! An advantage! I had that look myself. I recognized it, I knew these people.

But I wasn't getting anywhere with them. By midnight the crowd had thinned out. The lights were blinked in warning and the generator was turned off. The last of the rubes drifted back into the hills. They held Kewpie dolls. They held pinwheels.

I saw the acts going into their trailers to find some supper or drink some wine. I sat across the road with my back against a tree. I wanted a job with the carney. It seemed to me the finest possible way to live.

A while later a truck came along running without headlights and it turned into the dark lot. I sat up. I heard the truck doors slam. A few minutes later an old car and three men got out and walked into the carney. Other men arrived on foot, in jalopies. A few lights had gone back on. I crossed the road. There was some kind of renewed commerce, I didn't understand. I saw the belly dancer standing in the door of her trailer her arms folded a man at the foot of the steps tipped his cap. I saw the girl who sold tickets outside her booth she was looking into a hand mirror and primping her hair. At the back end of the lot in the shadow of the trees a line of men and boys outside a trailer. I went there and got on the end of the line. A man came out and talked in low tones to the others. I heard something moaning. Another man went in. From the trailer came these sounds of life's panic, shivers and moans and shrieks and crashings and hoarse cries, the most awesome fuckmusic I had ever heard. I got closer. I hadn't seen before sitting on a chair at the foot of the trailer steps that same woman attendant from the afternoon who kept a close and watchful eye on the crowd in front of Fanny the Fat Lady.

I LED HER FROM THE TRAILER TO THE TENT IN THE afternoon and back to her trailer at the end of the night. She placed her hand on my shoulder, and walking behind me at arm's length with a great quivering resettlement of herself at each step, she made her stately trustful way down the midway.

Once she hugged me. She was surprisingly gentle I did not share the popular lust for her I was embarrassed and maybe frightened by that mountainous softness I pulled away. Right away I saw I'd made a mistake. Fanny had a cleft palate and on top of that the sounds she made were in Spanish but I could tell her feelings were hurt. I moved to her and let her hug me. She put her warm hand on the small of my back. I thought I felt the touch of an astute intelligence.

She was truly sensitive to men, she had a real affection for them. She didn't know she was making money, she never saw the money. She held out her arms and loved them, and it didn't matter what happened, if they came in the folds of her thighs or the creases in the sides of her which spilled over the structure of her trunk like down quilts, she always screamed as if they had found her true center.

I decided that between this retarded whore freak

and the riffraff who stood in line to fuck her some really important sacrament was taken, some means of continuing with hope, a ritual oath of life which did not wear away but grew in the memory of her around the bars and taverns of the mountains, catching her image in the sawdust flying up through the sunlight in the mill yards or lying like the mist of the morning over the clear lakes.

On the other hand it was common knowledge in the carney that fat ladies were the biggest draw.

I got along with all the freaks, I made a point to. It was as if I had to acclimate myself to the worst there was. I never let them see that I had any special awareness of them. I knew it was important not to act like a rube. After a while they stopped looking at me with the carney eyes and forgot I was there. Some, the Living Oyster for instance, were taken care of by members of their families who lived with them and probably got them their jobs in the first place. There was about them all, freaks and family, such competence that you almost wondered how normal people got along. There was a harmony of malformation and life that could only scare the shit out of you if you thought about it. The freaks read the papers and talked about Roosevelt, just like everyone else in the country.

But with all of that they lived invalid lives, as someone in the pain of constant hopeless bad health, and so their dispositions were seldom sunny.

The Fingerlings were mean little bastards, they were not really a family but who could tell? They all had these little pug faces. They used to get into fights all the time and only the dwarf could do anything with them. They used to torture Wolf Woman. What she had done to arouse their wrath I never knew. They liked to sneak up on her and pull out tufts of her hair. "That's all right," they screamed, scuttling out of her way. "Plenty more where that came from!"

And every day the rubes paid their money to see them and then went off and took a chance on Fortune's wheel.

I had great respect for Sim Hearn. He was the owner of the enterprise. He was pretty strange himself, a tall thin man who walked with a stoop. Even the hottest days of the summer he wore an old gray fedora with the brim pulled way down, and a white-on-white shirt with a black tie and rubber bands around the sleeves above the elbows. He had stick arms. He was always sucking on his teeth, alighting on a particular crevasse with his tongue and then pulling air through it. *Cheeup cheeup!* If you wanted to know where Hearn was on the lot, all you had to do was listen. Sometimes you'd be doing your work and you'd realize it was you he was watching, the *cheeup cheeup* just behind your ear, as if he'd landed on your shoulder. You'd turn and there he'd be. He'd point at what he wanted done with his chin. "That," he'd say. He was a stingy son of a bitch even with his words.

I was fascinated by him. Sucking his teeth and never speaking more than he had to gave him an air of preoccupation, as if he had weightier matters on his mind than a fifth-rate carney. But he knew his business, all right. He knew what towns to skip, he knew what games would go in one place but not another, and he knew when it was time to pull up stakes. We were a smooth efficient outfit under Sim Hearn. He'd go on ahead to find the location and make the payoff. And when we drove into town he'd be waiting where we could see him sitting behind the wheel of his Model A with one arm out the window, the rubber band around the shirt sleeve.

His real genius was in freak dealing. Where did he get them? Could they be ordered? Was there a clearing house for freaks somewhere? There really was—a theatrical agency in New York on lower Broadway. But if he could, Sim Hearn liked to find them himself. People would come up to him and he'd go with them to see what was hidden in the basement or the barn. If he liked what he saw, he named his terms and didn't have to pay a commission. Maybe he had dreams of finding something so inspiring that he'd make his fortune, like Barnum. But to the afflicted of the countryside, he was a chance in a million. I'd go to work one morning and see some grotesque I hadn't seen before, not necessarily in costume at show time but definitely with the carney. Sometimes they didn't want to display themselves in their own neighborhoods. Sometimes Hearn's particular conviction of their ability was lacking or maybe he hadn't figured out how best to show them. They required some kind of seasoning, like rookie ballplayers, to give them their competence as professionals. One would be around awhile and disappear just as another would show up, I think they were traded back and forth among the different franchises of this mysterious league.

But when a new freak was introduced, that evening everyone would shine, the new one would tone them all up in competitive awareness, except for Fanny, secure and serene in her mightiness.

Herewith bio the poet Warren Penfield.

Born Indianapolis Indiana August 2 1899.

Moved at an early age with parents to southern Colorado.

First place Ludlow Consolidated Grade School Spelling Bee 1908.

Ludlow Colorado Boy of the Year 1913.

Colorado State Mental Asylum 1914, 1915.

Enlisted US Army Signal Corps 1916.

Valedictorian US Army Semaphore School Augusta Georgia.

Assigned First Carrier Pigeon Company Seventh Signal Battalion

First Division, AEF. Saw action Somme Offensive

pigeons have the shit shot out of them feathers falling over

trenches blasted in bits like snowflakes drifting through the

concussions of air or balancing on the thin fountain of a scream.

Citation accompanying Silver Star awarded Warren

Penfield 1918: that his company of pigeons having been

rendered inoperable and all other signal apparatus including

field telephone no longer available to him Corporal Penfield

did stand in an exposed position lit by flare under enemy

heavy fire and transmit in extended arm semaphore the urgent

communication of his battalion commander until accurate and

redemptive fire from his own artillery indicated the message

had been received. This was not true. What he transmitted

via full arm semaphore under enemy heavy fire was the first

verse of English poet William Wordsworth's Ode Intimations

of Immortality from Recollections of Early Childhood as follows

quote: There was a time when meadow grove and stream the

earth and every common sight to me did seem apparelled in

celestial light the glory and the freshness of a dream. It is not now as it hath been of yore—turn wheresoe'er I may by

night or day the things which I have seen I now can see no more endquote.

So informed Secretary of Army in letter July 4 1918, medal

enclosed. Incarceration US Army Veterans Psychological

Facility Nutley New Jersey 1918. First volume of verse

The Flowers of the Sangre de Cristo unpaged published
  by
the author 1918. No reviews. Crosscountry journey to
Seattle Washington 1919. Trans-Pacific voyage 1919.
Resident of Japan 1919–1927. Second volume of verse
  Child
Bride in a Zen Garden unpaged published in English
by Nosaka Publishing Company, Tokyo, 1926. No reviews.
Deported Japan undesirable alien 1927. Poet in residence
private mountain retreat Loon Lake NY 1927-1937.
Disappeared presumed lost at sea on around-
the-world airplane voyage 1937. No survivors.
Third volume of verse *Loon Lake* unpaged published
posthumously by the Grebe Press, Loon Lake NY
  1939
No reviews.

Y OU ARE WHAT? SAID JACK PENFIELD, LEANING
over the table to hear better. His brow lowered and his
mouth opened, the face was poised in skeptical antici-
pation of the intelligence he was about to receive. Or
had he received it? In his middle age he no longer
wanted to be the recipient of good news of any kind.

And if some was forthcoming he quickly rendered it ineffective, almost as if it were more important that the world be grimly consistent at this point than that it would offer a surprise. You are what?

The boy of the year, his son said.

What does that mean?

Oh Warren, his mother said, isn't that fine. She sat down beside her son, pulling the wooden chair next to his, and she faced her husband across the table. He would have to work on both of them now.

I don't know, Warren said. You get a certificate and five dollars at the spring ceremony.

Jack Penfield leaned back in his chair. I see. He got up and went to the mantel and took his pipe and tobacco tin and came back to the table and fixed up for a while while they watched. The large flat fingers tamped the tobacco in the bowl. The hand of the life-long miner with its unerasable lines of charcoal in the knuckles and under the nails. He lit his pipe. You know, he said, when I come up this evening there was a man with a rifle on Watertank Hill.

Please Jack his wife said.

What you going to do with the money lad?

I don't know.

That's more'n a day's wages. Are you proud?

I don't know.

You won't make four dollars when you come below. Did you know that?

Yes.

If there still is a mine. Are there any other english-speaking there aren't are there?

I don't think so.

Well then you had to be boy of the year didn't you.

Please Jack.

Didn't you.

I suppose.

The only one they can call up to the platform and trust to say thank you properly. No polack wop or damned greek knows to say thank you for makin me boy of the year does he?

I don't know.

And your ma's going to find a clean shirt for you that day won't she. And she'll comb her hair back and put the comb in it and go with the tears of thanks in her eyes for the company school and the company supply and the company house and the company boy of the year.

You poison everything Neda Penfield said. You make everything bad, you make a child feel bad for being alive. There's nothing worse than that. There's no evil worse than that.

But he minded less than his mother thought he did. He wanted his father to talk this way. It was very helpful to him. The consistency of their positions was all he asked, that his pa be unyielding and full of anger, that his ma be enraged or worse frightened by her husband's spiritual tactlessness. Warren knew they were poor and lived lives the color of slag. He knew there was nothing beautiful in Ludlow but he was eager to get up each morning and test the day. He knew the real evil was his own, the eye and ear that took in everything and suffered nothing. He accumulated meaningless useless data that nevertheless bewitched him. The thick bulbed vein in his father's hand, for instance, in contrast to the thin greenish vein in his mother's. The characteristic smell of the house and the privy were noted and recorded. There were certain objects he liked very much. His mother's tortoise-shell comb, the teeth broken off in several places. The coal stove, whose shape was like a naked woman, her long neck disappearing through the roof. He liked to see underwear drying on the line the wind animating it to a maniac dance. Sometimes he thought of the flapping long johns as a desperate signaling of imprisoned or tortured people. He was absorbed by the sun rising and the sun setting or the rain when it fell from rock to rock. He was excited by any kind of violence, a parent hitting a child a man hitting a woman. When he happened to see such things he would be suffused with a weird heat. His heart would beat furiously and then he'd feel sickened and would feel like throwing up. Until he broke into a cold sweat. Then he would feel all right again. He listened now with eyes downcast but in some contentment to their argument, enjoying the words of it, the claims and counterclaims, agreeing with each in turn they were so well matched and spoke so well the images that flew through his mind on their words.

I GOT OUT OF BED AND ROLLED MY CLOTHES AND shoes into a bundle. I grabbed the money from the bureau. I unlatched the door quietly and closed it behind me. There were no other guests at the Pine Grove

Motor Court. A thin frost lay on the window of her car. The wind blew.

I threw the bills into the wind.

I found a privy up the hill behind the cabins and next to it an outdoor shower, the kind you pumped the water for yourself. I stood in the shower of cold spring water and looked up at the swaying tops of the pine trees and I watched the sky turning gray and heard through the water and the toneless wind the sounds of the first bird waking.

I dried myself as best I could and put on my clothes. Shivering, stippleskinned, I struck off through the woods. I had no idea where I was going. It didn't matter. I ran to get warm. I ran into the woods as to another world.

All morning I went up and down the hills of timber. Sometimes I'd hear the sound of a truck or a car and it would shock me. I'd veer off to get as deep in the woods as possible. It was difficult to keep my sense of direction, difficult to put life behind me. I'd come along into a clearing and find the remains of a fire or an empty wine bottle. Traces of human life everywhere: stone fences, old trails, dirt roads grown over. I found a busted inner tube, yellowed sheets of newspaper with dates on them from the early summer.

But I saw no one: any stiff in his right mind would get out of the Adirondacks before autumn.

By the late morning I was so hungry I changed course and went downhill till I found a paved road. I walked along the tree line for several miles and came to a country store with a gas pump and some chickens in a coop. Stood in the trees and waited to see a black Model A or perhaps a carney truck or even a state police car. The odds were against it, but I was not thinking odds. The carney was a territory in my mind. It loomed out further than I had gone or maybe could go.

There were no cars. I slid down the embankment of loose earth behind the store and went around front and stepped in the door like any customer. I had my savings of the summer, twenty-six dollars, in my shoes; in my wallet I carried three dollars more. I bought a loaf of wax-papered bread, some slices of baloney, a bottle of Grade A milk and a package of Luckies. The store lady, short and wide and with thick dirty eyeglasses, treated me as if it were the most normal thing in the world for someone to come along from nowhere, as maybe it was.

I went down the road till it curved out of sight of the store, and then I ran back up into the woods and found a tree in a spot of sun and sat there and made my lunch. Then I went to sleep for a while, while the woods were still warm, but it was a mistake because I suffered terrible dreams of indistinct shapes and shadows and awful sounds of violence. Someone crying, sobbing, and it turned out to be me. I jumped up and got going again.

I went deeper and deeper into the woods and sometime at the height of the afternoon wandered into a stand of ancient pine with a porous forest floor of brown pine needles that was so soft you couldn't hear your own footsteps. It was dark in here, there was an umber twilight in lieu of the day, and there seemed to be no usual busy life at all, no birds, no insects, just this dark place of unnatural quiet. Looking up, I could hardly find anything green. Yet it was not threatening, the solitude was so complete, the stillness so perfect that I felt as if I had come into some vast, hushed

cathedral of peace. Not even a Father. I stopped walking and stood very still and listened for I don't know
what. And then, right in my tracks I sat down and for a
while was as still as everything else.

I thought of Fanny the Fat Lady's warm hand on the
small of my back.

By early afternoon I was traveling again on roads,
only jumping off to the side when I heard a car coming, or taking to the woods in order to skirt a town. I
went along that day with no destination in mind, no
plan of action except to follow the rise, and go for the
altitude. I had no food left and did not feel I needed
any. I came out to a broad plateau and looking out
ahead of me realized I had gone past the region of
towns and now, for my arrogance, had no hope of supper unless I found a farmhouse somewhere.

The open ground was uncultivated, mile after mile.
I was on a crumbling two-lane road with grass growing
in the cracks and this suggested to me the unlikelihood
of a ride coming along. Still I kept going.

And then with the sun turning red as it dropped
toward the evening, I saw to my left, perhaps fifty
yards into an open space of tall weed and tangled
brush, a single-track railroad embankment. Behind the
embankment was a curved outcropping of shiny flaked
rock. I got up on the embankment for a professional
survey: I had happened upon a one-track spur line of
some sort. I figured that as it curved in an arc around
the rock hill, there was a fair chance it would be going
slowly enough to hop. Coming down from the
roadbed, I found a bare patch of ground spotted with
oil. And beside the charred remains of a fire I saw a
flask of clear glass and a lady's shoe with the heel torn

off. So others had stopped here in their great study of the outdoors—it was a station of sorts.

I gathered a great bundle of kindling, but I was too tired to build a fire. I lay on my back with my hands behind my head and I watched the sky. The sun had gone down but the sky was still blue, a very pale blue, with a few high clouds still golden with sunlight. Soon I was lying in the dusk and feeling the chill of the evening but the sky was sunlit and blue and so far away in its warmth that I felt I was looking at it from a grave.

I fell asleep that way and sometime during the night was aroused by a train whistle. I lay there listening for it again in case I had only been dreaming. Again I heard it, this time somewhat closer. I stood up and tried to pound some circulation into my stiff hulk. The train was coming without question now. I had no idea what time it was, the sky was black, starless. I thought I could hear the locomotive. I moved toward the embankment and waited. I could hear the engine clearly now and knew it was moving at a slow speed. The first I saw of it was a diffuse paling of the darkness along the curve of the embankment. Suddenly I was blinded by a powerful light, as if I had looked into the sun. I dropped to my knees. The beam swung away from me in a transverse arc and a long conical ray of light illuminated the entire rock outcropping, every silvery vein of schist glittering as bright as a mirror, every fern and evergreen flaring for a moment as if torched. I rubbed my eyes and looked for the train behind the glare. It was passing from my left to my right. The locomotive and tender were blacker than the night, a massive movement forward of shadow, but there was a passenger car behind them and it was all lit up inside. I saw a porter in a white jacket serving drinks to three men sitting at a table. I saw dark wood paneling, a lamp with a fringed shade, and shelves of books in leather bindings. Then two women sitting talking at a group of wing chairs that looked textured, as if needle-pointed. Then a bright bedroom with frosted-glass wall lamps and a canopied bed and standing naked in front of a mirror was a blond girl and she was holding up for her examination a white dress on a hanger.

Oh my lords and ladies and then the train had passed through the clearing and I was watching the red light disappear around the bend. I hadn't moved from the moment the light had dazzled my eyes. I'd heard of private railroad cars but was not prepared. I was under the impression I would see it again if I waited. I waited. I heard it going down the track and listened until I couldn't hear it anymore. Into my vacated mind flowed all the English I never knew I'd learned at Paterson Latin High School. Grammar slammed into my brain. In an instant this vision of incandescent splendor had left me more alone and terrified than I knew it was possible to be.

I got a fire going and made it as large as I could, I threw everything I could find into it, it was a damn bonfire and I crouched beside it trying to get warm I made an involuntary sound in my throat for my dereliction, my loneliness, the callow hopes of my life. Who did I think I was? Where did I think I was going? What made me think it was worth anything to stay alive?

The fire blazed up. I wanted to get in it.

At the first light of the morning I climbed the embankment and set out down the tracks in the direction the train had gone.

COMPARE THE PRIVATE RAILROAD CAR SITTING on the Santa Fe siding one night in 1910 in front of the mine near Ludlow Colorado whose collapsed entry was being dug away by rescue crews. Late at night by the glow of torches they began to bring out the dead hunky miners, some so impregnated by coal dust they looked like ancient archaeological finds of considerable significance. Some had been blown to pieces and were assembled on the cold ground by thoughtful colleagues who matched the torn halves of pants legs or recognized what head went with what trunk. The boy followed these deliberations and remarked on the sepulchral interest of assembling pieces of bodies matching and discarding, trying this arm here that foot there on the dark ground, the chill of the October night on the slag hills, the black mineral mountains looming darker than the night sky, the boy noticing the darkening stains around the bodies as blood blacker than coalwater. Some miners were brought out intact, uninjured and looking only slightly stunned to have breathed all the available air until there was no more. Some faces had the look of irritability that comes when something small has gone wrong. Others had eyes rolled into their heads in exasperation others had sor-

rowed into death and by some curious self-embalm-
ment of the skin left the tracks of their tears like shining falling stars through their grizzled faces. The
rescue work was commanded from the private railroad
car, a property like the mine and like the miners of the
Colorado Fuel and Iron Company, and in the car a
self-sufficient unit with bedrooms kitchen small library
and a row of partners' desks were three or four officers
of the firm some in gartered shirt sleeves efficiently
dealing with the wives making settlements pushing
waivers across their desks proffering pens matching the
tally sheets to the employment records and in general
dealing so efficiently with the disaster that the mine
would be back in action within the week. The only
thing that threatened this work performance was the
occasional embittered woman who would come in
screaming and tearing her hair and cursing them in her
own language. They would nod to one of the private
peace officers and the troublesome woman would be
removed. Gradually in his inspection of the disaster
the boy found his way into the car and in the moment
before he was ejected he observed one of the company
officers, a stolid man impassively wiping the spittle
from his cheek. The brass plate at his desk informed
the boy of F. W. Bennett Vice President for Engineering. Warren felt the rough hand of the armed guard on
his neck and then the coolness of the night air as he
flew from the top of the rail-car step to the graveled
ground. His knee was embedded with bits of stone as
the miners had been peppered with coal fragments, so
he understood that feeling. To understand what it
meant to be buried alive in a mountain he sat later
with his eyes closed in the night and his hands over his
ears and he held his breath as long as he could.

EVERY DAY TO SCHOOL SHE WORE HER FADED dress of flowers, horizontal lines of originally cheery little tulips row upon row. It came below her knees and there the cast off shoes, boots practically, hook-and-eye boots all cracked and curled, there the boots began, and so nothing of her was uncovered except the neck above the high collar of frazzled lace, and the wrists and the hands and the incredible face that struck my heart like a jolt every time I raised my eyes to look at it.

Migod. When it was possible to feel that way.

Wasn't it. I used to wake up before dawn and wait impatiently for the light to come into the window so that I could jump out of bed and get ready for school. I would sit on the front wooden step and wait for her to come down the canyon. She would smile when she saw me.

Were you her best friend?

We were each other's only friend. Her English was very bad. The theory of the teacher with all these immigrant kids was that if you spoke English loudly enough they would eventually understand. They all sat there with their immense eyes and watched her every move. They never smiled, even when she scratched her head with her pencil and her wig moved up and down on her forehead. She taught them the pledge of allegiance phonetically.

I would like to have known you then.

You would not believe it, Lucinda, but I was very sensual.

I believe it.

No, you're smiling. But I was, I really was. I lived in such an alerted state that even the daylight sifting through a cloud would give me enormous shuddering response. My friend and I used to play after school in the hills above town. The sun would go down behind the Black Hills but we'd see it to the east still on the plains, moving away from us on the flat plains, racing away in a broad front like an army losing territory on a map. In the shadow in some gully or behind some rock she'd lie in my arms and look at me with her dark eyes, frightened and speechless by our strange intimacy, frightened but not spooked. She could say my name but not much else. She rolled the *rr*'s. Wadden.

Light me a cigarette, will you?

Is this boring?

No, it makes me sad, though. I know what happened.

I have in my life just three times seen faces in dark light, at dusk, or at dawn, or against a white pillow in which the fear of life was so profoundly accurate, like an animal's perfect apprehension, that it encompassed its opposite and became the gallantry to break your heart.

Go on.

One day I remember late in the summer, before we all had to leave Ludlow for the flats, we were playing up there at some run-off. Some black-water run-off falling off the rocks somehow, so filthy with coal dust that just putting your hand in it was enough to dye yourself black. She didn't want to get her one and only dress wet, she'd get a beating for that, so she tied it up around her waist and hunkered there by the stream to play. She wasn't as old as I. She was a younger person. She wore nothing underneath. It was very lovely. Because I had become still she became still. She let me touch her. She let me run my hand over her small back. I could feel the bones in her ass. I could feel the heat under her skinny thighs.

Was this when you became lovers?

Perhaps so. I mean I know we were at one time or another, I remember that it happened, but I don't remember the experience of it. What is that up ahead, Lucinda? It looks very dark.

It's nothing. A line squall.

HEAVE SAID HIS FATHER AND THEY SWUNG THE wooden chest up on the wagon bed. Now make it fast. He pushed up with his hands landed lightly on one knee and stood up beside the chest and worked it firmly between the bureau and the slatted side gate. He glanced up the canyon. They were coming along steadily now, mule-drawn wagons like his own or the two-wheeled handcarts which required the woman to throw her entire weight stiff-armed on the handle to keep it from rising and the man around the front braking with his bootheels dug into the ground.

She was nowhere in sight.

The sky was heavy almost black, it felt like evening

although it wasn't yet noon. A fine drizzle misted on the skin and made everything slippery to hold. Each drop of rain seemed to contain a seed of coal dust. If you rubbed the water on the back of your hand it smeared black. Hey his father shouted keep your wits boy! He nearly fell backward as a cardboard box hit him in the chest. He grabbed it. His mother came out of the house with her arms full of pots and pans. His parents went in and out of the door bringing him things which he found a place for on the wagon bed. Gradually he realized he was constructing the model of a city. Seen from a distance, the boxes and headboards and chairs and chests were the skyline of some glorious Eastern city, the kind he had seen in the rotogravure, New York maybe, or St. Louis.

I have a comment here: I note the boy Warren Penfield's relentless faculty of composition. Rather than apprehend reality he transforms it so that in this case, for example, in the eviction of the striking miners from the Colorado Fuel Company's houses, the pitiful pile of his family's belongings on the wagon bed is represented as a vision of high civilization. No wonder his father is angered by his constant daydreaming. Jack Penfield perceives it as mental incompetence. How he wonders will his son survive the harshness of this life when he the father and she the mother are no longer there to protect him? As to book learning, Warren can do that passably well, but as to plain good sense the character of his mind is not reassuring.

Neda Penfield takes a different view but not without some irritation that the boy doesn't give her more support for it. Her view is that he is a rare soul, a finer being either than herself or her husband. By some benign celestial error he was born to them and to their

life of slag who would more properly have been the
child of a wealthy family going to the finest schools
and with every material and intellectual advantage. He
gives her qualms of course but she nourishes a private
and barely articulated conviction that he is not defi-
cient only latent, that his strength is there but still
wrapped up in itself still to unfold in its fullness when
the time is ripe. When will the time be ripe? His hands
and feet are large and clumsy, he looms next to her
sometimes like a giant he is at that stage of life when
the largeness of him seems to wax and wane according
to his own rhythms of confidence. She is aware as
mothers are of the changes in him the manhood beginning to shine and she is comforted. But the wisdom of
him has still to appear. Sometimes the light will hit his
amber eye and she will feel ill at ease, as if she is living
with two men rather than a man and a boy. Perhaps
Jack Penfield feels this too and anticipates the revolt of
his son, the loosening of his power over him the free-
ing of his son from himself till he has nothing but himself and then inevitably he will be subjected to his son's
power over him. Yet he is secretly proud too and likes
the boy's good looks. Warren is gentle and distracted
as ever only his ears and elbows and wrists and ankles
show the power of him still to come.

Neda Penfield would like Warren to win some sort
of scholarship and go away to the city to study. She
wants this desperately even though she knows her life
with her husband then would be hell. Jack Penfield
wants Warren in the mines. He wants him in the mines
to establish such rage that he will finally be in contact
with the circumstances of his life, he will wake up to it.
And then see what happens, then see what glorious
flights of power and genius the boy has in him perhaps

to become an organizer a great union orator a radical a leader of men out of their living graves of coal. Let the boy work in a crouch for ten hours hacking coal in the chilling blackness of the earth, crouching with his feet in brackish water, not knowing which bite of the pick will bring the roof down on him. Let him work for his three tons a day and bring them up to be short-weighted by the company. Then my son will justify me and sanctify my name and fulfill the genius of my line.

The wagon loaded, Warren gives a hand up to his father and after a moment the two of them teetering on the gate, he nimbly leaps down and suffers the inspection of his work. The father pushes this adjusts that but says nothing, which is the highest approval. Together they tie everything in a web of stout rope, Warren running around from one side of the wagon to the other hauling tight looping knotting and he thinks of a wonderful bridge with granite towers and steel suspension cables what bridge is that.

And then his mother comes out of the house her hands empty but for a summer straw hat, a wide-brimmed straw with a round crown, and not seeing any place to put it she places it on her head. It is such a gallant gesture, so incongruous with the rain and the state of their fortunes that the two men look at her startled and she pulls her shoulders back and defies them with her glance, her face peculiarly shadowed by the brim as if the sun was oddly proven, but they wouldn't laugh because both have perceived in one shimmering instant before the fact of her wearing that hat is established, the still alive girl and the undefeated kingdom of their family.

She took her place on the bench and looked straight ahead over the mule's rump. Jack Penfield went into the house and came out with the last thing, his new bolt-action Savage whose stock was oiled smooth and whose barrel was blue steel, and he placed this across his lap as he sat up behind the mule and took the reins.

And so with a lurch of the wheels they turned into the traffic of wagons winding down through the canyons. In front of the Colorado Supply Company two sheriff's deputies stood on the porch to watch the procession. They had Winchesters cradled in their arms. Some of the families passing them made loud remarks. Some of them sang their union song. Most of them looked straight ahead and went on down the street into the descent of the prairie, too cold or too realistic to bother with the trappings of the spirit.

The rain was changing its nature, getting heavy turning hard, and Warren sitting cross-legged on top of a bureau felt the sting of ice, like steel pellets. He held out his hand and received a particle of hail. He put up his denim collar. He was facing forward but for some reason swiveled on his rump and looked back at the street just as the wagon behind picked up the pace to fill in the slack in the parade and it was she in her dress of tulips faded sitting up on her wagon on a stool like a princess borne in her palanquin, her body moving forward and back, her head moving in the lag of her body's rhythm and he smiled and raised his hand and she smiled and raised hers, and they stared at each other their bodies gently bending and straightening in the rhythm of the mules' pace, the wheels creaking in the mud the traces rattling like ancient music of fanfares and the two of them staring at each other like royal lovers in a procession toward their investiture under the hardening rain through the canyon of slag going down to the plains.

THINKING ABOUT THAT GIRL STANDING IN FRONT OF the mirror and holding up the white dress on the train gliding past me out of sight, I came along the track before I even knew it into the main street of a mountain village.

It was noon on the church tower. A pretty lakeside village with a general store a gas pump a white hotel with rocking chairs on the porch, a bait-and-tackle shop. I wanted to keep going but there was a cop on the corner. Casually I crossed the street and went into a diner and ordered the baked ham and brown beans in a crock and coffee. When I finished I ordered the same thing again. The waitress smiled and the chef himself looked out through the porthole of the kitchen door to see this prize customer.

I got out of that village without trouble resuming my walk just beyond the station crossing, following the rails that forked off into a narrower cut of trees. The track went through some woods circled around a small mountain lake and then it started up a grade a long slow winding grade, I was not already in love with her but in her field of force, what I thought I felt like some stray dog following the first human being it happened to see.

In the late afternoon I came to a miniature station house of creosoted brown logs complete with ticket window and potbellied stove. It was empty. Out the back door was the sidetracked private railroad car.

I climbed aboard. Each room had a narrow door with brass handle opening onto the corridor going down one side along the windows.

Here was the room of grand appointments where the men were drinking a card table of green baize and leather with receptacles for poker chips, a bar with bottles and glasses in fitted recesses, a Persian rug of rich red tone, paneling of dark wood, books in the shelves The Harvard Classics. A faint odor of cigar smoke. I brushed the tassels of the lampshades with the back of my hand.

Everything in this room, unlit and still, seemed more awesome than from the distance of the night, for it was quite clearly owned. That was the main property of the entire car, not that it was handsome or luxurious but that it was owned.

In the girl's bedroom I sat on the plump mattress newly made up with fresh sheets thick quilt of satiny material there was no sign of her of course not a thread not a bobby pin but as I thought about it the faintest intimation of a scent, a not unfamiliar scent, I inhaled deeply, a variety common enough to have previously informed the nostrils of a derelict somewhere before in his wandering one summer night in the carney perhaps.

The afternoon light came through the window at a low angle between the trees it suddenly faded the car darkened I left. Outside, the sky was showing stars as it does earlier than you think it should in the last of summer.

I was so blue. I was sorry I'd found the car, if I hadn't found it I could have thought about it for the rest of my life. If any. But now I felt let-down stupid at a loss what to do. The breeze had a chill and I supposed I couldn't do better going back as I'd come, so I followed the one road from the small station as it ran uphill into the woods.

Long before I got there, probably from the moment I left the village, I'd been on private property. They were the same hills and forest and stone of the natural world, they looked like the Adirondacks, but I was walking in fact on a map of fixed color, crimson perhaps.

The road inclined gradually around the side of a mountain, one side dropping away to show the darkening sky.

And then, below, a broad lake came into view, a lake glittering with the last light of the day. I stopped to look at it. Something was moving, making a straight line of agitation, like a tear, in the surface.

A moment later a bird was rising slowly from the water, a bird large enough to be seen from this distance but only against the silver phosphorescence of the water. When it rose as high as the land it was gone.

The rest of my survey I made in darkness, by the light of stars. I had come on some isolated reservation, and its center was a cluster of buildings on the mountain overlooking this same lake: a lodge of two stories, and several smaller outbuildings, barns, stables, garages. Even in darkness I could tell that the buildings, like the little station house at the bottom of the trail, were uniformly of log construction.

My vantage point was from the land side, a rise in

an enormous rolling meadow beside a tennis court fenced in wood and mesh. I did not try to move closer to see in detail what was in the light of the lodge windows, all ablaze everywhere, as if great crowds were inside. I knew there were no crowds. The wind amplified in gusts the strains of a dance band. When the song was over, it began again. It was a Victrola record of a tune I recognized, "Exactly Like You."

The perverse effect of this music and the lighted windows was of a repellent and desolate isolation.

Now the wind came up stronger across the meadow, it was off the lake and carried the water's chill. I looked up to the treetops of the wood behind me and saw them prancing and bucking in the way of a hard life of eminence. I was fixed by my own pride from going to the back door of this establishment and asking for a place to stay or a meal. I didn't know if I had the stamina for a night on these grounds, but it was as if I was reflecting the clear arrogance of whoever owned this place and traveled to it by imperial railroad, for I was goddamned if I would ask him or them for anything.

I didn't want her to see me like this!

I remember squatting behind the little tennis shack and keeping myself company with my cigarettes. I smoked one after another and made a community around their glow.

Now I'll tell what I don't remember. I don't remember the sound they must have made, the uncanny sound as it separated itself from the wind in the trees, of group exertion, breath chuffing across twenty or thirty hanging tongues, yelps of murderous excitement. Was the moon out? I rose from my crouch seeing something like an earthwave coming toward me, as if the ground were advancing in a sort of rolling quaking upheaval. This gradually distinguished itself as the furred musculature of shoulders and chests and legs, and I think now I must have seen the face of the lead dog, flung into moonlight, its maddened red eyes like the tracers of those launched fangs. If I didn't see it I've dreamed it a thousand times.

Goddamnit, if city boys knew any animals at all it was dogs. But these were like nothing I'd ever seen. Not that I had the leisure for contemplation. I held up my forearm and his teeth tore it like a piece of paper. Together we rammed into the side of the tennis shack. And then the others were up, tossing themselves at me in their fury but with great inefficiency, they turned on each other snarling for getting in each other's way though they were effective enough to my pain and screaming terror. I was kicking at them and flinging them off going for the throat trying to tear my throat out, I was kicking and waving my arms and fists and howling like a dog myself and knowing that if I went down I faced something more than the end of my life—shit—the extenuated appreciation of its end, piecemeal, my life taken from me chunk by chunk drop by drop every nerve shrieking.

I think I can imagine some faint memory of the odor of those dogs, feel the closeness of their life, their wild heartbeat! I hear their snorts and the snaps of teeth on air, I remember the toothtumblers lock once the flesh is found, the quick release and regrip down to the bone.

I recall without difficulty the intimate apprehension of prey in the jaws of a maniac life beyond all appeal.

Somehow I was vaulted or inspired upward in some acrobatic backward tumble through the un-framed shack window. I took one of the dogs with me, slamming it fixed in my wrist against the inner wall of the shack while the heads of the others ap-peared outside the window, a fountain of faces leap-ing and falling back in rage in frustration. But then one gripped the sill with its paws and began to pull itself up till its own weight would get it inside, I grabbed a tennis racquet hanging in its press and swung toward that head down on those paws. The dog fell out of sight and the other, who had come in with me, stunned loose from its slam against the wall, I now caught on the back with the racquet edge in its heavy press and broke its spine. They were not uniformed pedigreed hounds, they were every kind and make, and this one, a smaller mongrel, I lifted howling and threw to the others.

Things immediately got quiet. I heard the yelps and moans and grunts of appeasement, the soft sound of flesh being fanged. The small moonlit square of night I saw from the floor of the shack was peaceful with stars. Maybe I heard human voices, or the firing of a rifle or a gun, but I'm not sure. I lay there and as the blood flowed from me I lost consciousness.

•

Adirondacks.

Region first known for wilderness industries trapping
    hunting.

Earliest roads were logging trails out came the great
    trees

chained to sledges. In the winter blocks of ice were
    sawn

from the frozen lakes and carried in procession on fun-
    icular tracks

uphill to the railroad depots for shipment to the cities.

In early spring the tapping of the huge sugar maples

and the sap houses sweet blue smoke hanging over the
    green valleys.

In summer the natives grew small corn and picked wild
    berries

and grilled trout on open fires by the edge of rock
    rivers.

But one summer after the May flies painters and poets
    arrived

who paid money to sit in guide boats and to stand mo-
    mentously

above the gorges of rushing streams.

The artists and poets patrons seeing and hearing their
    reports
bought vast tracts of the Adirondacks very cheaply
and began to build elaborate camps there thus invent-
    ing
the wilderness as luxury.
Loon Lake a high mountain retreat cratered as purely
    cold and
clear in the mountains as water cupped in your hands.

IN THE MORNING THE OLD MAN, BENNETT, GAVE
them all woolen ponchos and took them for a speedboat ride on the lake. She sat up front between him
and Tommy. Tommy put his arm around her but she
preferred to lean forward in the lee of the windshield
where she avoided the wind if not the cold space it left
as it blew by.

The little flag in the stern flapped like a machine
gun. In the back seat there was no protection at all and
they were truly unhappy. The cigarette was whipped
out of Buster's mouth and taken in the air over the
wake by a black-and-white bird, some sort of gull. She
saw that, having turned to smile back at them, her
knee just touching the old man's pants leg, and Buster,
looking startled, saw it too. It seemed to fall away into
the sky. He faced her stupidly, his mouth still open and
a piece of cigarette paper pasted on his lower lip.

She knew Bennett was showing off for her, rearing
the mahogany speedboat through the waves as if it
were Buck Jones' Silver. The sky was very low and the

tops of the hills around the lake were shrouded in clouds. The clouds drifted through the trees and she was startled by that intimacy. She thought clouds should stay up in the sky where they belonged.

They had come to the closed end of the lake. The old man throttled down and the boat settled flatter in the water. There were marshes here and dead strip-lings poking out of the water. He headed straight for the trees and she felt Tommy clench up until a notch appeared in the shoreline. They went into a channel at slow speed and rode serenely by a beaver lodge of wet dark sticks and mud. The old man pointed it out.

She imagined the beaver pups inside their lodge lying on shelves just out of reach of the wavelets lapping their feet.

Then they were out in an even bigger lake with the hills somewhat farther away and a broad stretch of sky higher over everything. It turned out the old man owned this lake too. She wondered if he trained the crazy bird who came down from the sky for a cigarette.

Later, in the boathouse, Buster was so relieved at having survived travel on water that he told everyone about the bird.

That was a loon, the old man said, a kind of grebe. They all respectfully considered this intelligence.

You knew that didn't you Buster, Tommy said.

They put their ponchos back on the wall pegs and reclaimed their fedoras. There were other speedboats in the boathouse, each in its own berth. There were racks with wooden canoes. It was a brown log boat-house with casement windows in the same style as the big house up the hill.

There was a man there to take care of everything.

Bennett led the way. She noted how easily he moved up the path, his back straight, beautiful white hair. These people knew as no one else how to take care of themselves. He was dressed for the outdoors, with boots and a red plaid flannel shirt.

She held Tommy's arm and enjoyed the warmth of the land on her back. It looked as if the sun might burn through the clouds. She felt good. She felt like dancing. She watched her own feet walking in their strap shoes. They were grown-up-looking feet. She was arm in arm with Tommy, pulling him in close, trying to match strides up the hill. She watched his small black wing-tipped shoes pacing along, their shine ruined, and the cuffs of his pin-stripe flapping dust from the ground.

Up ahead the party was met by a fat guy. He saw her and stood as if struck by lightning. He had been coming down to the lake but turned now with another glance at her over his shoulder and ran along behind the old man.

She held Tommy's arm, held him back and let them all go out of sight up the hill.

You've got to be joking, Tommy said.

She rubbed against him. She kissed him and ran her tongue over his lips and leaned back from him holding her groin against him and looking into his eyes right there in the mountains of the Adirondacks.

Well the kid's impressed, Tommy said.

She nodded while looking into his eyes. The tip of her tongue appeared in the corner of her mouth. He disengaged her arms and stood back from her.

That's how much you know, he said.

IT'S WHO SHE IS, THINKS WARREN, DEFINITELY, NOW dressed in flimsies and struggling with the torments of her class but it's her, the same girl, returned to my life, changed in time, true, changed in place, changed let us be honest in character, but how can I doubt my feelings they are all I have I have spent my life studying them and of them all this is the indisputable constant, the feeling of recognition I have for her when she appears, the ease with which she comes to me regardless of the circumstances, for I have no particular appeal to women, only to this woman, and so the recognition must be mutual and it pushes us toward each other despite our differences, and our inability to understand each other's language, and here it has happened again though I am indisputably older fatter and more ridiculous as a figure of love than I have been before. Always I am older. Always we do not understand each other. Always I lose her. Oh God who made this girl give her to me this time to hold let me sink into the complacencies of fulfilled love, let us lose our memories together, and let me die from the ordinary insubstantial results of having lived.

WHAT HE INTUITS FROM THE COOLNESS OF HER CONversation or the moods that come over her is that she did not expect to find herself in her present situation. She is not devious and did not plan this. She seems to take each day as it comes and is clearly forged in her being by the race of men she's had to deal with. In short, they are equals. The realization sends him to the bottle with a shaking hand.

Naturally she would think he was part of the old man's retinue. It was a natural assumption. At drinks that evening they're alone. Can I tell you a story? he says. Outside, the rain is heavy, the kind of rain that tamps down the wind. Smoke from the big fireplace drifts into the room like a wisp of cloud come in from the mountains.

I've lived here for six years. I'm a poet and the Bennetts are my patrons. But I found this place on my own and when I came here it was to kill him.

The old man?

Yes.

She has to this point only half listened but now he is rewarded by her direct gaze. She sips her Manhattan. She is wearing pleated linen slacks and a thin blouse half buttoned. She likes to show herself.

I swear to the lordourgod I will make her see who I am.

People I loved died because of the policies of one of his companies. He owns lots of companies.

You know what he's worth?

Worth? What can it matter. I haven't got a dime myself, he says conscientiously, as if he'd made it his life's achievement. Millions, billions, the power over people. So I was going to kill him. I got through the dogs with just a tear or two and introduced myself out on that terrace there through the dining room one morning with my knife in my pocket.

She turns and looks through the big bay windows. She turns back.

But you didn't, she says.

ONE NIGHT WHEN THE DOGS ARE IN THE NEIGHBOR-hood he takes two wineglasses and a bottle of his table red and closes his door and half walks half runs over to her cottage.

I thought you might need some company, he says.

He follows her inside. She wears a robe. She is barefoot. He realizes she answered the door without breaking stride. She is pacing the room. Her arms are folded across her breasts.

The doors to her terrace are closed and locked. The curtain is pulled shut. The room smells of cigarettes. He pours the wine.

Later they are sitting on the floor beside the bed. He has been telling her about his life. He has recited some of his work. She has listened and smoked and held out her glass for wine.

Listen, he says holding his hand up, forefinger pointed. The dogs are gone. She smiles and accepts this as something he's done. Sitting Indian style, she leans forward and touches his face. Her robe has fallen open over her thighs like a curtain rising. He kisses her hand as it is withdrawn. I've loved three times in my life, he says. Always the same person.

I don't know what that's supposed to mean, she says. But I see I've got a live one here.

Then she is lying on the floor in his arms reading his face with judicious solemnity, her eyes gathering up the dim light of the room so widely open that he feels himself pouring into them. Because her spirit is strong he is surprised by the frailty of her. She is a small per-

son. Her breasts are full and her thighs rather short.
He can feel her ribs. Her buttocks are hard with a thin
layer of sweet softness over them, like a child's ass.
Her mons hair feels lightly oiled. He touches her cunt.
She closes her eyes. A queer bitter smell comes off her
body. He kisses her soft open mouth and it's just as he
knew, she is here and he's found her again.

Like many large overweight men he has surprising
agility. She is obviously entranced. But the lack of
practice is too much for him.

She says with characteristic directness: Is that the
whole show?

He laughs and one way or another maintains her
interest. Eventually he is ready again. Later he will try
to remember the experience of being in her and will
find that difficult. But he'll remember them lying on
their backs next to each other and the feel of the hard
nap of the carpet on his sweaty skin. He'll remember
that when he turned on his side to look at her the
silhouette of her body in the dark was like a range of
distant hills.

Yes, she said, as if their fucking had been conversation, sometimes nothing else will do but to drive as flat
out hard and fast as you can.

Annotated text *Loon Lake* by Warren Penfield.
If you listen the small splash is beaver.
As beaver swim their fur lies back and their heads
    elongate
and a true imperial cruelty shines from their eyes.
They're rodents, after all.
Beaver otter weasel mink and rat
a rodent specie of the Adirondacks
and they redistrict the world.
They go after the young trees and bring them down—
whole hillsides collapse in the lake when they're
    through.
They make their lodges of skinned poles, mud and
    boughs
like igloos of dark wet wood
and they enter and exit under water and build shelves
out of the water for the babies.
And when the mahogany speedboat goes by
trimmed with silver horns
in Loon Lake, in the Adirondacks,
the waves of the lake inside the beaver lodge lap gently
against the children's feet in the darkness.

Loon Lake
was once the destination of private railroad cars
rocking on a single track
through forests of pine and spruce and hemlock
branches and fronds brushing the windows of cut glass
while inside incandescent bulbs flickered
in frosted-glass chimneys over double beds
and liquor bottles trembled in their recessed cabinet
    fittings
above card tables of green baize
in rooms entered through narrow doors with brass
    latches.

If you step on a twig in a soft bed of pine needles
under an ancient stand of this wilderness
you will make no sound.
All due respect to the Indians of Loon Lake
the Adirondack nations, with all due respect.
What a clear cold life it must have been.
Everyone knew where he stood
chiefs or children or malcontents
and every village had its lover whom no one wanted
who sometimes lay down because of that
with a last self-pitying look at Loon Lake
before intoning his death prayers
and beginning the difficult business of dying by will
on the dry hummocks of pine needles.
The loons they heard were the loons we hear today,
cries to distract the dying
loons diving into the cold black lake
and diving back out again in a whorl of clinging water
clinging like importuning spirits
fingers shattering in spray
feeling up the wing along the rounded body of the

thrillingly exerting loon
taking a fish
rising to the moon streamlined
its loon eyes round and red.
A doomed Indian would hear them at night in their
    diving
and hear their cry not as triumph or as rage
or the insane compatibility with the earth
attributed to birds of prey
but in protest against falling
of having to fall into that black water
and struggle up from it again and again
the water kissing and pawing and whispering
the most horrible promises
the awful presumptuousness of the water
squeezing the eyes out of the head
floating the lungs out on the beak which clamps on
    them
like wriggling fish
extruding all organs and waste matter
turning the bird inside out
which the Indian sees is what death is
the environment exchanging itself for the being.
And there are stars where that happens too in space
in the black space some railroad journeys above the
    Adirondacks.

Well, anyway, in the summer of 1936
a chilling summer high in the Eastern mountains
a group of people arrived at a rich man's camp
in his private railway car
the men in fedoras and dark double-breasted suits
and the women in silver fox and cloche hats
sheer stockings of Japanese silk

and dresses that clung to them in the mountain air.
They shivered from the station to the camp
in an open carriage drawn by two horses.
It was the clearest night in the heavens
and the silhouettes of the jagged pines on the moun-
    taintop
in the moonlight looked like arrowheads
looked like the graves of heroic Indians.
The old man who was their host
an industrialist of enormous wealth
over the years had welcomed to his camp
financiers politicians screen stars
European princes boxing champions and
conductors of major orchestras
all of whom were honored to sign the guest book.
Occasionally for complicated reasons
he received persons strangely undistinguished.
His camp was a long log building of two stories
on a hill overlooking Loon Lake.
There was a great rustic entrance hall
with a wide staircase of halved logs
and a balustrade made of scraped saplings
a living room as large as a hotel lobby
with walls papered in birch bark
and hung with the mounted heads of deer and elk
and with modern leather sofas with rounded corners
and a great warming fireplace of native stone
big enough to roast an ox.
It was a fine manor house lacking nothing
with suites of bedrooms each with its own shade porch
and the most discreet staff of cooks and maids and
    porters
but designated a camp because its décor was rough-
    hewn.

Annotate old man who was their host as follows: F(Francis) W (Warren) Bennett born August 2 1878 Glens Falls New York. Father millionaire Augustus Bennett founder of Union Supply Company major outfitter army uniforms and military accessories hats boots Springfield rifles insignia saddles ceremonial swords etc to Army of the United States during Civil War. FW Bennett a student at Groton thence Massachusetts Institute of Technology Boston graduating with a degree in mine engineering. Bought controlling interest Missouri-Clanback Coal Company St Louis upon graduation. Took control Missouri & Western Railroad 1902. Founding partner Colorado Fuel Company with John C. Osgood Julian Kleber John L Jerome. Surviving partner associate of John D. Rockefeller Colorado Fuel and Iron Company, vice president of engineering. Immense success Colorado and Missouri speculative coal-mining ventures suggested use of capital abroad. Took over National Mexican Silver Mining Company. Founder Chilean-American Copper Company. Board of Directors James Steel Co., Northwest Lumber Trust, Baltimore, Chicago & Albuquerque RR Co., etc. Trustee Jordan College, Rhinebeck N.Y. Trustee Miss Morris' School for Young Women, Briarcliff Manor NY. Member Knickerbocker, Acropolis, New York; Silks, Saratoga Springs; Rhode Island Keel, Newport. Marriages Fanny Teale Stevens, no issue; Bootsie van der Kellen, no issue; Lucinda Bailey, no issue. Died 1967 Lausanne Switzerland.

And this party of visitors were really romantic gangsters

thieves, extortionists and murderers of the lower class
and their women who might or might not be whores.
The old man welcomed them warmly
enjoying their responses to his camp
admiring the women in their tight dresses and red lips
relishing the having of them there so out of place
at Loon Lake.
The first morning of their visit
he led everyone down the hill
to give them rides in his biggest speedboat
a long mahogany Chris-Craft with a powerful inboard
that resonantly shook the water as she idled.
He handed them each a woolen poncho with a hood
and told them the ride was fast and cold
but still they were not prepared when under way
he opened up the throttle
and the boat reared in the water like Buck Jones'
    horse.
The women shrieked and gripped the gangsters' arms
and spray stinging like ice coated their faces
while the small flag at the stern snapped like a machine
    gun.
And one of the men lipping an unlit cigarette
felt it whipped away by the wind.
He turned and saw it sail over the wake
where a loon appeared from nowhere
beaked it before it hit the water
and rose back into the sky above the mountain.

Annotate boat reared in the water like Buck Jones'
horse as follows: Buck Jones a cowboy movie star si-
lents 1920s and talkies early 1930s. Others of this spe-

cie: Tom Mix, Tim McCoy, Big Boy Williams. Buck
Jones' horse palomino stallion named Silver. Others of
this specie: Pal Feller Tony.

The old man rode them around Loon Lake, its islands
through channels where beaver had built their lodges
and everything they saw the trees the mountains
the water and even the land they couldn't see under
     the water
was what he owned. And then he brought them in
     throttling down
and the boat was awash in a rush of foam
like the outspread wings of a waterbird coming to rest.
Two other mahogany boats of different lengths
were berthed in the boathouse
and racks of canoes and guide boats upside down
and on walls paddles hanging from brackets
and fishing rods and snowshoes for some strange rea-
     son
and not a gangster there did not reflect
how this dark boathouse with its canals
and hollow-sounding deck floors
was bigger than the home his family lived in
when he was a kid, as big as the orphan's home in fact.
But one gangster wanted to know about the lake
and its connecting lakes, the distance one could travel
     on them
as if he was planning a fast getaway.

Just disappearing around the corner out of sight
was the boathouse attendant.
And everyone walked up the hill for drinks and lunch.

Drinks were at twelve-thirty and lunch at one-thirty
after which, returning to their rooms,
the guests found riding outfits laid across their beds
and boots in their right sizes all new.
At three they met each other at the stables
laughing at each other and being laughed at
and the stableman fitted them out with horses
and the sensation was particularly giddy when the
    horses
began to move without warning ignoring them up
    there in the saddle
threatening to launch with each bounce like a paddle
    ball.
And so each day the best gangster among them real-
    ized
there would be something to do they could not do
    well.

The unchecked walking horses made for the woods
no one was in the lead, the old man was not there.
They were alone on these horses who took this wide
    trail
they seemed to know.
They were busy maintaining themselves on the tops of
    these horses
stepping with their plodding footfall through the soft
    earth
of the wide trail.
By and by proceeding gently downhill they came
to another shore of the lake, of Loon Lake,
and the trees were cut down here and the cold sun
    shone.
They found themselves before an airplane hangar

with a concrete ramp sloping into the water.
As the horses stood there the hangar doors slid open
there was a man pushing back each of the steel doors
although they saw only his arm and hand and shoe-
    tops.
And then from a gray cloud over the mountain
beyond the far end of the lake an airplane appeared
and made its descent in front of the mountain
growing larger as it came toward them
a green-and-white seaplane with a cowled engine and
    overhead wing.
It landed in the water with barely a splash
taxiing smartly with a feathery sound.
The horses nickered and stirred, everyone held on
and the lead gangster said whoa boy, whoa boy
and the goddamn plane came right out of the water
up the ramp, water falling from its pontoons
the wheels in the pontoons leaving a wet track on the
    concrete
and nosed up to the open hangar
blowing up a cloud of dirt and noise.
The engine was cut and the cabin door opened
and putting her hands on the wing struts a woman
    jumped down
a slim woman in trousers and a leather jacket and a
    silk scarf
and a leather helmet which she removed showing
    light-brown hair cut close
and she looked at them and nodded without smiling
and that was the old man's wife.

Annotate old man's wife as follows: Lucinda Bailey
Bennett born 1896 Philadelphia PA. Father US Under-

secretary of State Bangwin Channing under McKinley.
Private tutoring in France and Switzerland. Miss
Morris' School for Young Women. Brearly. Long Island School of Aviation practicing stalls tailspins
stalled glide half-roll snap roll slow roll rolling eight
wingovers Immelmann loops. Winner First Woman's
Air Regatta Long Island New York to Palm Beach
Florida 1921. Winner Single-Engine National Women's
Sprints 1922–1929. First woman to fly alone Long Island—Bermuda. Woman's world record cross-country
flight Long Island to San Diego 1932, twenty-seven
hours sixteen minutes. First woman to fly alone Long
Island to Newfoundland. Winner Chicago Air Meet
1931, 1932, 1933. Glenn Curtiss National Aviatrix
Silver Cup 1934. Lindbergh Trophy 1935. Member
President's Commission on the Future of Aviation
1936. Honorary Member US Naval Air Patrol 1936.
Lost on round-the-world flight over the Pacific
1937.

She strode off down the trail toward the big house
and they were not to see her again that day
neither at drinks which were at six-thirty
nor dinner at seven-thirty.
But her husband was a gracious host
attentive to the women particularly.
He revealed that she was a famous aviatrix
and some of them recognized her name from the news-
     papers.
He spoke proudly of her accomplishments
the races she won flying measured courses
marked by towers with checkered windsocks

and her endurance flights some of which
were still the record for a woman.
After dinner he talked vaguely of his life
his regret that so much of it was business.
He talked about the unrest in the country
and the peculiar mood of the workers
and he solicited the gangsters' views over brandy
on the likelihood of revolution.
And now he said rising I'm going to retire.
But you're still young said one of the gangsters.
For the night the old man said with a smile
I mean I'm going to bed. Good night.
And when he went up the stairs of halved tree trunks
they all looked at each other and had nothing to say.
They were standing where the old man had left them
in their tuxes and black ties.
They had stood when he stood the women had stood
    when he stood
and quietly as they could they all went to their rooms,
where the bedcovers had been turned back and the
    reading lamps lighted.
And in the room of the best gangster there
a slim and swarthy man with dark eyes, a short man
very well put together
there were doors leading to a screened porch
and he opened them and stood on the dark porch
and heard the night life of the forest and the lake
and the splash of the fish terrifyingly removed from
    Loon Lake.
He had long since run out of words
for his sickening recognition of real class
nervously insisting how swell it was.
He turned back into the room.

His girl was fingering the hand-embroidered initials
in the center of the blanket.
They were the same initials as on the bath towels
and on the cigarette box filled with fresh Luckies
and on the matchbooks and on the breast pockets of
      the pajamas
of every size stocked in the drawers
the same initials, the logo.

Annotate reference the best gangster there as follows:
Thomas Crapo alias Tommy the Emperor. Born Ho-
boken New Jersey 1905. Hoboken Consolidated Grade
School 1917. New Jersey National Guard 1914–1917.
Rainbow Division American Expeditionary Force
1917–1918. Saw action Château-Thierry. Victory
Medal. Founder Brandywine Importing Company
1919. Board of Directors Inverness Distribution Com-
pany. Founding partner Boardwalk Amusement Com-
pany 1920. President Dance-a-dime Incorporated.
Founder Crapo Industrial Services Incorporated, New
York, Chicago, Detroit. Patron Boys Town, March of
Dimes, Police Athletic League New York, Policeman's
Benevolent Society Chicago. Present whereabouts un-
known.

Annotate reference his girl as follows: Clara Lukács
born 1918 Hell's Kitchen New York. School of the Sisters of Poor Clare, expelled 1932. S.S. Kresge counter
girl (notions) 1932–1934. Receptionist Lukács' West
29th St Funeral Parlor 1934. Present whereabouts un-
known.

The gangster's girl was eighteen
and had had an abortion he knew nothing about.
She found something to criticize, one thing,
the single beds, and as she undressed
raising her knees, slipping off her shoes
unhooking her stockings from her garters
she spoke of the bloodlessness of the rich not believing
    it
while the gangster lay between the sheets in the ini-
    tialed pajamas
arranging himself under the covers so that they were
    neat and tight
as if trying to take as little possession of the bed as
    possible
not wanting to appear to himself to threaten anything.
He locked his hands behind his head and ignored the
    girl
and lay in the dark not even smoking.

But at three that morning
there was a terrible howl
from the pack of wild dogs that ran in the mountains—
not wolves but dogs that had reverted
when their owners couldn't feed them any longer.
The old man had warned them this might happen
but the girl crept into the bed of the gangster
and he put his arm around her and held her
so that she would not slip off the edge
and they listened to the howling
and then the sound nearer to the house
of running dogs, of terrifying exertion
and then something gushing

in the gardens below the windows.
And they heard the soft separation
together with grunts and snorts and yelps
of flesh as it is fanged and lifted from a body.
Jesus, the girl said
and the gangster felt her breath on his collarbone
and smelled the gel in her hair, the sweetness of it,
and felt the gathered dice of her shoulders
and her shivering and her cold hand on his stomach
underneath the waistband.

In the morning they joined the old man
on the sun terrace outside the dining room.
Halfway down the hill a handyman pushing a wheel-
    barrow
was just disappearing around a bend in the path.
I hope you weren't frightened, the old man said, they
    took a deer
and he turned surprisingly young blue eyes on the best
    gangster's girl.
Later that morning she saw on the hills in the sun
all around Lake Loon
patches of color where the trees were turning
and she went for a walk alone and in the woods she saw
in the orange and yellowing leaves of deciduous trees
the coming winter
imagining in these high mountains
snow falling like some astronomical disaster
and Loon Lake as the white hole of a monstrous me-
    teor
and every branch of the evergreens all around
described with snow, each twig each needle
balancing a tiny snowfall precisely imitative of itself.

And at dinner she wore her white satin gown
with nothing underneath to ruin the lines.
And the old man's wife came to dinner this night
clearly younger than her husband, trim and neat
with small beautifully groomed hands and still young
    shoulders and neck
but brackets at the corners of her mouth.
She talked to them politely with no condescension
and showed them in glass cases in the game room
trophies of air races she had won
small silver women pilots
silver cups and silver planes on pedestals.
Then still early in the evening she said good night
and that she had enjoyed meeting them.
They watched her go.
And after the old man retired
and all the gangsters and their women stood around
in their black ties and tuxes and long gowns
the best gangster's girl saw a large Victrola in the
    corner
of the big living room with its leather couches and
grand fireplace
the servants spirited away the coffee service
and the gangster's girl put on a record and commanded
everyone to dance.
And they danced to the Victrola music
they felt better they did the fox trot
and went to the liquor cabinet and broke open some
    Scotch
and gin and they danced and smoked
the old man's cigarettes from the boxes on the tables
and the only light came from the big fire
and the women danced with one arm dangling holding
    empty glasses

and the gangsters nuzzled their shoulders
and their new shoes made slow sibilant rhythms
on the polished floors
as they danced in their tuxes and gowns of satin at
        Loon Lake
at Loon Lake
in the rich man's camp
in the mountains of the Adirondacks.

HE WAS A WHISTLING WONDER WITH HIS FACE AND
arms and legs in bandages and bandages crisscrossed
like bandoliers across his chest. Every now and then
they looked in on him with the same separation of
themselves from the sight as rubes looking at the
freaks. They all wore green.

  They told him the dog packs were well known in the
region, several of them told him that, as if it were a
consolation. He had difficulty speaking through his
pain and swollen tissue, so that they could not be exactly sure what he thought of them and their fucking
dogs.

  The elderly country doctor was eager to see what
complication might set in to try him beyond the resources of his medicine.

  There were pills for the pain but I took as few as I

could. It seemed important to me to stay awake, to know what was going on. Maybe I thought the dogs would come back. The room was damp. There was a small window high on the wall. I was in the basement of one of the log buildings I'd seen and it seemed to me not a very safe place to be. Also it was as bad as the original event to dream of it again drugged in a kind of dream prison and struggling for consciousness. Pain was better. It came in spasms and with the sharp point of imprinted teeth, it tore along in clawing sweeps down my chest and seemed sometimes to raise the bandages from the skin. I tried to consider it objectively, like a scientist sitting in a white coat looking through a microscope. Ahh, peering at each little cell-point of pain. Remarkable!

And since I was in pain, I thought of my mother and father. I thought of myself bedridden in Paterson. They look at me lying there flushed and wheezing, a boy impossibly exercised just by the act of living, and go off to work at their machines.

A man looked in on me each morning and made a grunt of disgust or scorn just like my father had although heavyset not at all like my thin and gaunt father but in the same role, with the same wordless eloquence. He wore a kind of uniform of dark green shirt and matching pants.

And for my mother a woman in pale green uniform and white shoes and opaque brown hose with a thick seam down the back. An impassive porky being with hands that worked at high speed setting down trays pounding pillows carrying off urinals while she thought her own thoughts.

I could tell that each of them felt badly used to be taking care of some tramp who had wandered onto the grounds. It was an affront to the natural order which made service to people bearable because they were higher than you, not lower.

I responded with a pride of my own which asked for nothing and gave as little indication of need as possible. And I never thanked them for anything. As I felt better I grew contemptuous as if, coming into this province of wealth, I had adopted its customs. Or perhaps it was more serious, perhaps it had been injected in the saliva of the dogs.

On the other hand I had only the word of these people that the dogs didn't belong to the owner of this place. And even if they didn't, they certainly ran to his advantage. My rage flared as if it were the last wound to be felt and the slowest to heal.

As time went on I understood that I lay in a room of the staff house where perhaps fifteen or twenty people lived who wore the green livery, forest-green for the outdoor workers, the paler shade for the indoor. They all looked somewhat stolidly alike, as if related.

I was alert to find a friend and I did. She was a girl of the pale green set, a young maid in the big house who shyly looked in on me, advancing each time a little farther into the room until finally she showed up in mid-morning one day when everyone else was working. She had seen we were the same age and that was enough.

Her name was Libby. She didn't think of not answering any question that occurred to me.

This place was called Loon Lake. It was the domain of the same F. W. Bennett of the Bennett Autobody Works. Did I know the name? He was very rich. He owned thirty thousand acres here and it was just one of his places. He owned the lake itself, the water in the lake, the land under the water and the fish that swam in it.

"But not the dogs," I said.

"Oh, no," she said, "those are wild-running, those dogs. It's the fault of the people who own them and can't feed them anymore. And then they go off and forage and breed wild and hunt in packs."

"The people?"

"The dogs. All through the mountains it's like that, not just here. Does it hurt?" she asked.

"It don't tickle."

A tremor went through her. She held her arms as if she was cold.

"Tell me, does your F. W. Bennett have a wife?"

"Oh, sure! She's famous. The Mrs. Bennett who wins all the air races. Her picture's in the papers. Lucinda Bennett?"

"Oh, her," I said. "The one with the blond hair?"

"No, she's a brunette." Libby touched her own hair, which was brunet too. Like all her features it was ordinary. She was possessed of a sort of plain prettiness that caused you to study her and wish this feature or that might be better.

"Brunettes are my favorite," I said.

She blushed. She was a simple innocent person, she granted me her own youthful face on the world without knowing who I was or where I came from. In five minutes I had her whole history. Her uncle, one of the groundkeepers, had gotten her the job. She made twelve dollars a week plus room and board. She was fervent in her gratitude. She spoke in what I could tell was the communal piety of the staff. How nervously lucky they would have to feel, how clannish in their good fortune exempt in these mountains from an afflicted age. Mr. Bennett and Mrs. Bennett came or went separately or together or had guests or didn't, but the place was maintained all year round including the dead of winter.

"Don't you get lonely up here?" I said.

She thought a long time. "Well, I send six dollars to my father in Albany."

Not realizing this was enough for me to feel chastened, she frowned and cast about in her mind for justification. "You'd be surprised who comes here," she said. She brightened "You get to see famous people."

"Who?"

"Why, big politicians, and prime ministers from England. And Jeanette MacDonald? She was here in the spring! She's beautiful. I saw her clothes. She gave me five dollars!"

"Who else?"

"Oh well, I never saw him, it was before I came. But Charlie Chaplin."

"Sure," I said. "On roller skates."

She looked then suddenly frightened. Who would doubt her word? She turned and left the room, and I thought to myself well that's that. But a short while later she returned, softly closing the door behind her. She held a large leatherbound book to her chest and looked at me over the gilt edge with bright excited eyes. "I better not get caught," she said.

It was the Loon Lake guest book. She fixed the pillows so I could pull myself up and she sat on the side of the bed and opened the book to a page marked "1931." Her index finger ran down a list of signatures and stopped and she turned her eyes on me as I saw whose signature it was: Charles Chaplin had made an elegant scrawl, and next to it, where there was a space for comment, he had written: "Splendid weekend! Gay company!"

Vindicated, Libby watched with pleasure as I became absorbed by all the names, right up to the present: signatures of movie stars, orchestra leaders, authors, senators, all famous enough to be recognized by me, but also signatures I recognized only vaguely, or only sensed as names of magnitude, like the name F. W. Bennett, names that had been given to things, names painted on the big signs over factories or carved in the stone over the entrances of office buildings. I couldn't stop looking at them. I felt I could learn something, that there was something here, some powerful knowledge I could use. But it was in code! If only I could understand the significance of the notations, I'd have what I needed I'd know what I'd always dreamed of knowing—although I couldn't have said what it was. I touched the signatures, traced them trying to feel the ink. It was some mysterious system of legalities and caste and extended brilliant endeavor—all abbreviated into these names and dates of proud people from all over the world who had come here to this secret place in the mountains.

I became aware of this girl Libby in her pale green uniform. She sat very close to me, the starched front of her uniform rose and fell with her breathing. When I glanced up from the book I found her face near mine, her head bowed and her eyes on the page, but her consciousness all directed to me. Her full lower lip was impressed into a suggestion of voluptuousness by her front teeth. She had thick wavy hair. What sweet appropriate modesty of being. Her trust was part of it, or so I understood—the willingness of the others of us to find a place and live our lives within it, making our

trembling alliances and becoming famous and powerful
to each other.

I turned back to the book. Some of the people there
were such big shots they needed only one name to
identify themselves. Leopold, one of them had written. Of Belgium.

I said to Libby, "Hey, how long have I been here,
anyway?"

"We were taking off the summer covers and putting
the rugs down," she said. "It was that night. I never
hope to hear what I heard that night."

"Well, when was it, please?"

"Two weeks ago."

"Wasn't someone here then? Didn't you have visitors?"

She looked at me and then looked away. She
glanced at the book. She wanted it back.

"I saw the train, Libby. People were on it. Is anyone
here now?"

She shook her head.

"Well, how come I don't see anything that recent in
the guest book?"

She was silent a long while. I knew I was extending
her loyalty. I gazed at her and waited for my answer.
She looked discouraged. "Not just anyone gets to
sign," she said finally.

"Is that right?" I said. She wouldn't look at me now.

"I think someone's calling you, Libby."

"Where?" She went to the door, opened it and listened. I leaned over with a painful lunge to the bedside stand. In the little drawer was a fountain pen. I
unscrewed the cap, shook a blot on the floor, spread
open the guest book and signed my name with a flour-
ish.

"What are you doing!" Libby said. Her hand was on her cheek and she stared at me in horror.

"Joe," I wrote. "Of Paterson. Splendid dogs. Swell company."

I fell back on the pillow. By signing the guest book, did I mean to be going on my way? I felt the pretense, as well as any other, washed away in a wave of weakness and despair.

The girl grabbed the book and ran.

She had a friend, as it turned out, a man who lived on the grounds as a kind of permanent houseguest. He came to look at me later that day, peering in the door with an expression of wonder very odd in a full-grown middle-aged adult.

He was a large heavy man. He was bearded. His hair was overgrown and unkempt. His eyes were blue and set in a field of pink that suggested a history of torments and conflicts past ordinary understanding. His weight and size seemed to amplify the act of breathing, which took place through his mouth. His nose looked swollen, a web of fine purple lines ran up his cheeks from the undergrowth, and all the ravage together told of the drinker.

He said his name was Warren Penfield. He wanted to speak about moral responsibility.

He padded around the room in a pair of old tennis sneakers. He wore baggy trousers belted below his stomach, and an ancient tweed jacket with patches at the elbow. Beneath the jacket was what seemed to be a soft graying tennis shirt part of the collar folded under he didn't seem to be aware of this.

"I can understand your feeling better than you can, young man. I spend my life understanding feelings, yes, my own and others, that's what I do, that's what poets do, that's what they're supposed to do."

"You're a poet?"

"I'm the poet in residence here," he said, drawing himself up slightly trying to tuck his shirt in glancing then at me from the corner of his eye.

I thought I would never know the end of the subtle luxuries with which the wealthy provided themselves.

"So I can understand your feelings. But I also understand poor Libby's, good God she's one of the few decent people around here, and now she's in fear for her job. Do you realize what it would mean for her to lose her job? Of course I'll do what I can, the Bennetts aren't here right now, fortunately, I'll think of something, yes, I'll speak to Lucinda, I suppose I can, but that's not the point. You should have realized the girl was responsible for anything you did. She was nice to you, she made you her friend, she shared something she knew, and that's how you repaid her."

I liked him enormously. I was smiling I was admitted into his realm of moral concern without passport credentials references of any sort. There I was a hobo boy lying on this cot in this weird place suppurating, for all he knew, in my dereliction, not a pot to pee in, and he was trying to recall me to my honor. He assumed I had it!

He saw me smiling and started to smile too. Then we were laughing.

"Of course it was wicked, a good wicked joke, God knows I can enjoy a joke at his expense. I wish there were more of them. Incidentally, he himself is not totally devoid of humor, you know."

"Who?"

"Bennett. I've studied him a long time. He's a very

capable human being. Quite charming at times. The mistake most people make is to jump to conclusions before they even meet him."

"Well, I'll try not to," I said and we laughed again.

At that moment my mother-keeper came in, took my tray, gave Penfield a dirty look, and left.

"Dreadful woman," he said. "They all are. Except for Libby, of course. They despise me. I'm more than they are but I have no place as they have. They play all sorts of tricks on me, I have to beg for my meals. But when the Bennetts are here they'll invite me to dine and then I'm served like I'm the king of England."

I saw that he suffered from this, as from everything, in a state of expressive self-magnifying complaint.

"Well, I suppose I should go. How do you feel, by the way?"

"Lousy."

He pulled up his jacket sleeve and showed me on the inside of his left arm a pale scar from the wrist to the elbow. "You're not the only one, I want you to know. They treed me seven years ago when I came here one night—just like you."

ONE MORNING ON HIS BED AT THE FOOT A folded suit of dark green. He dressed in it and looked for the first time into the hallway outside the room where he had been since he was carried there on some door was a mirror and there he was thin pale-faced boy pale as a sheet, with a sparse stubble on the rim of the jaw, a head of uncombed hair looking too big for the body, and a hunch as if he were still flinching from the teeth, from the snarling face of the mountainous night.

Something has leaked out through the stitches and some of the serious intention of the world has leaked in: like the sense of high stakes, the desolate chance of real destiny.

There was a distant railroad track with telephone poles regularly spaced down the side of my neck over the clavicle across the breastbone. There was another spur line on either arm and the right leg.

I had no feeling in the fourth finger of my right hand.

Thus I found myself on a brilliant morning raking leaves in the shadow of the great sprawling lodge house of the auto magnate F. W. Bennett. I was not to consider myself employed, however. My Loon Lake parents would as frankly have sent me on my way but they did nothing without the approval of their employer, who was still to return.

I felt weak in the knees, I couldn't have gone anywhere anyway. I was glad to hold on to the rake.

The lodge house was two stories on the land side, three on the lake side—the land dropped precipitously from the crest of the hill—and its walls were logs, uniformly brown, set with casement windows and crowned with a wood shingle roof of many angles and regularly spaced dormers. The trees oak maple elm, and though it was still September, a heavy leaf fall everywhere behind the meadow of my encounter, a burning wood of orange and gold and behind this on a distant mountain, ageless stands of evergreen against the bright blue sky.

As the morning advanced the sun was warm on my back. The air was sweet. I felt better. I was one of three or four workmen. A small truck with slat sides moved slowly among us to receive our leaves. We moved around to the back of the house and swept the leaves from two terraces, the upper with tables and chairs for dining, the lower with cushioned wooden wheeled lounge chairs for the view and the sun.

The lake out there a definite mountain lake, a water cupped high in the earth, its east and west shores hidden from view by intervening hills, its south shore across the water filled with pine and spruce that rose up straight on the mountainside in a kind of terror.

The lake glittered with fragments of sun, and flying over it were a couple of large black-and-white loons, big as swans. There was a boathouse down at the water in the same style as the main house. A dock going around the boathouse. A swimming float fifty yards out.

Between the terraces and the water line was a steep hillside garden of wild things, and through its paths we raked away the unwanted leaves from the bushes and plants.

I looked back up the hill to the house and felt the imposition of an enormous will on the natural planet. Stillness and peace, not the sound of a car or a horn or even a human voice, and I felt Loon Lake in its isolation, the bought wilderness, and speculated what I would do if I had the money. Would I purchase isolation, as this man had? Was that what money was for, to put a distance of fifty thousand acres of mountain terrain between you and the boondocks of the world?

The man made automobile bodies, and they were for connection, cars were democracy we had been told.

The wind rose in a sudden gust about my ears, and as I looked back to the lake, a loon was coming in like a roller coaster. He hit the water and skidded for thirty yards, sending up a great spray, and when the water settled he was gone. I couldn't see him, I thought the fucker had drowned. But up he popped, shaking and mauling a fat fish. And when the fish was polished off, I heard a weird maniac cry coming off the water, and echoing off the hills.

A while later I followed the workers going along the hillside with their rakes through the trees past the stables to the staff house for lunch. The people of the light and dark green ate in a sort of bunkhouse dining room with long tables and benches. The food was put out on compartmented metal trays as in a cafeteria.

Fifteen, twenty of them looking at me as I hesitated

with my tray and then slid into a place next to Libby, who smiled and looked with some satisfaction to the rest of the table. I was inspected by a heavyset man with thick black eyebrows I took to be the uncle she had mentioned. I gave back a clear-eyed friendly face don't worry I'm no threat not me. After that I was ignored. I studied them all covertly: there were two, possibly three families of Bennett servants here. They did not make conversation. I had a palpable feeling of the politics of the place, the suspicious credential I had as a victim of the dogs. It wasn't enough to crack their guild. They seemed confident of that.

Well, screw them, they couldn't even understand that I wanted no part of it. When I was strong enough, a day or two, I'd be on my way down the railroad track and leave it to them to work out why. I still had the dollars I'd come with, stained brown with my blood but no less negotiable. Nobody here, not even Libby, knew my full name or had asked where I came from or where I'd been going.

The force of self-distinguishing which I found so foolish among stiffs and hobos was what I ran on. When you are nobody and have nothing, you depend on your troubles for self-respect. I had paid heavily for the bed and board. I wasn't one of them, I was a paying guest.

I finished and walked out while they were still drinking their coffee. I'd be damned if I'd lift a rake or anything else. What could they do, fire me? I stood on the porch and thought about leaving right away, immediately.

And it was at this moment that I saw over the rise to the meadow two people on the tennis court—one of them a girl with blond hair.

I fixed my eyes on her and walked forward already confirmed in expectation by the agonized heave of my heart.

Mr. Penfield the resident poet, an absurd roundish figure in white shorts and a shirt stretched dangerously by an enormous belly, was showing from his side of the net the proper form of the forehand. Once twice three times he stroked the air. His lithe student, trim in a tennis dress, watched him while holding her racquet on her shoulder.

Penfield now hit a ball to her. Careless of all his advice, she swung at it with a great wild lunge and poled it far over the fence across the meadow. I saw tennis balls lying like white flowers everywhere.

He reached into a round basket for another ball and hit it gently, and again she took a furious swing and the ball flew over the fence. Once more he hit to her and she spun herself around missing the ball entirely. He said something to her. She glared at him, dropped the racquet and left the court.

She strode across the grass toward the main house. She tossed her visor away unpinned her hair fluffing it to the breeze ignoring him as he stood on the court and called after her in a voice half reproach half apology, "Clara! Clara!"

But she went over the crest of a slope and descended by degrees until only her head could be seen moving toward the house. Mr. Penfield hurriedly collected the tennis balls lying about the court. I did the same thing in the grass. We met at the court gate. His large bleary face gazed upon mine.

"She can't bear to be taught," he said, admitting me with a stunning lack of ceremony to his thoughts. "All I said was 'Take a level swing, don't worry about hitting hard.'" He looked again in the direction she had gone. He smiled. "But what game can it be, after all, in which one doesn't hit one's hardest!"

He thrust into my hands the racquet and pail of balls and hurried off after her, moving lightly on the balls of his feet with that ability of some fat people to be quick and graceful. I stepped onto the court and picked up her racquet. I took everything to the shack not even thinking of it as the site of my grisly misfortune. I had forgotten misfortune. I headed back to the staff house, from one moment to the next, a worried probationary in my dark green shirt and pants no thought further from my mind than leaving. I wanted a job! Their job! Just as they knew I did. I would take up the rake or any other tool they had in mind oh God it was Clara, that was her name, Clara the girl on the train, no question about it, twice now the sight of her had stopped my heart.

I DIDN'T KNOW WHAT WOULD HAPPEN IN MY LIFE BUT I knew whatever it was it would have to do with her, with Clara. I thought even having her name was an enormous inroad of intelligence. Was she a Bennett? But wouldn't they know their games, weren't they trained to their tennis and their riding? This one, so blazingly beautiful and pissed-off, knew nothing, this one standing pigeon-toed and swinging stiff-armed at balls so incredibly breath-takingly awkward and untrained—no, she was not a relation. Was she a guest? If so, where were the others, she had come with a train, maids in waiting! an entourage! but they were nowhere about, only the resident poet Penfield ambled after her like her pet bear. Was she related to Penfield?

I would do anything be anything to know her and know about her. Dressed in dark green, a spy! I worked to show them how worthy I was, how useful, to show them how I admired what *they* were and how I wanted to be like them and one of them. How much time did I have? Only until the big man arrived, I had only that time to prove I shouldn't be thrown out on my ass.

Of course I couldn't express to Libby even the most idly curious question about this princess living on the grounds. But she had loved showing me the guest book and I thought from her same peasant identification with Bennett wealth she would enjoy the wonder on my face as she secretly showed me the main house, where they lived and had their lives and Charlie Chaplin and the one-named kings sat down to dinner.

The Bennetts not at home there was a bending of the rules: on Saturday night two Loon Lake station wagons pulled out leaving a skeleton staff.

On Sunday afternoon with the sun coming through the trees at low angles to light the rooms, through rectangles of sun along dark corridors, Libby and I tiptoed about the vast upstairs with its hall alcoves of casement windows and window seats and bookshelves and its suits of rooms, each with its generous shade porch, and Adirondacks chairs and sofas.

Whatever empty room I saw led my mind to the next room, the next turn in the corridor, everywhere the light off the lake cast its silvery shimmer on the walls or in my eyes as we passed open doorways.

One wing was closed off. "We can't go there," Libby said.

"Why not?" I asked, casual as I could be.

"It's the Bennetts' wing, where they stay."

"Is someone there?"

"No. But I wouldn't feel right about it. Rose and Mary take care of it," she said.

She led me down a back stair through a kitchen with two black steel ranges and pantries of provisions and several iceboxes each crowned with its humming cylindrical motor.

Through a room of glass cabinets filled with sets of china and drawers of silver service.

Through the hexagonal dining room, three walls of glass and a table hexagonal in shape to seat thirty people.

To the huge living room, the grandest room of all, with tan leather couches built into the walls, the walls hung with the heads of trophy. There were two different levels of game tables and racks of magazines and clusters of stuffed chairs all looking out enormous windows to the lake.

I found myself tiptoeing, with a sense of intrusion, my chest constricted—and something else—the thinnest possibility of destructive intent, some very fine denial on my part to submit to awe. "Of course this is just one of their places," Libby said. "Can you imagine?"

One or two steps up and we were in the entrance

hall. The walls were of dark rough wood. We stood under a chandelier made from antlers. I gazed up a wide curved staircase of halved logs polished to a high shine, with balusters of saplings. I gazed at this as at the gnarled and swirling access to a kingdom of trolls.

"Don't you love roughing it?" I said to Libby, running her up the staircase. "What!" she cried, but laughing too, entirely subject to my mood. In the long upstairs corridor I placed her hand on my arm and strolled with her as if we were master and mistress. I led her into one of the suites and flinging open the glass doors of the porch, I extended my arm and said, "Let us enjoy the view that God in his wisdom has arranged for us, my deah." She swept past me giggling in the game and we stood in the sun side by side looking over the kingdom.

"Do you mind if I smoke, old girl?" I said in my best imitation of wealthy speech. "No? Why, thank you, I think I'll light up one of these monogrammed cigs with my initials on them."

She was animated with pleasure, how easily she could be made to live! I kissed her to show her how the wealthy kissed, their noses so high in the air that their lips never met, only their chins. Then of course I kissed her properly. She was confused, she drew back blushing, she had thought it her secret that she was sweet on me.

Whatever I wanted from poor Libby I couldn't explain what I was doing solely to gain it. We had the run of the house and pretended to be masters. For those few minutes the upstairs maid and the hobo boy were the Bennetts of Loon Lake.

Libby took my hand and showed me a storage room where F. W. Bennett kept his stock of outfits that he provided his guests as gifts: riding habits and boots, tennis flannels, bathing suits, a goddamn haberdashery.

I stood in front of a full-length mirror and took off my greens and put on a pair of tan tweed knickers with pleats, ribbed socks, brown-and-white saddle shoes, my size, a soft white shirt, and a white sweater with an argyle design of large gold and brown diamonds across my chest.

I was stunned by the magnificent youth that looked back at me from the mirror. All the scars and deeper marks of hard life were covered in fine fashion. The face, a bit gaunt but unlined, the hair I combed back hastily with my fingers. He made a passing aristocrat! Well, I thought, so a lot of the effect comes from the outside, doesn't it? I might be a Bennett son!

And then I felt again my child's pretense that those two gray sticks in Paterson were not really my parents but my kidnappers! Who knew whose child I was!

I dreamed of recognition from her from Clara. It was her nearness that made me so crazy, and bold with Libby. So feverish so happy.

And as for Bennett I thought, He is no more aware of me than of some unfortunate prowler mauled by the wild dogs. But here I am, wearing his clothes, wandering freely through his house. Here I am, Mr. Muck-a-muck, and you don't even know it!

Then Libby came back from the female supply store and she was wearing jodhpurs and a silk blouse and a riding helmet perched none too securely on her thick hair and she wobbled in a pair of shiny boots too wide in the shank for her thin legs.

"You look swell, Libby," I said. She turned around with little shaky steps and gave me all the dimensions.

Her gray eyes shone, her mouth stretched in her tremulous overbitten smile. I danced her out of there down the corridor doing a fast fox trot full of swirls while I hummed the tune I had heard the night I came, "Exactly Like You," Libby laughing and worrying at the same time, telling me to hush, looking back over her shoulder, giggling, falling against me every other step, brushing my cheek with her lips. And the light lay like a track along the carpet and shone in golden stations of the open doors.

THERE BEING NO SIGN OF HER IN THE MAIN HOUSE I knew she was staying in the smaller lodge perhaps a hundred yards west, into the woods and halfway down the hill to the lake.

I think I must have spent some while calculating how to get there, figuring out a pretext and then a script for the conversation we would have. But one evening, during the staff meal, one of the woodfolk, a grandmotherly one, said to me, "That Penfield called. You're to go over to the cottage."

"Who, me? What for?"

"How should I know?" she said. "I'll be glad when you're gone and them with you."

I finished my meal as slowly as I could, feigning the

attitude of the workingmen of dark green. I washed my tray and lit a cigarette and sauntered back to my room.

I latched the door and changed from my work clothes to the knickers and shirt and sweater and ribbed socks and saddle shoes. Poor Libby, all happiness drained like the color in her face when I told her I was keeping these things. Shouldn't she have known that the fellow who'd write in the guest book would do that? Anyway, she understood the firm basis of our relationship, that whatever trust she placed in me I would betray.

And as for Mr. Penfield I knew in my bones I didn't have anything to fear from him. He had a way of canceling himself out if you let him talk long enough.

I washed my face and combed my hair and got out of the staff house without being seen.

Already dark on the path, the first stars coming out. Joe drew a sharp breath and tried to calm himself. He was trembling. He had followed her, navigating by her star, and by that means had been sleeping in a bed and eating well and indulging his self-regard for several weeks. An edited view but fervently held.

In his mind, his feelings were enough. He didn't need intentions, plans, the specificity of hope. Presenting his heart was enough.

"Here he is—and look at him!" Penfield said at the door. He held a bottle of red wine in one hand and a glass in the other. "Come in, come in!"

It was a low-ceilinged cottage with a living room and kitchen and stone hearth all in one. I tried not to look at her she was sitting on the sofa Indian style wearing a robe of white satiny material and it had fallen open across her thighs. I tried not to look she was not looking at me but taking a mighty pull from her wineglass head up neck beautiful pulsing neck.

"Here he is, Clara—Joe of Paterson, the man I wanted you to meet." A glass was put in my hand.

"Miss Clara Lukaćs," he said.

Pointing me at a chair, he crossed his ankles and sank his bulk down on the floor at her feet.

They were both facing me and to my right and their left a fire was going in the fireplace. The light flared and dimmed on their faces as some kind of wavering attention, I thought, especially from her she had not asked to meet me how absurd to have thought that. I sensed some purpose not entirely complimentary in the summons. Yet Penfield was smiling amiably indicating to me to drink and so I did, with the odd conviction that I had never tasted wine before. I had ridden the cars with the bums of three states worked with freaks and was wicked and shameless but in this moment it was my inexperience that shone.

What was the conversation? Mostly his, of course, the brilliant singsong of the failed poet, but how could I have been listening with the attention such beautiful words demanded, people from my world didn't talk with such embellishment such scrollwork. I had never before met someone who admitted to the profession of poet but believed it by the way he spoke. I kept my eyes on his face but it was her I looked at, this restless cat of inattention sitting quite still and staring into her wine careless of exposed limbs the inner thigh the rounded knee small cream cracked hummock of the underknees she sat quite still but her mind pacing from one wall to another, an expression on her small fair face of grief or petulance I couldn't tell. But how she felt was of overriding importance to me, how she felt!

—then and every moment after—was my foremost concern, what I lived by. This was her quality and I think she was unconscious of it, that her presence occupied great moral space around her though she was surprisingly small, a small-boned slight thing with narrow shoulders. There was nothing stately about her except the alarming size of her moods. I studied her face with a fervent rush of recognition, a fair skin with a rouge of chapped cheeks, quick green eyes prominent upper lip everything framed in marcelled bleached blond hair I had friends playing as a child with such faces in Paterson I heard the fluent yowl of injustice from this face.

Mr. Penfield speaking of injustice explained how much more modest were his own rooms over the stables than this full cottage in the rustic log style. On the other hand he wrote well there he said in his way of negating his every point of view by obliging himself to express its opposite.

Then he recites some lines about the place, about Loon Lake. The glass in one hand, the bottle in the other, he sits with legs outstretched he is in his dirty sneakers with no socks his tweed jacket with the elbow patches his tennis shirt with the soft collar turned under on one side, he produces a deep melodious voice for his lines not his normal voice I was embarrassed by this sudden access to performance but she was not. She paid attention to his poetry as she had not to his conversation. But no audience was as responsive to Mr. Penfield's words as he was. His red eyes grew large with a film of tears.

I augment my memory with the lines actually printed in a private edition, the last of his three privately published volumes all recording different times of his life in the different places the same person. "The loons they heard were the loons we hear today"—in his deep reader's chant—"cries to distract the dying loons diving into the cold black lake   and diving back out again in a whorl of clinging water   clinging like importuning spirits   fingers shattering in spray   feeling up the wing along the rounded body of the   thrillingly exerting loon   beaking a fish   rising to the moon streamlined   its loon eyes round and red."

And I, resonantly attuned to her, alive to the firelit moment—somewhere I had gotten at great cost, with the scars to show it, from such profound effort, the kind of unceasing insistence on my life's rights that was only now so exhausting in my release from it. As this absurd fat drunkard sang his words they seemed the most beautiful I had ever heard. But perhaps any words would have done. I heard them and I didn't hear them, I had no idea he had just written them I thought they were from some book already done, I heard the feeling they inspired in me, that I was living at last! That it was the way it should be, I was feeling Penfield's immense careless generosity, the boon of himself which granted me without argument everything I was struggling for, all of it assumed in the simple giving of words, so moving to this scruffy boy.

It was the moment of dangerous specification of everything I thought worth wanting. After the loon flew off whose red eyes were much like his own he cleared his throat and he poured wine all around although I'd barely sipped mine. He emptied the bottle on his turn and struggled to his feet for another bottle which he uncorked while continuing to speak and again he sat down with the new bottle as attached to his hand as the old.

I tried not to look at her. I saw the glance from under her brows toward the ceiling, the impatience, and then I began to feel the force of the occasion which was that somehow I was enlisted to help divert, distract or pacify Clara Lukács. That was the meaning of the self-dramatization of the man, that we were in some overburdened instant, with our backs to it, grounding our heels, digging in.

And then he was telling us about the war, of all things, a veteran, migod, would he bring out the poppies? But soon we were inside his images, listening like children, the mule-drawn caissons sinking in the mud, the troops in greatcoats and tin helmets riding the mules' backs, kicking their boots sharply against the mules' flanks, the bracing of backs on six-foot wheels, spokes like baseball bats tires of steel, each soldier alone and miserable inside his coat, charred trees beside the road the sky showing through city hall, gusts of acrid air blowing from the front, and here is Corporal Penfield riding the signal wagon, flag tubes strapped to his back like quivers, a helmet tilting over his eyes because the strap is too loose, and on his lap the crate covered with a khaki blanket shifts perceptibly, the pigeons whirring with each dull boom lighting the sky like lightning miles ahead.

He was dangling a medal. He had taken it from his pocket. He handed it to me. The colors of the ribbon had bled, there was thread and lint attached to it, but it was a Silver Star and it was his.

I leaned forward put it in her hand leaning forward over the bear rug between us, our hands grazed I felt the heat of her hand.

And there in our minds as we looked at the palpable proof was Signal Corporal Penfield during the battle of the Somme dispatched urgently to semaphore the artillery to drop some heavy stuff on the encircling Huns.

"The field telephone didn't work, there wasn't even a damn pigeon left." He paused to wet his throat. "So I took the old semaphore flags and went up to the top of a hill where I could be seen, because even though it was night the star shells were like the Fourth of July and it was brighter than day. I could see out over no man's land. I sent my message"—here he lifted his arms, attached to the glass and bottle and did a half-hearted pantomime—"and a while later the artillery came in on target, and that's what I got the medal for."

"You're a hero," she said, smiling. She dropped the medal in his lap and then raised her glass to her lips.

"No, but, love, you haven't heard the end." He dropped his chin to his chest. "I was so terrified I didn't send the message I was supposed to. What I semaphored was the first verse of a poem."

"What?" I said.

"'There was a time when meadow, grove, and stream,   The earth, and every common sight,
      To me did seem   Apparelled in celestial light,
      The glory and the freshness of a dream,' and so on," he said. "And a while later the shells came in on target. It was very strange."

She was laughing. "In the war—in the battle?"

"Surely you know it," he said. "The Intimations Ode? Didn't you have it in school?"

"But why?"

"I don't know why. Maybe I thought I was going to die. Maybe it seemed to me the only appropriate thing *to* say. Anyway, after I got the medal I wrote a letter to the Secretary of the Army returning it and telling him it was more properly William Wordsworth's."

"But it wasn't a medal for poetry," I said, and immediately felt like a fool.

"Apparently not, Joe of Paterson. Apparently not. I had to go for psychiatric tests. They pinned the medal on my bathrobe. They kept me under observation for ninety days in Nutley, New Jersey."

"Where?" she said, happily laughing. He looked up at her, victorious in her amusement. "Oh, Warren, you old fuck, where?" She threw back her head and laughed and laughed, I gazed at her throat, her neck, it was a moment in which I could look at all of her as she sat in her white satin robe, she bending forward now in her laughter, the robe unfolding like unfolding wings so that I could see her breasts.

Then I realized Penfield was looking at me, with his head lowered, with raised eyebrows, a characteristic expression, I knew at once, full of sadness, full of self-acknowledgment, and as she reached out and touched his head he too began to giggle, he was in love with her, and soon they were both laughing and I was laughing, but trying not to for some reason, feeling badly that I laughed, feeling ashamed.

I hadn't realized how drunk they were. A few moments later, in silence, she put her glass down and reached out, holding his head in her arms. He looked up at her, and behind her shingle of hair he kissed her, his hand with the bottle going up involuntarily, another semaphore, and I heard her sob, and then both of them were crying.

* * *

I tried to leave, but they wouldn't allow it. All at once they were very physical with me, placing themselves on either side of me and leading me back to the middle of the room. Penfield went to stoke up the fire. She led me to my chair and pressed my shoulders firmly with her small hands and then sat across from me and studied me solemnly. Until this moment her primary awareness had been of Penfield, she had not quite acknowledged me, as if one person at a time, and only one, could occupy her mind. She was always to be this way, intense and direct with whatever she fixed upon, and whatever the affront to those on the periphery. It was not snobbishness or anything like that—she was in fact reckless of her self-interest in a situation, and that I think was the center of her force and effect. She knew nothing about courtesy in the sense of not being subject to it. She blazed through her feelings and suffered the consequences.

I began to realize as we talked that she was no older than I was. I was stunned—I was not yet twenty—I equated power and position in the world with age.

"You live here?" she said. "How do you stand it?" I rubbed my palms on my knickers. I looked with alarm at Warren Penfield, who said, "Clara, he's my surprise for you," and came back to his place on the floor.

She had a throaty voice with a scratched quality. Her diction was of the street. "Whats 'at mean!" She gazed at me, her eyes widening, and I was certain, as if a chasm were opening around me, that she was as fraudulent in this place as I was. I drank off my wine.

"You remember the night you heard the dogs?" the poet said to her, and leaned forward to refill my glass. "Joe here is taking each day as it comes—like you, Clara."

I saw realization light her eyes. She went to the fire and sat down before it with her back to us. I don't remember much of what happened after that. I drank more than I should have. The fire looming her shadow across the low-ceilinged room. Later we heard the rain falling, a heavy rain that seemed to do something to the draught. Wood smoke came into the room on gusts. At this point we were all standing, I had removed my shirt, and she was tracing the scars on my chest and arms and neck with her fingertips.

I could smell her, the soap she used, the gel of her hair. The firelight flared on our faces as if we were standing with the poet in his war.

"He told me it was a deer, that they took a deer," she said. "That was a lie."

"Yes," Penfield said, watching her fingers.

"What class," Clara said. Tears were suddenly coming down her cheeks.

"I could help you leave," Penfield said. His eyes closed and he began moving his head from side to side like someone in mourning. "I can get you out of here. We can leave together." His sentences became a hum, a soft keening, as if he were listening to some private elegy and had no hope of an answer from her.

"That son of a bitch," she said with the tears streaming. "I wouldn't give him the satisfaction."

Certain contracts having quietly been made in mountains
certified convicts having mislaid their companions
I direct you eight hundred Mercator miles west
to the autobody works on the flat landscape
dawn whitening the frost on the corrugated shed roofs
the smokeless stacks the endless chain-link fence
the first trolley of the morning down Division Street
discharges workers in caps and open jackets but not
workers.
The pickets roused from their sleep huddled by steel-
drum fires
the cops awakened in their cars rubbing their misted
windshields
the second trolley of the morning tolls down Division
Street
discharges workers or workers at first glance
but somehow not resembling the strikers grouping un-
easily
in front of the main gates of the autobody works.
The cops make calls from phoneboxes on the corners
the third trolley of the morning grinding its flanged
wheels

on Division Street stopping the arrivals stepping down
now
seen in the light their expressions of newly purchased
loyalty
appearing as an unaccustomed cause in their shrewd
appraising eyes
the insignia of their dereliction, jackets with pockets of
pints
shoes tied around with rope, medals of filth,
mercenaries with callused fingers discovering
the cobblestones pried so easily
by ones and twos and hefted as many as until the
tracks
of the trolleys of Division Street stand up from unpaved beds.
Open trucks arrive filled with the faces not of workers.
This army can take the city apart and put it back together
if it so wishes or perhaps wrap the electrified lines
stringing the utility poles overhead around each individual striker
until he may go self-powered into eternity.

Cops start patrol-car engines drive quietly away
certain black sedans now arrive between arrivals
of the crowded streetcars and trucks some men in
overcoats appearing
among the seeming workers resembling only slightly
now the pickets
with the eyes of lepers staring at them
no saints present on this wet gray morning to kiss
them,
so numerous now they do not even have to look at
whom they will face

when they walk over them into the plant and throw the
        switches.
And primly planning the action deploying forces
is a slim and swarthy man in overcoat and pearl-gray
        fedora
a dark-eyed man short but very well put together
friend of industrialists, businessman who keeps his
        word
and capable of a gracious gesture under the right con-
        ditions.
Only now, as with a gloved hand he beckons one of the
        strikers
an aged man with white hair and rounded shoulders
who has called out brothers don't do this to your
        brothers
to meet him between the lines alone in no man's land
does a small snapshot of rage light his brain.
He impassively demonstrates the function of the cob-
        blestone
a sudden event on the workingman's skull who has met
        him
surprised now at the red routes of death mapped on his
        forehead
turning to share this intelligence with his brothers
hand lifted too late as the signal for the engagement to
        begin.

AND THEN THE LIFE QUICKENED, SUDDENLY THE people in green were scurrying about purposefully, there even seemed to be more of them, and I knew without being told that the master of Loon Lake, Mr. F. W. Bennett, was in place.

One morning I was mucking out the stables. Two horses were made ready for riding. The wide doors swung open admitting a great flood of light, the horses were led out, and I caught a glimpse of her in jodhpurs, velvet riding jacket, she was fixing the strap of her riding helmet. The doors closed. I climbed over the stall gate and ran to a window. A bay flank and a shiny brown boot moved through my field of vision. I heard a man's voice, a quiet word of encouragement, and then she, on her lighter mount, passed my eyes, the boot not quite secure in the stirrup.

I ran to the doors and put my eyes to the crack: the back and head of white hair were all I could see of Bennett before Clara's figure loomed up on her fat-assed horse, she didn't roll with its footfalls but took each one bumping, her black riding helmet slightly askew.

And then horses and riders passed behind some trees and were gone.

I raked shit.

In the evening I went to Mr. Penfield's rooms and we listened to the scraps of dance music carried from the main house on the wind.

"I suppose I'll be out of here tomorrow," I said.

"What?" He had been staring into his wineglass.

"When it comes to his attention."

"You can't be sure, Joe of Paterson. I have made a great study of the very rich. The one way they are accessible is though their whim." He swallowed some wine. "Yes. I have not told you this, but six or seven years ago when I came up here at night along the track, as you did, I knew where I was going. I had traced Frank Bennett to Loon Lake and I intended to kill him."

"I have the idea myself," I said. He didn't seem to hear me.

"Mr. Bennett was amused. I was invited to remain on the grounds and write my poetry. Yes. And now you see me."

"I do," I said. "I see you."

"I know what you think. You think living this way year after year and not going anywhere, not doing anything, I have lost my perspective. It's true! It's true! So that everything that happens, every, oh God"—his eyes go heavenward, he swallows some wine—"small thing, is monumentally significant. I know! I lie in wait like a bullfrog lying in wait for whatever comes along for his tongue to stick to. Yes. That's the only part of me that moves, my tongue."

He dropped his chin on his chest and stared at me with his bleary red eyes. "You want to hear me croak?"

"What?"

He emitted the sound of a bullfrog, never had I heard such a blat of self-disgust I didn't want to. It was not one night like this but several I remember, sitting in his living room over the stables, piles of books on the floor, a desk covered with papers, composition notebooks the kind I used in school, clumps of dust on the floors, ashtrays filled to overflowing, ashes on the carpet, on the window seat, he drifts back and forth back and forth between the wine bottles and the window, and all the while Miss Clara Lukács dances rides swims dines in the provinces of Loon Lake, mysteriously advanced now to the rank of its mistress.

"I don't think it's a small thing," I said. "I think it is monumentally significant."

"Yes," he says, and he pulls his chair closer to mine, "this is not the first acquaintance. And it has nothing to do with who I am or the way I look, it's always the same—the immediate recognition I have for her when she appears, and the ease with which she comes to me whatever circumstances I'm in, whatever I've become. Because I have no particular appeal to women and I never have, except to this woman, and so the recognition must be mutual and it pushes us toward each other even though we don't talk the same language. And so, you see, now again, even though I'm indisputably fatter and more ridiculous as a figure of love than I ever was. And even though"—his eyes brimmed—"she is faithful to nothing but her own life."

I didn't know what he was talking about.

He struggled out of his chair and ran to his bookshelves, and not finding what he wanted, he disappeared into a closet from which came the sounds of crashing and falling things.

He stumbled out with a book in his hand. He blew

the dust off. "I want you to have this," he said, "my first published work, my first thin volume of verse"—he smiled unsmiled—"*The Flowers of the Sangre de Cristo*." He did not hand me the book but examined it closely. "I printed it on a hand press and bound it myself in Nutley. It was my project for recovery, you see. The signatures in this one are out of order. But no matter, no matter."

He pressed the volume on me now and looked in my eyes as if hoping to see the wisdom that would flow into them from the book.

"Just a minute," he said. He ran back into the closet there was a terrible crash I jumped up but he came out coughing in a cloud of chalky dust waving his second published work. "This one too," he said, slamming the closet door. He swallowed a great draught of wine and slumped back in his chair wheezing from the exertion.

I held the two slim volumes, the second included a Japanese woodprint as frontispiece. "Don't read them now, don't ask me to watch you as you read them," he said.

I held the books, I could not help granting him the authority he craved as profound commentator on his own life—he was an author! Never mind that he published his books himself, I was impressed, nobody I ever knew had written a book. I held them in my hand.

Apart from everything else and despite the shadows of the wishes in my mind the vaguest shadows of the implementation of the wishes, I am moved to be so set up in the world with such a distinguished friend. I know he is a posturing drunk, how could I not recognize the type, but he has made me his friend, this poet, and I have a presence in the world.

He tells me his one remaining belief.

"Who are you to doubt it," he says angrily, "a follower of trains in the night!"

I don't doubt it I don't. I have listened to his life, heard it accounted indulged improved incanted and I believe it all. It is a life that goes past grief and sorrow into a realm, like the life of a famous gangster or an explorer, where sudden death is the ordinary condition. And somehow I'm invited to engage my instinct not to share his suffering but to marvel at it, a life farcically set in the path of historical and natural disaster it comes to me as entertainment—

The war before the war before the war
Before the rise of the Meiji emperor
Before the black ships—

his great accomplishment was his own private being the grandness and the depth of his failed affections each of his representations of himself at the critical moments of his past contributed to the finished man before me

Child Bride in a Zen Garden by Warren Penfield
In a poem of plum blossoms and boats poled down a
    river
Behind a garden wall the sun lighting its pediment of
    red tile
A fourteen-year-old girl aches for her husband.
One bird whistles in the foliage of a tree that stands on
    crutches.

Small things are cherished, a comb a hand mirror a
	golden carp
in a pool no more than eight inches deep. Curved
	wooden foot-
bridges of great age connects the banks of ponds. But
	everywhere
we know on the map are mountains with vertical faces
and thunderous waterfalls, escutcheons of burning
	houses
and suicidal armies, history clattering in contradistinc-
	tion to
the sunlight melting itself in the bamboo grove.

Oh the fifty-three stations of the Tokaido. On the em-
	bankment
above the rich paddy travelers crouch under slants of
	rain.
Messengers run with their breechcloths flapping. Mer-
	chants
beat their donkeys. Boats with squared sails make
directly for shore. Paper lanterns slide down the
	waves.
Rain like the hammers of sculptors works the curved
	slopes
of water. When the sky clears at sunset fifty-three pre-
	fecture
officials arrive in the stations of the Tokaido. Fifty-
	three
women are prepared for them. Sunlit legends will be
	made tonight.
Beans are picked from the gardens, plump fowl
	slaughtered, and in castles above the road unem-
	ployed warriors duel the firelight.

They weep they curse they raise wine cups to honor.
    Saints
of the wrong religion go unrecognized in the darkness
    beyond the
lighted windows of the inns. And at the end of the
    Tokaido
at the top of an inaccessible mountain sits the emperor
    himself,
a self-imperator, a self impersonating a self in splendor
in his empty room its walls painted with long-legged
    waterbirds,
its floor covered with ministers lying face down attend-
    ing him.
The emperor is lacquered, his sword is set with suns,
    while
in another room doctors dispute the meaning of his
    stool.

Oh compact foreign devils flesh of rice
Everywhere we are smaller than the landscape.
I sit on the wood promenade overlooking my garden
    and I
am the real emperor. The small twisted tree is very old
    and has a
name. The rocks like islands in the sea of raked
gravel have names. The gravel waves break upon the
    rocks.
A girl with suncast eyes cries on the other side of the
    ancient
wall. I run across the gravel sea
and spy on her through the gate. Her blue-black hair is
undressed, like a child's. She sits on a bed of moss, her
bowed neck as long as a lady's of the court. The words
    rise

and fall in my throat growling and humming and making tunes.
I am breaking the laws of my religion. She is alert now
to
the aviary of our language and stares at me with her
wet mournful
eyes, the track of one tear surmounting the pout of her
lip
and disappearing in the corner of her mouth. I speak
and she
shifts to her knees, deferentially places her hands flat
upon
her thighs. The soles of her feet are pale. She listens.
She is as still as the fieldmouse in the talons of the
hawk.

Oh the fifty-three stages of the Tokaido. The old monk
and the girl
clamber up on the rock path. Along the path falls a
stream
so vertically on rocks that the water, broken into millions of
drops, bounces pachinko pachinko like pellets of steel.
We find a ledge overlooking the ocean. I aspire to
goodness.
I aspire to the endless serenity of the realized Buddha.
In the sun on the rock ledge I remove her clothing. I
remove my clothing she averts her eyes. We hunker in
the
hairless sallow integument of our kind. Her haunches
are
small and muscular. Her thighs are slender. Her backbone

is as ordered as the stones of a Zen garden. I see reflected
in the polished gray rock under her the entrance to her
life.
It is like the etching of a fig.
Raising my hand in the gesture of tenderness, I see her
chin
lift in trust and at that moment I fling myself at her
and she falls into the sea.
She falls in a slow spiral, wobbling like a spent arrow.
I feel her heart beating in my chest.
I feel all she is, her flesh and bone, her terror in the
sky.

THE FIELD OF HIS ACCOMPLISHMENT WAS HIS OWN
private being, the grandness and depth of his failed
affections. Each of his representations of himself at the
critical moments of his past contributed to the finished
man before me. He proved everything by his self-dep-
recation, his sighs, his lachrymose pauses, his prodi-
gious thirst for wine, and he proved it in the scene or
two with Clara, when, at an hour he somehow always
knew, he would get me to help him over to her cottage
not five minutes since she had come in herself, her
make-up and hair and dress all showing the use of the
evening, and she in some sort of sodden rage. What
excited Mr. Penfield was the idea of rescue. He wanted
to save her, take her away, carry her off. It was the
pulsating center of his passion. And she seemed now
not to understand, as if they spoke different languages,
hers being Realism.

"War-rin," she would say, "do I have to spell it out?"

"Oh God," he'd cry, lifting his eyes, "oh God who made this girl, give her to me this time to hold, let me sink into the complacencies of fulfilled love, let us lose our memories together and let me die from the ordinary insubstantial results of having lived!"

"Goddamnit," Clara shouted, and then, appealing to me, the audience, a role I embraced as I would any she chose, "what does he want from me? Oh Jesus! Joe," she'd say when, invariably, he broke down, "why did you bring him? Take him home. Get this fucking drunk out of here."

ANOTHER NIGHT OR THE ONE AFTER, I WENT over to her cottage alone. I supposed it was midnight. No light on. It didn't matter. I sat in the shadow of her porch and I folded my arms and waited. A strong wind blowing over the mountains and sounding in the trees around the cottage. The trunks of the pine trees swayed and creaked. I sat with my back to the door and drew up my knees. I might be hearing her in her rut, singing somewhere with the wind going past an open window. That was all right. That was all right. If the poet could have her on her terms and the rich man on his, I could have her on mine. My revelation. Maybe she traveled like a princess on a private train, maybe poets thought they recognized her, but I knew her accent, she was an Eastern industrial child, she had come off streets like my streets she was born of the infinite class of nameless workers my very own exclusive class. Jesus, I had pressed against girls like her in the hallways, I had bent them backward on the banister, I had pulled their hair I had lifted their skirts I had rubbed them till they creamed through their underpants.

I reached over my head and tried the doorknob. Open. I decided to wait for her in comfort. I turned on a light. The wood smoke lay under the low ceiling. The hearth was cold. I put in some paper and kindling and got a fire going and stood with my back to the fire.

The green livery had as little regard for her as they did for Penfield. The place was a mess. Not that she'd care. I looked in her bedroom. Her clothes everywhere, stockings twisted and curled like strips of bacon, step-ins in two perfect circles on the floor as if disengaged in a meditative moment, or flung across a lampshade as if drop-kicked.

Poor Mr. Penfield. I knew what he couldn't possibly know. I knew what made his sympathies obsolete. Clara and Bennett had had breakfast together on the morning after he arrived. I managed to be raking leaves at the foot of the terrace wall under their line of sight. It was a bright windy morning and the clouds actually were below us over the lake and drifting through the trees on the mountains. "I think clouds should stay in the sky where they belong," Clara said, "don't you?" And Bennett had laughed.

Clara held a relentless view of the world. There

were no visible principles. Every one of her moods and feelings was intense and true to itself—if not to the one before or the one after. She lightened and darkened like the times of the day.

I smoked a cigarette from the monogrammed cigarette box. Clearly, in my aspiration it was FWB I would have to contend with. FWB, the man who was paying for everything. Conceivably this gave him an advantage.

I mashed out the cigarette, stretched out on my back before the fire, put my hands under my head and closed my eyes.

I slept in that position for several hours. I remember coming awake with the fire out and sunlight glowing on the windows. The silhouettes of branches and leaves wavered on the log wall and a reddish gold light filled the room. I heard the sound of an airplane. It grew louder and then with a rise in pitch it receded and grew faint. I lay there and it got louder again and finally so close and thunderous that the cups rattled in the sink. Then the sound receded once more, the pitch of the engine rising. I went to the window: a single-engine plane with pontoons was banking over the mountain on the other side of the lake. I watched it, a seaplane with a cowled engine and an overhead wing. As it banked, its dimensions flared and I saw a smartly painted green-and-white craft zooming over the water and then lifting its nose and banking off again, the sun flashing on its wings. It was very beautiful to see. Again it was coming around. I ran outside. I watched several runs, each one was different in speed or angle of descent, it looked as if the pilot was practicing or doing tests. You didn't often see airplanes this close.

And then as the show continued here was Clara

Lukaćs coming through the woods from the main house. She wore a white evening gown. She carried her shoes in her hand. She peered up through the trees, she turned, she walked backward, she stopped, she stood on her toes. She moved through patches of light and shade, and reaching the little clearing in front of the cabin, she took me in with a glance and turned to see the plane in its run.

It was very low this time. It drifted down the length of the lake and then dropped below the tree line.

"Are *you* here?" Clara said. She passed into the house and I followed. She stood in the middle of the room with her hands on her hips, and realizing she still held her shoes, she flung them away. At this moment the phone rang. It was in the bedroom and she ran in as if she was going to attack it.

"What!" I heard her shout by way of greeting. A pause. "Yeah, well, I wouldn't count on it!" she said and slammed the phone down.

I waited a minute. When she didn't come out, I moved to the doorway. She was sitting on the edge of her bed in some distraction slipping off one shoulder strap, then the other, shrugging her gown to her waist. Losing all volition, she dropped her hands in her lap and sat hunched over without glamour or grace. Her hair was matted and tears streamed down her cheeks.

She had no degrees of response, she lived hard, and the effect of her crying on my heart was calamitous. Her eyes were swollen almost immediately, her breasts were wet with her tears. Her looks collapsed as if they were a pretense.

"Hey," I said. "Come on. Come on."

After a while she stood up and let the gown fall to her ankles. She had nothing on underneath. She was big-breasted for such a thin narrow-shouldered girl. She stepped out of the gown and went into the bathroom and a moment later I heard the shower running. Her behind was small and firm, if a bit on the flat side. The prominence of her backbone made me smile. It made me think of the scrawny backs on sunburned little girls who came to the carnival in their bathing suits and convened at the cotton candy.

While she showered I found a percolator and put up some coffee. She came out wrapped in a white bath towel with a big maroon *FWB* monogrammed on the front. She accepted a mug of coffee and sat on the couch with her legs folded under her and held the mug with both hands as if for warmth. She had washed her hair, which lay about her head in wet curls, she was no longer crying but the exercise had left her eyes glistening and as she looked at me I wondered how I could have found anything to criticize. I had never in my life seen a woman more beautiful.

"This place is getting on my nerves," she said. "How do I get out of here?"

"I'll take care of it, leave it to me," I said without a moment's hesitation. Without a moment's hesitation. She glanced at me as she sipped her coffee. I waited for my justice. I wondered if I had taken her too literally if she would laugh now crack my heart with her laughter. But she said nothing and seemed satisfied enough by my assurance. Sun filled the room. She put her cup on the floor and curled up on the sofa with her back to me.

Drops of water glittered in her hair. After a while I realized she had gone to sleep.

I ran out of there determined not to be amazed. I should concentrate on what I was going to do next.

Amazement would set me back. I wanted to sing, I
was exhilarated to madness. But the way to bring this
off was to think of my brazen hopes as reasonable and
myself as a calm practical person matter-of-factly making a life for himself that was no more than he de-
served.

T HEN BENNETT HIMSELF WAS SUDDENLY IN FULL
force in my life like a storm that had arrived.

I found myself that same morning with three or four
of the groundkeepers, each of us with a pick or shovel
on our shoulders, we were hurrying to a site in the
woods off the main bridle path. Bennett was waiting.
He was standing on a hill of some sort. His horse was
tethered to a tree along the trail. "Come up here," he
called.

We climbed up the face of an enormous boulder imbedded in the ground. "I've always wondered about
this," he said. "I want it exposed."

The foreman of us, an older man long in the Bennett service, took off his cap and scratched his head.
"You want us to dig this rock up?" he asked.

"Dig around it," Bennett said. "You see here? This
is the top of it, we're standing on top of it. That's what

this rise is. I want the whole thing uncovered, I don't know why it's here."

The workmen had trouble believing what he wanted. Bennett didn't get mad. Instead, he took one of the picks and started going at it himself. "You see?" he called out, breathing hard between swings of the pick. "Work it away, like this. You see that, how it extends? Goes all the way over here."

"Here, Mr. Bennett," the foreman said. "Don't you be doing that. You, you," he said to us. "Get to work."

So we started digging out a boulder that might be the size of a dirigible. Bennett watched each of us to see that we understood.

"That's the way," he said. "That's what I want."

He was sturdy and vigorous. Moved around a lot. A short wide-shouldered man with a large head. His hair was white but very full and combed as I combed mine, to a pompadour. He was well-tanned. Blue eyes. A handsome blunt-faced old bastard in a riding outfit.

I had expected someone older, more restrained.

He climbed down off the rise and for several minutes crashed around in the woods nearby to see if he could find another rock like it. "You see," he shouted, "it's the only one. Damnedest thing!" he called out as if we were all colleagues on some archaelogical expedition.

Then he mounted his horse and rode off in the direction of the stables. As soon as he was out of sight the foreman leaned on his shovel, took off his cap and wiped his forehead with the back of his hand. "Jesus Mary and Joseph," he said.

We all sat down on the boulder.

But a while later two more diggers came along

flushed from their dens, and soon there were a half-dozen of us standing shirtless in the woods swinging our picks and shovels at this mountainous stone.

It was interesting to me how the impulse of the man transformed into the hard work of the rest of us. By our digging we suggested something really important was going on, someone passing by would look at us and think it was serious—we ourselves were proof of the seriousness of the thing.

I had expected not to like F. W. Bennett. But he was insane. How could I resist that? There was this manic energy of his, a mad light in his eye. He was free. That was what free men were like, they shone their freedom over everyone.

I didn't want to think what he did with Clara. I could not dream that she could matter to him in any way at all that I would recognize. I swung my pick. All the intelligence I had of him, from his house and his lands and his train and his resident poets, had not prepared me for the impersonal force of him, the frightening freedom of him.

In the late afternoon we knocked off work, having unearthed the boulder to its southern polar slope. It sat now in an enormous trench at the bottom of which were packed several other stones. It looked as if it weighed several tons. On the way back we stopped in front of the main house to report these findings. Bennett stood on his front porch. He was very pleased. "We'll take it as far down as it goes, boys," he said. "And tomorrow we'll look for markings. I want to see if it has markings."

Apparently as he gazed at these dirty and sweat-stained workmen he saw in the face of one something that might have been disbelief.

"You, Joe," he said to me, "you think it's just a rock, don't you?"

I was so stunned that he knew my name I didn't know what to say.

"Come inside. I want you to see something." He turned and went in the house.

Someone reached over and took the pick from my shoulder. I heard a snicker. I followed F. W. Bennett into his front hall and went past the stairway of halved logs to the sunken living room.

There was a shimmering light on the ceiling, a reflection of the lake. But the floor was in shadow. In one corner, on a table, was a book with line drawings of primitive stone monuments: in all cases one large boulder rested on three or four smaller ones.

"You see?" he said. "I'm not as crazy as you think. They put down these megaliths, or dolmens, for their fallen chiefs."

He strode around the room lecturing me on the burial practices of ancient Indian tribes of New England. He compared them to the ancient burial practices of the Western desert tribes. Indoors he seemed older. He was vigorous and moved constantly but his voice was somewhat hoarse, it suggested age.

I stood in my filthy dark greens wondering how I was going to get out of there.

A maid came in holding a phone on a long cord. She brought it to his side and held it for him on her palm while he picked up the receiver. "Yes?" He continued to move about, and the maid in her light green uniform followed him dutifully where he went, dealing with the cord so that it wouldn't snag on the furniture. He was getting information. He asked short questions —How many? What time?—and listened to lengthy answers. I looked out the bay wall of windows. The late afternoon shadows made the lake a brilliant dark blue water.

On the terrace a woman was arranging flowers in a vase. I realized I was looking at Lucinda Bailey Bennett, the aviatrix. The small shock of seeing someone famous.

"You don't know how to work cameras, by any chance?"

The phone was gone. Bennett was talking to me.

"I've got all this equipment here but I can't get the hang of it myself," he said. "I want to take proper pictures of the excavation and send them out to see if I'm right."

"I don't know anything about cameras," I said.

"I thought you were smart . . . Well," he said, "I wanted to take a look at you, anyway, to see if you belong with me on a permanent basis. What's *your* opinion?"

"You mean a job?" I said.

"That's what I mean. You think you ought to be hired?"

I swallowed. "No," I said.

"No?" He seemed amused.

"I couldn't live here," I said. "It's not for me."

He laughed out loud. "You seemed to have adapted well enough. From what I understand you've made the place your own."

Something outside had caught his eye. He stepped onto the terrace, closing the glass doors behind him, and stood calling down the hill to somebody at the boathouse.

My muscles were tight and my hands clenched. I tried to loosen up.

Mrs. Bennett glanced through the window to where I was and said something to her husband. He turned to her smiling and said something back and she looked again in at me briefly, a half smile on her face. She was a very elegant, honest-looking lady, very well composed, with brown hair cut short, no make-up or anything like that, she wore a loose sweater and a longish skirt and low-heeled shoes. I thought you would not be able to tell, if you didn't know, that this slim handsome woman with her flowers knew how to fly the hell out of airplanes.

And then it came to me he was telling her who the boy inside was. The one and only Joe of Paterson. She was so elegant I realized that what I had written in anger and pride was from another point of view pathetic. I felt betrayed, like a child who gives out his most precious secret and hears it laughed about.

I turned to leave. I thought how powerful this Bennett was if I could be made to feel so bad from just a moment or two of his attention.

"Just a minute, Joe," he called. "I'm not finished with you."

He went past me into the front hall and then down the corridor of the other wing of the house. He opened a door and beckoned to me.

A large room filled with books, cabinets with silver cups, photographs of Mrs. Bennett standing in front of airplanes, Mr. Bennett in a railroad engineer's cap waving from the controls of a steam locomotive, photographs of cars and horses and presidents and governors and film stars. There were globes on stands and big dictionaries on lecterns, a ticker-tape machine under glass—a whole life of glory was in this room.

Bennett sat down behind his desk and took a manila

folder out of a drawer and studied the papers in it for several minutes while I stood before him.

Without looking up, he said, "Are your injuries healed?"

"I suppose."

"Have you been in touch with your parents?"

"My parents?"

"They signed a waiver," he said, removing a document from the folder. "You mean you haven't talked to them? I am not at fault for the injuries you incurred on my property. They received two hundred and fifty dollars."

"How do you know my parents?"

"We looked through your billfold. You might have been on your way out."

I was too stunned to speak.

"They haven't called or written to see how you're getting along?" He shoved a paper along the desk and I saw at the bottom the shaky signature of my father. "I'm not lying to you," Bennett said. "By right that's your money."

I shook my head.

"You don't want to work for me. Fine. You can go home and if you're smart you can use that money to make money. Buy something and sell it for profit. Anything, it doesn't matter. Some of the great fortunes in this country were built from less."

I pictured my father in the kitchen, coming to terms with this legal paper that had to be signed. Finding my school pen somewhere in a drawer and the bottle with Waterman's ink. Testing the penpoint on the oilcloth that covered the table and then rubbing the ink off with his thumb before it dried. My mother standing at the sink, washing the dishes, disguising the moment of the waiver in their lives as one more ordinary moment.

"No," I said. "It's theirs."

"I'll tell you," Bennett said. "I always respect a man's decision. Never try to argue him out of it. You're not staying here and you're not going home. That leaves you back on the road, doesn't it? Back on the bum. Well, I say why not, if that's what you want. But be sure you can handle it. Just be sure you've got the guts. So that if you have to steal or take a sap to someone's head for a meal, you'll be able to. Every kind of life has its demands, its tests. Can I do this? Can I live with the consequences of what I'm doing? If you can't answer yes, you're in a life that's too much for you. Then you drop down a notch. If you can't steal and you can't sap someone on the head when you have to, you join the line at the flophouse. You get on the bread line. If you can't muscle your way into the bread line, you sit at the curb and hold out your hand. You're a beggar. If you can't whine and wheedle and beg your cup of coffee, if you can't take the billy on the bottoms of your feet—why, I say be a poet. Yes" —he laughed at the thought—"like old Penfield, find your level. Get in, get into the place that's your nature, whether it's running a corporation or picking daisies in a field, get in there and live to it, live to the fullness of it, become what you are, and I'll say to you, you've done more than most men. Most men—and let me tell you, I know men—most of them don't ever do that. They'll work at a job and not know why. They'll marry a woman and not know why. They'll go to their graves and not know why."

He was standing at the window gazing out with his hands behind his back, gently slapping the back of one hand into the palm of the other. "I've never understood it, but there it is. I've never understood how a man could give up his life, give it up, moment by moment, even as he lives it, give it up from the second he's born. But there it is. Bow his head. Agree. Go along. Do what everyone's doing. Let it leach away. Sign it away. Drink it away. Sleep it away."

He was standing at the window meditating, eclipsing the window light so that the dark bulk of him was apparent. He was stocky and short-legged with a large head, like a mountain troll. "Well," he said, "you're brash enough. Where are you going?"

"I don't know. As far as I can get."

He came back to his desk and wrote something on a piece of paper. "You happen to need something—this is a private number, not to be given out, you understand?"

He folded the paper and handed it to me. He gave me a quick glance, one eyebrow arching over the lighted eye of shrewdness. "But don't leave until I've got my dolmen," he said, turning and picking up his telephone.

THE FIRST CHANCE I HAD I HURRIED TO PENFIELD'S. He was the only one who could help me with Clara's escape. That was his word, escape. Clara would leave because with unforgivable haste she'd been removed from the cozy confidences of Loon Lake's master bedroom. But it wouldn't do to tell him that. He thought he was in torment for her sake. He brooded about rescuing her. That's the way poets are, I said to myself. They see what no one else can see, and what is clear to everyone else they don't see.

I found him in bed. His breath rasped. His skin was a strange pink-gray color and it shone in a glaze of perspiration. He stared at me mournfully from his pillows, his blue and bloodshot eyes swimming in helplessness.

Oh God. That was all I needed.

I went out and found Libby in the staff house.

"I'll have nothing to do with you," she said.

"It's not me, Libby. It's Mr. Penfield. Something's wrong with him. I think he needs a doctor."

She looked at me with suspicion. She went ahead of me to the stables and ran up the stairs to keep as much distance between us as she could.

She took one look at the poet and without troubling to remove herself from his hearing said, "There's nothing wrong with him, he just likes to carry on."

"What do you know, Libby?" he cried out, stung.

"I know what a hollow leg is," she said. "Look at this place, it's enough to make anyone sick."

"Get out, get out!" Penfield shouted. "Will everyone torture me? Am I to die with the scorn of servants in my ears?"

She ignored him and with a great flurry went into action, picking up papers books dirty socks.

"Go away," he shouted. "Don't touch a thing, damnit, you're disrupting everything!"

She straightened his bedcovers and plumped up his pillows while he shouted at her to leave him alone.

Furious with both of us, she marched out.

"Joe, there's a bottle of wine under the window seat," Mr. Penfield said.

I wondered what was wrong with me to be so gullible to the claims of this man. He lived here at Loon Lake sloshing in self-pity, the best aspect of him, his gift for poetry, put to the use of unsound notions. Obviously this was the solution of his life. I couldn't change that if I tried. Nobody could.

I handed him the bottle and a glass. He sat up.

"Mr. Penfield, I've got to tell you something," I said, pulling a chair to his bedside. "But I need some information first. Who is Clara? Who were those people who came with her on the train?"

"Tommy Crapo," he said.

"Who?"

"Tommy Crapo. The industrial consultant." He drank off a half-glass of wine. "Don't you read the newspapers? Don't you look at the tabloids? Tommy Crapo who has his picture taken on night-club banquettes with beautiful women."

Color was coming back to his face. He emptied the glass and lay back on his pillows.

"Is he in the rackets?"

"Mr. Crapo is a specialist in labor relations. Yes. I think that's a fair description."

"Does he work for Bennett? Does he knock heads for Bennett?"

He stared at the ceiling. A moment passed. "Why do you ask? You think I should get Miss Lukács away from here, don't you?"

"Well, she's ready."

"What?" He was not used to being taken at his word. He was not equipped for action.

"Miss Lukács is ready to get out of here," I said.

"What?"

"She's ready to make her escape."

I have committed many sins in my life. This precise sin—the sin against poets—is without absolution.

He was out of bed and struggling into a worn maroon robe that had a few tassels left on the belt. I could hear each breath he took. He got on his knees to look under the bed for his slippers. He found them, stood, stepped into them, and then went slapping across the floor, back and forth from one corner of his apartment to another without purpose or intent but busy with agitation.

I sat him down in his reading chair and brought him a cigarette and lit it for him, he held it between thumb and forefinger, his hand shaking.

"What did she say?" he asked.

"She wants me to get her away."

"You?"

"She thinks if you leave together, you'll be too easy to follow. Like a hot car."

"What?"

"Crapo doesn't know me from Adam."

"Crapo is back?"

"He's on his way, Mr. Penfield."

"I see. I see."

"Miss Lukaćs says once she's safe she can get in touch with you."

"She said that?"

"I've worked out a plan but I need money and I need a car."

"Yes, yes, so that's the way it happens. I see. I see." He was not fooled, he was not a fool, the large protuberant eyes stared through me. "Yes, yes. To be absolutely realistic I'm not in the picture. That's all right, it's just, I'm reconciled. The two young ones. Yes."

He kept talking this way.

I had the uncanny feeling that he was translating what I told him into another language. Yet I could hear everything he said. He rose, he seemed to gain strength, he strode back and forth from the window to the door. "Yes, of course, there is more than I knew. Yes. I want this for her. It's just. I put my faith in you, Joe. Yes, take her away from here. Two young people! It's right. Yes, it's the only way."

"I'll need money and a car," I said.

"Of course. Leave it to me. I'll help you. I'll get you both out. You'll see, you'll see. I have resources. Yes. You'll find Warren Penfield comes through. I have resources. I have allies."

He seemed joyful. He clapped his hands together and glanced heavenward to express his joy. In this moment he would rather have died than reveal his anguish.

As I was leaving he stood at the door and pulled

back the sleeve of his robe. "Look here, Joe," he said. He held up his right arm. "The sign of the wild dog! Right?" He gave me a wan but demonstrably brave smile. I had to smile back. I rolled up my sleeve and showed my arm.

"That's right," he said. "You know what two men do who share the sign of the wild dog?" He touched his forearm to mine so that they crossed. "That's right," he said in a husky voice. "My pain is your pain. My life is your life."

Data linkage escape this is not an emergency
Come with me compound with me
A tulip cups the sun quietly in its color
Dixie cups hold chocolate and vanilla
Before the war after the war or
After the war before the war
A man sells me a Dixie cup for a nickel in a dark candy
    store.
The boy stands on the sidewalk in the sun
Licking the face of Joan Crawford free of ice cream.
A boy enjoys ice cream from a wooden spoon in the
    sun
before the war in front of the candy store on the
    corner
while he waits for the light to change. At this moment
    several
things happen. A horse pulling the wagon of a peddler
of vegetables trots by smartly golden balls of dung
    dropping

from the base of its arched tail. Then there was a whirring
in my ears and over the top of Paterson Grade School
Three
a monumental dirigible nosed into view looming so
low
I could see the seams of its paneled silver skin
and human shadows on the windows of its gondola. It
was not
sailing straight through its bow but shouldering the
wind shuddering
dipping and rising in its sea of air. It soared over the
roof
of a tenement and disappeared. At the same time
the traffic light turned green and I crossed from sun to
shade
noting that the not unpleasant odor of fresh horse ma-
nure
abruptly ceased with the change of temperature. In
front of
the shoe repair on Mechanic Street at the sidewalk's
edge
between a Nash and a Hudson parked at the curb a
baby girl
was suspended from her mother's hands her pants
pulled down.
It was desired of this child that she relieve herself there
and then
schoolchildren going past in bunches peddlers at their
cars
mothers pushing strollers and an older boy with ice
cream
stopping shamelessly to watch. And this beautiful little
girl

turned a face of such outrage upon me that I immediately

recognized you Clara and with then saintly inability to withstand

life you closed your eyes and allowed the thin stream of

golden water to cascade to the tar which was instantly black and

shone clearer than a night sky.

IN THE MORNING HACKING AWAY AT THE INDIAN-chief monument, I saw him going down the bridle path, going right by without so much as a glance at the strange work on the rock, walking a few steps, running, walking again hurriedly, on the trail through the woods.

I waited five minutes and then I dropped my shovel and sauntered off. "Where you going!" someone called behind me. I raised my hand to show I knew what I was doing and that I'd be right back.

This was the trail the riders took to get to another shore of the lake, a mile down from the main house. It was hoed regularly to keep it soft—I had done some of that myself. It went through stands of towering pine and over small clearings where the grass was turning tan and gold in the autumn, and then it dropped down into an area where the leaves were falling like snow-flakes. I felt the same turning season in me.

Where the trail cornered, along the shore of the wide lake, was an airplane hangar with a concrete ramp. Mr. Penfield sat on the ramp with his arms around his knees. He was looking at the water. The wind had whipped up a small white chop. Wavelets slapped at the concrete. He didn't seem to notice Lucinda Bailey Bennett coming out of the hangar and walking toward him. She pulled a big red trainman's handkerchief from the pocket of her overalls and wiped her hands.

I ducked around through the underbrush and came within a few feet of them. I could see inside: an engine was suspended from pulleys. A man was guiding it to a workbench.

"What do you do, Lucinda," said Mr. Penfield in a petulant tone. "Paint the innards like a new toy?"

"No, old bear. When I'm through, its innards will be dark and oiled, and refitted to tolerances that will take me to the top of the sky." She stuffed her handkerchief into the pouch of her overalls. "Why are you sulking? I thought you loved me."

"Since I gave up manhood to live here, I make no claims of that sort on anyone."

She smiled. "That's not the report I have."

"Oh, Lucinda," he said with a groan, and he turned to look up at her.

"So much suffering." She touched the back of her hand to his temple. "Poor Warren."

"How much better for me if when I came here my throat had been ripped out."

She sighed. "Yes," she said, "I suppose so."

After a moment she turned back and he lifted himself grunting to his feet. He lumbered after her. "Forgive me," he called.

"Oh, Warren, it's such a bore when you whine." She went into the hangar.

"Yes," he cried out bitterly. "Indeed. My agony does not divert." And he followed her.

I couldn't hear them now. The hangar was lit by electric lights that glimmered very faintly through the brightness of the morning. But I saw them moving around, she working and he talking with grand gestures. Every once in a while I heard the sound of his voice, and I knew Mr. Penfield well enough to know he was in good form, eloquent in his self-dramatization. I hoped so, because he was talking for me.

The man who'd been helping came out, lit a cigarette and went off along the trail. I moved to the hangar itself, staying out of sight of the doorway. I leaned my back to the wall.

"You have a good nature," I heard Mrs. Bennett say.

"Oh my dear!"

"Would you like to go on a flight? Probably not. But a really long flight. Just the two of us. Would you consider it?"

"What? Where?"

"I don't know. The Far East. Shall we do that? Fly across the Pacific."

"The Far East?"

"Yes, pooh bear. A long flight. You and I. Oh, that's a *good* idea! Who knows what might happen." She burst out laughing. "Warren, if you could see the expression on your face! The dismay!"

"Lucinda, what—How is it possible? Am I misunderstood?"

"Oh, foolish thing—I don't mean that! Good God!" She was merry now. "It's a practice made too thoroughly disreputable by its devotees, don't you think?"

* * *

That evening the four of them met for dinner. I stood on the terrace just out of the light cast through the windows and I watched them at their drinks. A fire blazed in the huge fireplace. Mounted prey gazed down at them. Clara was wearing a gown of sequined silver. She looked cheap. She sat staring at the floor, cowed, maybe even stunned into silence, by the nuances of civilization in that room. The gentlemen wore black tie, in which Mr. Penfield managed to look as rumpled and ill-prepared for life as ever. With his characteristic expression of appeal for love and under-standing he glanced habitually at the others, but espe-cially Clara. Lucinda Bennett smiled faintly and kept up her end of the conversation. Only F. W. Bennett seemed to be enjoying himself. He became so ani-mated he stood up to deliver his sentences. He went to a table behind the leather sofa and held up a large flat book opened, and resting on his arm, and he read from it and laughed and looked at the others for their reaction.

I went through the woods to Clara's cabin and found her luggage standing just inside the front door. There were three bags and a hatbox. I got all of them under my arms or hanging from my hands, and strug-gled up the hill to the garage on the far side of the tennis court. This was the old Loon Lake stable. It housed five cars. In the last stall was Mrs. Bennett's car, a rarely used gray two-door Mercedes-Benz with a canvas top and spare tires in the front fender wells. I looked for the ignition key where Mr. Penfield had told me to—in the bud vase on the right-hand side in the back. Yes. I packed the bags in the trunk, which was not large, and put the hatbox in the back seat. I turned on the map light and by its glow learned the

European-style shifting. There were four gears, and a diagram of their positions was imprinted on the mother-of-pearl knob of the floor shift. The dust on the seat cracked under me. I flicked at it with a chamois cloth. The odometer showed less than ten thousand miles. Then I saw it was not even miles, it was kilometers. Lucinda Bennett had told Mr. Penfield it was a 1933 model. Clearly, her interest in machines did not include cars. The license plate was up to date, however.

I swung open the doors as quietly as I could and got in and started the engine. I backed out. It was a noisy car—I later found it was only forty horsepower—and I drove it the few yards to the gas pump shushing it as if it were a baby. I filled it with Mr. Bennett's personal ethyl and then I gave each tire a shot of his air. I was wearing his knickers and argyle sweater and brown-and-white saddle shoes. I tried not to get them dirty.

I was ready to go. I waited behind the wheel. It was a snug little car. The seats were gray leather. The doors opened front to back. I went over some road maps. I sat there and got the feeling of the car and worried about driving it well, and wondered where to go and what I would say to Clara Lukács and what she would say to me. I worried that people seeing me behind the wheel would think I was rich. I didn't once reflect on the lately peculiar conforming of life to my desires. I didn't think of Lucinda Bennett's generosity or despair, or Mr. Penfield's, nor even reach the most obvious conclusion, that I was leaving Loon Lake in somewhat better condition than I had come. Calculating, heedless, and without gratitude, I accepted every circumstance that had put me there, only gunning my mind to the future, wanting more, expecting more, too intent on what was ahead to sit back and give thanks or to laugh or to feel bad.

I peered through the windshield. I watched the trees shaking in the night wind. I unlatched the canvas top and pushed it back a bit and looked at the stars, which seemed to shimmer and blur as if the wind were blowing through them.

Eventually she got there, hurrying along with Mr. Penfield holding her arm, while she held her gown off the ground to keep from tripping. She wore a fur jacket over the gown. He opened the door, but before she could slide in, he grabbed her and hugged her and started to gabble something. I saw all this with their heads cut off. I saw her push him away. "War-rin, please!" she said.

Then she was in the car beside me, in an atmosphere of fur and cold air, and she slammed the door. Penfield peered in, then ran around the front of the car to the driver's side. I started the engine and threw the toggle switch for the headlights. I adjusted the throttle. I rolled down my window and he thrust something in my hand, a wad of bills. "I wish it was more," he said. He gave us advice of many kinds, cheerful assurances, warnings about the road, the weather, appeals to keep in touch, phone numbers on bits of paper, promises, vows, thrown kisses—and to this fitful love song I put the car into first, and off we lurched down the road.

We were taking what was called the back road, away from the main house; there was a sudden bend, and Mr. Penfield, waving in the night in his black tie, veered out of my rear view.

I leaned forward, attentive to the clutching, and gradually, as we made our way bumping and sliding over this gravelly unpaved circuit through the Bennett preserve, I got the hang of it. We drove for quite a while. I glanced at her. In the glow of the dashboard I saw her young face.

I think now of that long drive down through the forest to the state road, dogs appearing from nowhere to gallop yelping alongside, their breath sounding metallic, like the engine; and disappearing just as suddenly, then again one or two of them, then for a mile a beating pack; and she saying nothing, only holding the leather strap by her window, looking out to the side, to the front, her eyes following them tracking them, the youth of her illuminated in the low light. Finally we outdistanced them all.

She sat back in her seat. She took a cigarette out of her purse and lit it.

"What do you think he'll do when he finds you gone?" I said.

"An interesting question," she said.

And so we descended from Loon Lake, Clara's clear eyes fixed on the farthest probe of the headlights, and I looking at her every other moment, in her composure of total attention, going with the ride.

E VERY MORNING SHE SWEPT THE DIRT PATH OUT-side the monastery wall. She always wore the same thing, a simple kimono and those wooden slippers, you know? She was fifteen or sixteen years old but her hair was cut in the bowl cut of young children. Hair as black as night. She never smiled, but when she glanced at me there was such a flash of recognition from my soul that I went weak with joy.

Oh, Warren.

I used to wake up before dawn and do my chores and manage always to be at the gate when the sun rose and she came to do hers. She was the daughter of some working family down the street. They sweep the streets there with straw brooms. The unpaved streets. They sweep the dirt, compose it. They compose everything, they pick the fallen leaves one at a time.

How did you get to her?

I wish you wouldn't phrase it that way, Lucinda. We knew each other on sight. We had to. My Japanese was less than rudimentary. Her English nonexistent. Only the upper class studied English. It was a great social distinction to know English. A workman's daughter couldn't aspire to that.

Light me a cigarette, will you?

I have in my life just three times seen a face in dark light, at dusk or dawn or against a white pillow, in which there is a recognizably perfect perception of the world, some matched reflection of the world in her eye's light as terrifying and beautiful in equal measure. Am I coherent?

A moral light? Is that what you mean?

She lives through her fear to her curiosity, there is a stillness of apprehension, like an animal's stillness of perfect apprehension of its predator, and it is gallantry to break the heart.

I wish we had known each other when we were young.

Her father and several uncles made up a delegation to complain about my conduct to the monastery officials, who of course did not have to be told. I had broken every rule in the book. At the moment both sides gathered to come down on us we slipped away together and took the train to Tokyo. We found a room.

Is this when you became lovers?

I suppose so. I thought I could support us by teaching American customs and manners to Japanese businessmen. They wanted that. They were studying us intently. They listened to jazz and danced the Charleston. You're not crying, are you?

It makes me sad. I know what happened.

I left the house one morning. I had an appointment to see someone at the U.S. embassy. It was a Saturday, the first day in September, 1923. As I walked down the street, I lost my balance but suddenly people everywhere were screaming. The streets were cracking open. I ran back, the city was falling down everywhere, I climbed over rubble, I saw her coming after me with her arms raised, the cobblestones heaved, the street broke open, it filled with water, I reached her and grabbed her hand just as the earth sank away and she fell in, she fell from my hands and where the earth had been there was a steaming lake. What is that up ahead, Lucinda? It looks very dark.

It's nothing. A line squall.

THE NIGHTS SEEMED TO RACE BY. THE WEATHER got colder. The freaks got nastier. We came one day to a town less promising than any I'd seen. It was shut down and boarded. One tavern and one store were open. I don't remember the name of this town, it was like a tree with just a branch or two still alive.

In a lot beside the boarded-up railroad depot Sim Hearn gave the signal and the carney put up for business. In the evening we turned on the lights and a few mountain people straggled in but most of the time the freaks talked to each other because nothing else was doing. The rides went around empty. I thought Sim Hearn had lost his marbles.

The next night the same thing, the wind blew through the booths and rattled the tent flaps, they sounded like over the mountains somewhere there was some gang war of Tommy guns going on.

I thought Sim Hearn was telling us the season was over by enacting the news. The cook built a fire on the ground and heated an ash can of water. He scrubbed his pots and pans with brown soap. Other people were packing. Mrs. Hearn grabbed my arm and we stepped behind a wagon.

"Hearn goes no farther," she said. "Look, a sweater I have for you so you wouldn't be cold."

She was a pain in the ass with her presents. She brought me cigarettes, oranges, she washed my clothes, all in secret of course. Nobody knew about it except the whole carney.

It chilled me to think Sim Hearn might know it. But his distance from me was unchanged and his peculiar authority maintained itself in my mind. It was as if no matter what I did to his wife I could never break through that supreme indifference. I decided no man was that godlike. I decided he didn't know. I wished he did know. Then I wouldn't be some nameless creature so low as to be beneath his line of vision.

The next morning we struck everything but the show tent. We raised the wood shutters on the wagons and nailed them shut. We pushed the wagons into an old car barn across the tracks from the depot. After lunch a few people left with their bags or bundles. Nobody said so long or even looked at anyone else. I think I was shocked. Despite all my other feelings about the carney, I could believe it was a privilege to be attached to it. It angered me that people would walk away as if Hearn Bros. had no more distinction than a mission flop.

On the other hand, why should it be different? Sim Hearn couldn't care less if any one of them lived or died and they knew that. He was going to take the trucks down to Florida for the winter and let them get down there on their own. If they showed up, he'd hire them; if they didn't, that was all right too.

Fanny the Fat Lady's wagon was in place and hadn't been moved. I saw Mrs. Hearn coming out of her trailer. "Fanny wheezes like calliope," she said.

"Well, why doesn't someone get a doctor?"

She put her hand on my cheek and looked in my eyes. "I worry to think someday if we are not together what will happen to you."

Several of the freaks were leaving in a group. I was told to take a truck and drive them about fifteen miles to a town called Chester, where there was a spur line to Albany. It was the afternoon, already getting dark. In the cab with me sat the woman who took care of Fanny. The whole ride she wept and blew her nose. She spoke to herself in Spanish as if her running stream of thoughts and sorrows came up over the banks every now and then. She thought I wasn't looking when she lifted her skirt and fingered the metal clip of her garter to make sure it was fastened properly. I saw tucked in the top of her stocking a wad of bills that looked like a lot of money.

I let off the truckload of freaks and their keepers in Chester, New York, and they hopped, climbed or were lowered from the tailgate. They went limping and scuttling into the waiting room carrying their bags like anyone. Why not? They were mostly immigrants, after all—the same people but with a twist who worked for pennies in the sawmills or stood on the bread lines.

But I imagined the stationmaster seeing through his grill this company of freaks in ordinary streetclothes approaching him with questions of schedule and tickets.

Why didn't I get on the train with them? Did I really want to drive a truck to Florida? Did I want to bang Mrs. Magda Hearn in more states of the Union?

I thought of the freaks as pilgrims or revolutionaries of some angry religion nobody knew anything about yet.

When I got back it was already dark. I could tell something was wrong, there were lots of cars there and wagon teams. I cut the engine, and stood on the running board. Beyond the lot was a hill that rose steeply, blacker than the sky, I could see its outline against the blue-black space of sky behind it. I thought I heard a scream. I listened—it was something else, a drumming of the earth or the sound of a rug being beaten. I walked toward the show tent, there was the dimmest light in there. A man stepped out of the shadow and put his hand on my arm. A flashlight shone in my eyes.

"Who's this?" a voice said.

And then I heard Magda Hearn. "It's all right. He's with the show."

My arm was still held and I could feel the consideration of this intelligence in the mind behind the light. The flashlight went off. I made out the figure of a state trooper, blocked hat and gun and Sam Browne belt. Then my arm was released, the marks of the fingers still on me, like the afterimage on the eye.

Magda Hearn was walking me toward the show tent. "Joe," she said, "I want you to see, to understand. And I wait for you in the car. Do you hear me?"

"What's going on?" I said. "What are the police doing here?"

"Joe, please to listen." She was whispering in my ear and in each cycle of her crippled gait, the sibilance rose and fell in waves of urgency.

Then I passed through the flaps.

The show tent had a few rows of wooden bleachers and a small ring where the ponies could run around and the bareback sisters, if they were so inclined, could do their turns. A cat act had been featured here for a while.

The bleachers were empty. One bulb burned from the tent pole. Eighty, maybe a hundred men stood in a circle in the dirt of the ring. I couldn't see over their backs but I heard the not unfamiliar night music, the grunts and gurgling moans and squeals of Fanny the Fat Lady. As the rhythm got faster the crowd shouted encouragement. Then I heard that peculiar basso thumping as if the earth itself was being drummed. Then an abrupt silence and the hoarse male roar of expiration. Whistles and cheers came from the crowd, men turned outward, I saw them drinking from bottles, exchanging money. Staggering through the ring, buttoning his pants, was a grifter I recognized. He sank down on his knees beside me, removed a flask from his back pocket and took a long pull.

Some sort of hot shame rose from the roots of my sex into my stomach and chest: it felt like illness. I pushed forward and saw Fanny on her back, arms and legs flung outward. She was naked. She lay twitching, each spasm jerking her flesh into ripples. She wheezed and fought for breath. The sweated slathered flesh was caked in dirt, but with white crevasses in the folds of her and a red blotch in the middle. I was pushed aside and spun around. A moment later another lover had fallen on her. The crowd yelled and jammed up around me. She was quickly brought to pitch, her great back rising and thumping into the earth, but this one didn't last long, and to great merry raucous hoots and jeers he stumbled out of the ring.

Almost immediately another rube was moving forward for his turn. I jumped him just as he unbuckled his belt. I knocked him down and kicked him in the groin. He yowled, doubling up and clutching himself and I took his place crouching beside Fanny, facing them all, my fists clenched. I was screaming something, I don't remember what, it stunned them for a second, and then they were laughing and taunting me and shouting at me to wait my turn.

Fanny lay there trembling in her agony and her eyes were rolled into her head. Her mouth was open and giving off gasping animal wheezes. Maniacally, I felt betrayed by her, as if life itself, the human pretense. I became enraged with her! In my nostrils, mixed with the sharp fume of booze, was an organic stench, a bitter foul smell of burning nerves, and shit and scum.

Then something flew out at me, a pint bottle, or a rock, and caught me low on the forehead. I went down, dazed, clutching my eyes, bright lights in my brain. I had fallen on Fanny, she was like some soft rotten animal carcass. Her arms helplessly went around me. I was panicked and tried to get free. My struggles were mistaken—I was pulled out of her grasp by my feet and dragged through the dirt and kicked and rolled and yanked to my feet and given a clout on the side of the head.

I found myself on my knees, behind the crowd. I was wet. Blood streamed in my eye. But the ceremony continued. There were men drooling there. There were onanists. There were gamblers betting on the moment of death. Later there were men leaping on her, on each other, squatting on her head, crawling over her, falling on her, shoving bottles in her. There were gallants calling for order, for some law of decency if all pleasure was not to be lost. And Fanny giving up a human appearance by degrees, trumpeting her ecstasies to the killing passion of the rubes.

From one only was there absolute quiet in this mayhem. I looked at him. His face was hidden in the shadow of his hat brim. You wouldn't know his connection with these spermy rites except for the indolence of his stance as he leaned against the bleacher supports with his bony arms folded and his ankles crossed. And I could swear I heard, through the hoarse cries and shouts and shrieking and orgiastic death, the thoughtful and preoccupied sucking of Sim Hearn's tongue on his teeth.

Riding over the mountain in the Model A, Joe became aware of where he was. She accelerated, the headlights brightened; she braked, the headlights dimmed. The bones of his legs sounded the ground pitch of the engine. Mrs. Hearn's face luminous in the night, she urged the car forward with her chin, her furrowed brow, her shoulders putting english on the turns. At the bottom of a hill she gunned it, halfway up plunged with her left leg, shifted to second, she came over the tops of the hills with her horn blowing, headlights making a quick stab at the night sky.

"Of course they never live long, such creatures—the heart won't beat for them...All summer Sim Hearn watches—he watches and then he sees the signs—she doesn't take breath as she should—from the bed she cannot lift herself...The people know Hearn—he gives something special at end of summer, a grand finale...The word goes through the mountains...Look where we are—we make time better than I hoped."

In the early hours of the morning she judged us safely away and turned into a motor court and paid for a cabin in the pines farthest from the road. Wedged into the rumble seat was my broken-down valise with everything I possessed in the world. She had packed it for me. I carried it and her frayed black Gladstone into the room. She locked the car and locked the cabin door behind us and pulled the shades and then pulled the light cord.

The bed had a khaki blanket but no sheets. Two lumpy gray pillows. Magda Hearn rummaged in her bag for a white cotton face towel. She spread the towel on top of the bureau. The room had the shit smell of old untreated wood. She removed from her purse a manila envelope and from the envelope removed a stack of greenbacks which she placed on the cotton towel.

"Sim knows to get the money out before the fun starts," she said. "To Albany to the bank he thinks I am going."

She wet her thumb on her lower lip and stood at the bureau counting the money. I sat down on the bed and took off my shoes and socks. She wet her thumb on the inside of her lower lip, pulling it down so that for a moment her teeth showed her expression went slack. She was a while counting.

"Fifteen hundred and eighty-four dollars!"

She dug in her purse and extracted a wallet and from this withdrew another wad of bills.

"And plus salary which he never paid!" she said in a tone of vengeful triumph. The thumb applied to the red inside of her lip. She counted aloud this time. "Two hundred I squeeze from you, you bastard!"

She opened her Gladstone, interrupting herself to press her lips strongly on my mouth.

She pulled the string tie of a small canvas coin sack and spilled a stream of coins on the bed.

She lay on the bed making separate piles of nickels and dimes and quarters and halves, the little piles collapsed and came together because she was shaking the bed with her guttural glee. She started over, she was keen on pennies, too—if there had been coins of smaller denominations, she would have counted them, too. She was ready to count coins forever and to bitterly calculate the suffering she had done for each one.

"Joe Joe Joe! Tomorrow we trade his car and its license and buy new. We drive to California you and me. We are in our new car on way to California before even he thinks is something wrong!"

She gave up the count and lay back on her back in the coins. She lifted her arms. "Come to me, come to Magda. You know what?" Kissing me, running hands on me, opening one by one the buttons on my fly. "To Hollywood we are going. I have read the magazines, I understand the movie business. I sell my life story. A film of my life! Everyone will know who Magda is."

She unbuckled my belt, she opened the buttons of my shirt. She kissed my chest and pulled the shirt down off my shoulders. "And who knows who knows, with your looks, my Joseph, with your body, why you cannot be movie star? And we will love each other and have great sooccess. Shall we?" Laughing, going down on me. "Shall we?"

She had no idea I had actually caught evil as one catches a fever, she didn't understand this, she thought my passion matched hers. I wanted to do for her what had been done to the Fat Lady, I wanted the force of a hundred men in unholy fellowship, I went at her like a murderous drunkard.

I fucked past her joy into her first alarm, I saw on her face under the weak glare of the hanging bulb the dilated eye. I was enraged by the flaws of her, the unnatural cleft of her left hip, one buttock was actually atrophied, the raised veins behind the knees, the hanging breasts like deflated balloons, the yellowed face with loosened folds of skin at the neck rising in parallel rows as she turned her head from me this stinking Hungarian hag this thieving crone bitch with the gall to think she had me for her toy boy her lover chuffing now like a fucking steam engine I brought the tears to her eyes she would acknowledge nothing she resisted and then the voice did come, and then the voice louder and more insistent, and finally she seemed to be urging me along as if we were together, the lying cunt in the Pine Grove Motor Court, our music mingling with the night wind in the pines the tree trunks creaking the million crickets. I ended and began again. We wrestled. She begged me to stop. Tears of mourning came from my eyes. I let her fall asleep. I woke her, made her moan. At one point the coins sticking to the wet ass, the wet belly, I invented a use of Magda Hearn so unendurable to her that she fell twisting from the trapeze, she flung herself off the bed—a moment's silence, then the sickening shaming sound of bone and flesh slamming into the floor, a grunt. I lay on my back on the bed not daring to look, I heard a small soprano cry, a deeper moan, a whispered curse. I lay still. After a while I realized I was listening to the snores of an exhausted human being.

I thought I saw the first crack of light under the window shade. I got off the bed and rolled my clothes and shoes into a bundle. I grabbed the stack of bills from the bureau. I unlatched the door quietly and closed it behind me. There were no other guests at the Pine Grove Motor Court. A thin frost lay on the windshield of the Model A. The wind blew.

With all my might I reared back and threw the bills into the wind. I thought of them as the Fat Lady's ashes.

I found a privy up the hill behind the cabins and next to it an outdoor shower. I stood in the shower of cold springwater and looked up at the swaying tops of the pine trees and watched the sky lighten and heard through the water and the toneless wind the sounds of the first birds waking.

I dried myself as best I could and put on my clothes in a tremble of stippled skin and turned my back on the cabins and struck off through the woods. I had no idea where I was going. It didn't particularly matter. I ran to get warm. I ran into the woods as to another world.

AT KAMAKURA HE CLIMBED THE SPIRAL STAIRS inside the largest Buddha in the world. In the head of the largest Buddha, on the ledge of its chin, sat a tiny Buddha facing in the opposite direction. Simple idolatry held no interest for him, but a religion that joked held genuine interest. He felt all at once the immense power of a communication that used no words. I acknowledge Warren's lifelong commitment—cancel lifelong commitment—fatal attraction for any kind of communication whether from words, flags, pigeons or the touch of fingertips in hope of a common language, but we must remember how we are vulnerable to the repetition of our insights so that they tend to come to us not as confirmation of something we already know but as genuine discoveries each and every time. And so he descended, and by degrees over a period of several days, drifted south along the route of the old Tokaido. He saw thousands of Buddhas lined up in trays in the tourist shops or ranked in legions at the shrines, some in lead, some in wood, some carved in stone and dressed in little knitted caps and capes. He came to see in this ubiquitous phenomenon the Buddha's godlike propensity of self-division, the endless fractioning of himself into every perceivable aspect, an allegory made by the people of Japan from the cellular process of life. Thus enlightened, he turned his eyes on the people in the streets and the narrow shopping arcades, old women in black slapping along on their sandals, black-haired children of incredible beauty staring at him with their thumbs stuck in their plump cheeks, giggling pairs of young women in brightly colored kimonos, old shopkeepers with wispy goatees bowing as he passed, thoughtful peddlers, and young men who stopped in their tracks to glare at him and bear themselves with brazen umbrage—they were all the Buddha too in his infinite aspect. Traveling down this avenue of thought lit only by stone lanterns filled with small stones in lieu of flames, he saw the true dereliction of the planet and realized anew that convictions of friendship, love, the assumption of culture, the certainty of calendars were fragile constructs of the imagination, and there was no place to live that was truly home, neither for him nor for the multitudinous islanders of Japan.

In this he-took-for-appropriate state of mind, Warren arrived one day at road's end, Kyoto, the strange city whose chief industry was meditation. He wandered from one monastery to the next, there were whole neighborhoods of them, but where, where was the sign that one was for him? He was afflicted with a fluttering humility, not daring even to make inquiries, hovering at this gate or in that garden or touching down for just a moment of indecision before the small window with the visitor admission in yen painted in black calligraphy on white cardboard stuck into the grate as if he were looking for a movie to see. Late in the afternoon, weary and full of self-condemnation, he

happened to stumble up the step of a wooden verandah overlooking one of these beautiful monastery gardens of raked gravel and moss and stone. Thus
launched, his large Caucasian person hurtled through a
rice-paper door, splintering its laths, and like an infant
being born, he found himself with the back half of him
still on the porch side of the door and the front half in
a room, looking with wide, even horrified eyes at the
benign polished wood Buddah sitting facing him with a
little altar of flowers on either side and the sinuous
smoke of incense appearing to squinch up its eyes. He
had made a terrible thunderous racket but nobody
came running, nobody came shouting, and after he
crawled the rest of the way into the room he set about
calmly picking up the pieces and preparing in his mind
the self-demeaning speech by which he would beg the
chance to make the most extended and profound resti-
tution. As it happened, the monastery was empty; he
was to learn it was the rare annual holiday of this particular establishment in which everyone was set free
for twenty-four hours. Only after searching the
grounds did Warren find an old caretaker willing to
come look and see the awful thing he had done. This
old caretaker was smoking a cigarette, which he held
in his teeth. He took in smoke with each inhalation
and with each exhalation smoke streamed out of his
nostrils. He gazed at the carnage, the plumes of smoke
from his nostrils indicating the depth and strength of
each drawn breath, and it seemed to fascinate him that
such a perfect and modest structure as a sliding paper
door should have been turned into this. He was a very
short, extremely bald old man, and he wore a torn
ribbed undershirt and a pair of dirty white muslin
knickers with flapping ties at the waist but the peculiar

thing was that he was not unpleasant to look upon, it did not create feelings of pity or fear or other degrees of patronization to look upon him. He picked up a broken length of lath and looked at it and asked a question in unintelligible Japanese. I'll pay for it, Warren said and removed from his pocket a wad of yen. He unfolded the bills and looked at the old man squinting at the money through the cigarette smoke. Warren peeled off one bill and put it in the man's hand. Then another. Then another. He kept waiting for a sign that he'd met the cost. He hesitated. The old man looked at him and peremptorily slapped his arm with the lath. Warren was so astonished he dropped the whole wad of bills in the old man's hand. The caretaker put the bills into the pockets of his voluminous knickers, looked up at the Caucasian and swatted him again with the flat of the stick, this time across the side of his face. Then he laughed, and in so doing released his cigarette, which fell from his teeth and lay on the wooden floor glowing. Immediately Warren, thinking the whole place would go up, stepped on the tobacco ember with his large shoe, only realizing in that moment the defacement he had committed by stepping with street shoes on the monastery floors.

But the caretaker had turned and headed back to his garden shed with its straw brooms and clay pots and small pyramids of gravel. Warren experienced the uncanny sense of a sharply learned lesson. He slept that night at a Western hotel in the downtown section of Kyoto and found in the nightstand drawer a volume in English that seemed to be the Buddhist equivalent of the Bible. Gautama was an Indian prince kept at home by his father so as not to see life in any aspect but its most luxurious. But one day he went out and saw a beggar, an old crippled man, a monk and a corpse. He was thus able to conclude despite his own royal existence that life was suffering. Why couldn't he have figured that out without leaving the palace? Warren wondered. If death exists, life has to be suffering. Did his father hide death from Gautama? How was that done? The book said the cause of all suffering was desire, the desire to have the desire to be. Perhaps a prince would never experience the desire to have, but how could he avoid the desire to be? If desire by its nature is not gratified before it realizes itself, does it not exist in palaces too? Does it not exist especially in palaces? Nevertheless, he liked the story. He trusted Gautama Siddhartha and the simplicity of his reasoning. Not many people could get away with that sort of reasoning. He trusted the eightfold path for defeating desire and transcending suffering.

Early the next morning Warren went back to the monastery. The place was a shambles. Doors and shoji walls were splintered and torn everywhere. There were recumbent bodies on the verandah, and in the garden a monk lay in a pool of vomit. All the walls were torn and hanging, bodies lay about as if dead. There was even a body lying across the crest of the tile roof. The monastery looked as if it had been bombed. But even as he gazed at this dismal scene he heard the sound of small tinkling bells coming from somewhere in the main monastery building, and though the bells were soft and delicate they had the astonishing effect of rousing the Zen Buddhists from their drunken stupor. One by one they groaned, rose to their feet and staggered off.

And then around the corner came a man in white holding a staff of temple bells. His head was shaved, he was stout, the folds of his neck were like ruffles of a collar. He walked right up to Warren and inquired in heavily accented English if he could be of help. I want to discuss with someone the possibility of enrolling here for Zen training, Warren said. Of course, the monk said. If you don't mind waiting more than two moments but less than six, I will approach the Master for you.

More than two but less than six, Warren thought as he waited in an anteroom beside the front gate. That's a few. Shortly thereafter he was escorted by the monk to a small room with a beautiful Bodhisattva *pratima* and a vase of flowers and straw mats and cushions, and without having to be told, even by himself, he dropped to his knees and bowed to the resident Master, who was seated and facing him with a face of genial amusement. It was the old caretaker. On the one day off of the year for all his followers and monks, he, in perfect realization, had stayed where he was. The Master was smoking a cigarette. Another monk came by and listened. He was laughing and telling the monk, in Japanese, about his first meeting with Warren. Gusts of smoke came out of him. As the story was elaborated, the Master rose and began to act it out, and there to Warren's astonishment was a perfect imitation of himself, the way he carried himself, his walk, the tone of his voice, the shock on his face as the lath slapped his cheek. The Japanese laughed till there were tears in their eyes. Soon Warren began to smile and then he too exploded into laughter. He would come to understand in the months to follow that the Master so perfectly realized whatever he chose to do, that a kind of magnetic field was formed in which whoever was in his presence drew on its power. That is why interviews with the Master were so highly prized. His perfection was an impersonal force that you could feel and hope someday to manifest from yourself on a continuous basis. If he laughed, it was perfect laughter, and you had to laugh too. If he chose to cry, everyone around him would have to weep. But where did it come from, how did it happen? All Warren could work out was that the Master lived totally to the fullness of his being each and every moment of his existence. He was completely of the moment, then and there, in which you found him. Nothing of him was deadened by the suffering of his past life and there was no striving or fear in him for his future.

Would the Master feel a need to write poems?

No, because poems are the expression of longing and despair. Yes, because if the Master is one in every instant with what he sees and hears and feels, the poem is not the Master's written need for the world singing in the Master.

No, because the poem is a cry of the unborn heart. Yes, because the poem perfectly embodies the world, there is no world without poem.

Your register apologizes for rendering nonlinear thinking in linear language, the apperceptions of oneness in dualistic terminology. However, there is no difficulty representing the absolute physical torture of Warren Penfield's commitment in Zen meditation. He could not physically accomplish even the half lotus, his spine threatened to snap, his legs seemed to be in a vise; even the mudra—the bowl-shaped position of the hands, the thumbs lightly touching, a simple relaxed representation in the hand of the flow from right to left, from left to right, the rocking crescent continuity of the universe intimations of stars and ancient Eastern recognitions—became under the torment of his distracted physically weeping thought a spastic hand clench, a hardened manifestation of frozen fear and anguish, the exact opposite of the right practice, the body imprisoned, the mind entirely personal and self-involved and then God help you if you nod off every now and then as who could not, sitting like a damn beer pretzel twelve, sixteen hours a day he comes along and hits you with the damn slapstick the goddamn yellow-skinned bastard the next time he hits me with that stick I'm going to get up and wrap it around his goddamn yellow neck and break a goddamn Buddha doll over his goddamn shaven head this is not right thinking but tell me Gautama enlighten me if what you say is true why is it so difficult to attain wouldn't it all make a lot more sense if everyone could do it if everyone could be it without even thinking without being anything less before, without the death of my darling, and men drowning in the cold black coalwater of collapsed mines miles of coalstone sinking slowly upon their chests, or bullets perforating them like cutout coupons supposing I do attain it, supposing I find the right understanding what then what happens outside me how do I help Local 10110 of the Western Federation of Miners, Smelters, Sheepdippers and Zenpissers, and then there's the food, look what we wait for when at last the cute little tinkly bell rings and we may unpretzel ourself and try to regain the circulation in our swollen limbs, little bits of pickled leather, or some absolute excrescence of the lowest sea life lightly salted or a congealed ball of rice dipped in some rank fermented fluid that smells to me like the stuff we dipped the pigeons in to kill the lice.

* * *

No, there is no problem expressing the inner record of Warren Penfield's quest for enlightenment: the whining despair, the uncharacteristic epithet, the rage, the backsliding giving up and consequent self-nauseation, the stubborn goings on, all of this silent, in a temple hall of inscrutable meditators, all of whom reminded him of the immigrant kids to the Ludlow Grade School around him totally serene and insulated in their lack of language the feeling what do they all know that I don't know why don't the storms of self taste fire and thunder across their brainbrow, why aren't they as sick and unsure of their dangerous selves as I am of mine, leading then to the false Zen-like casuistry as, for example, if we are to press ourselves on the world sticking to it like a decal, if I am one with the rocks the trees the stars why is my memory invalid and why then are the images of Clara on our beds of slag in the cool mountain dusk of Colorado forbidden me, I am my memory and the images of my past are me, and if I am the rocks and stones and trees, Wordsworth, rocked round in earth's diurnal course with rocks and stones and trees, why are my phantoms less real why are the ghostvoices of my mama and papa less real why is the mud of the Marne less real why must I exclude exclude, if everything is now and mind is matter is not everything valid is not meditation the substance of the mind as well as its practice?

Nor is it difficult to render the casually developed outer circumstances of this monastic life, the old Master becoming at some times demonic in his teaching, a destroyer of ego, of humble ordinary lines of thought, an army of right practice, right understanding overwhelming the frail redoubts and trenches of Warren's Western mind. One day they were in the temple and he came in screaming, naked, climbed the Buddha like a bee alighting on a flower and bending it with its own honeygravid weight and they watched shocked and stunned as a beautiful polished wood Buddha toppled to the floor under the Master, an act of profound desecration with sexual impact, and the Buddha lay split like a log, a piece of wood the aperture of an earthquake and nothing was ever said of it again. He was a violent old man, one day Warren was admitted for his counseling and the Master threw a cup of cold green tea in his face and that was the lesson of the day. One day he lectured them all, a particular holy day and he shouted at them saying you were all Masters when you first came through the gate and now look at you, I have more respect for the horse that pulls the shitwagon than I have for you—screaming and growling and trilling in the Japanese way of singsong, Warren prostrate with all the rest. But everyone took it as material to be pondered and worked out, it was only a style of pedagogy and only someone stupid enough to take emotions seriously would be shocked threatened or angered by the serene antics of the realized Buddha spirit of such a great Master. Warren finally reached the preliminary kindergarten stage of getting his own koan, a paradoxical question to form the empty mind of meditation. Each devotee received his own koan like a rabbit's foot to stroke and treasure, an unanswerable question to torment him month after month, perhaps year after year, until enlightenment burst over and he was able to answer it when the Master gently asked it of him the hundred millionth time. Warren walked in bowed, kneeled on the straw mat. The Master was smoking and making each breath visible as a plume of cigarette smoke and Warren knew the standard koans, the famous ones, there were actually collections of them like college course outlines but the one given to him he had never heard before or read anywhere and it was delivered by the Master with a shake of his head, sigh and a glance of helpless supplication at the ceiling: Penfield-san, said the Master, if this is a religion for warriors, what are *you* doing here? Warren thanked him, bowed and backed out of the room even though the Master looked as if he was going to say something more. Later in his first pondering of this infinitely resounding question he squatted by his favorite place, near the garden gate beyond the gravel garden, and saw through the slats as for the first time the beautiful little girl who swept the street.

I DROVE OUT OF THE MOUNTAINS THROUGH THE night and found the way to Utica, New York, coming into city streets in the rain at three o'clock, passing freight yards, warehouses. She was asleep, I didn't want to wake her, I bumped the car gently across the railroad tracks and headed south and west toward Pittsburgh.

I wanted to log as many miles as I could before Bennett got up in the morning.

By dawn I was clear-eyed exhausted, feeling my

nerves finely strung, the weariness in the hinges of my jaws, you are never more alert. Red lights in the dawn at intersections between fields, I saw the light of dawn shoot clear down the telegraph wires like a surge of power, I passed milk trucks and heard train whistles the sun came up and flooded my left eye suddenly it was day commerce was on the roads we had survived Loon Lake and were cruising through the United States of America.

I woke her for breakfast, we walked into a diner—some town in Pennsylvania. Clara in her fur jacket and long dress and Junior in his knickers and sweater. Someone dropped a plate. Clara is not awake yet—a hard sleeper, a hard everything—she sits warming her hands on her coffee cup, studies the tabletop.

"This won't do," I said, steering her by the arm to the car.

"What?"

"It's asking for trouble."

I found an Army-Navy Surplus Store. I bought myself a regular pair of pants, work shirt, socks, a wool seaman's cap and khaki greatcoat. I bought Clara a black merchant marine pullover and a pea jacket. I made her change her clothes in the back of the store. Then I did.

Mr. Penfield had pressed upon me about eighty dollars in clean soft ones and fives, bills that looked as if they had spent years in a shoe box. I added to this the forty dollars or so of my own fortune. The clothes had come to twenty-eight, and another dollar and change for breakfast.

"What kind of money do you have?"

"Money?"

"I want to see what our cash assets are."

"I don't have any money."

"That's really swell."

"Look in my bag if you don't believe me."

"Well, how far did you think you could go without money?"

"I don't know. You tell me."

It was the best of conversations, all I could have wished for. I scowled. I drove hard.

We took the bumps in unison, we leaned at the same angle on the curves. I didn't know where we were going and she didn't ask. I drove to speed. I stopped wondering what she was feeling, what she was thinking. She was happy on the move, alert and at peace, all the inflamed spirit was lifted from her. She had various ways of arranging herself in the seat, legs tucked up or one under the other, or arms folded, head down, but in any position definitive, beautiful.

Come with me

Late that afternoon we were going up a steep hill along the Monongahela, Pittsburgh spreading out below us, stacks of smoke, black sky, crucible fire. By nightfall I was numb, I couldn't drive another mile. We were in some town in eastern Ohio, maybe it was Steubenville, I'm not sure. On a narrow street I found the Rutherford Hayes, a four-story hotel with fire escapes and a barber's pole at the entrance. I took a deep breath and pulled up to the curb.

In the empty lobby were the worn upholstered chairs and half-dead rubber plants that would have been elegance had I not been educated at Loon Lake. I had never stayed at a hotel but I knew what to do from the movies.

I got us upstairs without incident and tipped the

bellboy fifty cents. "Yes, suh!" he said. I chain-locked the door behind him.

We had a corner room with large windows, each covered with a dark green pull shade and flimsy white curtains. Everything had a worn-out look, a great circle of wear in the middle of the rug. I liked that. I liked the idea of public accommodation, people passing through. Bennett could keep his Loon Lake. I looked out the window. We were on the top floor, we had a view of greater Steubenville. In the bathroom was a faucet for ice water.

Clara, who had been in hotels before, found the experience unexceptional. She opened her overnight bag and took over the bathroom. I smoked a cigarette and listened to the sounds of her bathing. I kept looking around the room as if I expected to see someone else. Who? We were alone, she was alone with me and nobody knew where we were. I was smiling. I was thinking of myself crouched in the weeds in the cold night while a train goes by and a naked girl holds a white dress before a mirror.

This was a double bed I had booked and she hadn't even blinked. That would seem reason to hope. But for Clara Lukács there was no necessary significance in sleeping beside somebody in the same bed. She came out of the bathroom without a stitch. I undressed and turned out the light as cool in my assumptions as I could be. A high whine of impatience, a kind of child's growl, and a poke of her elbow was what I got when I happened to move against her in the dark. Just testing.

She curled up with her back toward me, and those vertebrae which I had noticed and loved were all at once deployed like the Maginot Line.

* * *

In the morning she woke out of sorts, mean.

"What in hell am I doing here?" she muttered. "Jesus," she said, looking at me. "I must be out of my mind."

I was stunned. My first impulse was to appeal.

"Look at him, hunky king of the road there. Oh, this is great—this really is great." She snapped up the window shade and looked out. "God damn him," she said. "And his wives and his boats and choo-choo trains."

She began to dress. She held up blouses, skirts, looked at them, flung them down. She sat abruptly on the bed with her arms full of clothes and she stared at the floor.

"Hey," I said. "I told you I'd get you out of there and I did. Didn't I?"

She didn't answer.

"Hey, girlie," I said, "didn't I? You have a complaint? You think you're some hot-ass bargain?"

"You bet I am, hunky, I can promise you."

"Well then, go on," I said. "Go back to your fancy friends and see what they do for you. Look what they already done."

I got out of bed, pulled on my pants and socks, and stuck my feet in my shoes.

"Where are you going?" she said.

"Here," I said, taking out my wallet. I crumpled a couple of singles and threw them on the floor. "That and a twitch of your ass will get you back to the loons."

"You're not leaving," she said. "You're not leaving me here!"

"You can go back to your career fucking for old men," I said. I put on my shirt and combed my hair in the mirror over the dresser. "It's probably as good as you can do anyhow."

The mirror shattered. I didn't know what she had thrown. When I went for her she was reaching for the Gideon Bible to throw that. I grabbed her arm and we knocked the bedside lamp to the floor. I pinned her to the bed. She tried to bite me. I held her by the wrists and put my knees on each point of the pelvis.

"You're hurting me!" I moved back and let go of her. She lay still. A queer bitter smell came from her. It was anger that aroused her, confrontation was the secret.

But when I found her she was loving and soft and she shrank away softer and more innocent of her feelings than I had dreamed.

I held her, I loved the narrow shoulders, the small-boned frailness of her, the softness of her breasts against me. I was kissing her eyes, her cheeks, but she cried in the panic of the sensation, her legs couldn't find their place, she was like a swimmer kicking out or like someone trying to shinny up a pole.

I wanted her to know the sudden certainty declaring in me like God. I was where I belonged! I remembered this!

But she didn't seem to be aware of how I felt, there was this distracted spirit of her, her head shook from side to side with bursts of voice, like sobs, as if someone was mourned.

Our lovemaking was like song or like speech. "Don't you see," I asked again and again, "don't you understand?" And she shook her head from side to side in her distraction. I couldn't overcome this. I became insistent, I felt my time running out, I felt I had to break into her recognition. It's you, I wanted her to say, and she wouldn't say the words.

And then the tenderness was gone and I was pounding the breath from her, beating ugly grunts of sound from her, wanting her to form words but hearing savage stupid gusts of voiceless air coming from her.

In my moment of stunned paralytic grief I groan I go off bucking I think I hear her laugh.

For several days we made our life sleeping till midmorning and getting on the road and driving again till the sun went down and we could find a bed. We drove through boarded-up towns, we ate blue-plate specials and we slept in rooming houses with linoleum on the floor and outhouses in back or in small motor-court cabins with the sound all night of the trucks rolling past. Night and morning we made love it was what we did our occupation our exercise. But always with great suspense in my mind. I never knew if it would happen again. I didn't have the feeling anything was established in her. She fucked in a kind of lonely self-intensification. She slept without touching me, she slept with no need to touch or hold me, she went off to sleep and it was as if I weren't there.

I would think about this lying in the dark while she slept. I was there for her, I was what she assumed, and I was willing to be that, to be the assumption she didn't even know she was making. And then one day she'd discover that she loved me.

Once in a while, usually in the numb exhaustion of daybreak, I'd look into her face and see an aspect there of acknowledgment I wanted in the gold-washed green eyes. There would be humor in them. The lips slightly swollen and open, the small warm puff of breath. She'd giggle to see neither of us was dead and she'd give me a cracklipped kiss a soft dry kiss with the hot pulp of her lip against mine.

She liked to be inside her appetites and her feelings. Whatever they were. One day in a rainstorm I skidded off the road. I was frantically spinning the wheel, I couldn't see through the rain, it had turned white, opaque, but Clara was laughing and shrieking like a kid on a carnival ride. We thudded into a ditch. Water softened the canvas top and began to leak through and we sat at a tilt as if in a diving plane, in clouds. I thought we might drown. Then we felt the car rise, somehow the water floated us free, and when the storm passed over, we gently drifted a half mile or so in the flood like some stately barge down a stream. She loved it, she loved every second of it, her fingers gripping my arm, the nails digging into my skin.

Sometimes we went out at night walking some main street to a local movie. She liked to stop in a tavern and drink ten-cent beers, she liked the looks she got, the sexual alert that went off every time she walked into a bar or a diner. One time someone came over to the booth and started to talk to her as if I weren't even there. It seemed to me unavoidable what I had to do. He was an amiable fellow with a foolish grin, but with the strength in him of belonging in this bar, of being known in this bar, this town, he looked down and saw my knife, the tip making an indentation in the blue shirt and the sprung gut. He was genuinely astonished, they don't use knives in boondocks of the Midwest, he backed off with his palms up.

She had turned pale. "What's the idea, do you know what you're doing?" She spoke in a soft urgent whisper leaning toward me over the table.

"I do," I said, "and if you don't stand up and get your ass moving I'll do the same to you."

Outside I grabbed her arm. She was in a cold rage but I had the feeling, too, that I had done right, that I had shown her something she wanted to see.

"You know something?" she said as I hurried her along to our room. "You're crazy, you know that?"

I thought they were the first words of love I'd heard from her.

In Dayton, Ohio, I saw in the rear-view mirror the unmistakable professional interest of a traffic cop as we drove away from his intersection.

"I have not been smart," I said. "I suppose my mind has been on other things."

I made a sharp turn into a side street and started looking for the poor part of town.

"What's the matter?"

"A German convertible with bud vases and New York plates. You don't often see that in these here parts."

She thought awhile. "Is this a hot car?"

"In a manner of speaking."

Soon enough we were going through the dingy sections where the bums were standing on the sidewalks and the garbage spilled into the streets. The Buckeye State Used Cars enterprise looked grim and satisfactorily seedy, I turned in there and commenced a negotiation. The man with his fat dirty fingernails showed me there was not even a book on such a car. I said that was because it was so expensive they didn't figure anyone could afford it. He said maybe so, but how could he sell a car where you could not get the parts if they broke? I said nothing ever broke on a car like this. He said how could he take ownership on a car that had no papers? I said it was my family's car and since when did you walk around with papers on your own family's car? He said why did I want to sell my family's car? I said I was running away to get married and needed cash. "How are you going to run if you don't have no car anymore?" he said. "I'm going to buy a modest well-tuned vehicle from you," I said, looking with bright honest earnestness into his face.

He walked around the car several times. He glanced at Clara in the front seat, I had told her to put on her fur jacket. "That is my fiancée," I said to him softly, "of whom they don't approve." I could see him thinking: They wouldn't go after their own kid.

Come with me

Combust with me

"Someday," Clara said over the noise, "maybe you'll be able to buy it back, or one like it."

"What?"

"I said someday you could hope to get it back."

"I've got my car," I said, pounding the dashboard. "I've got papers for it. I've got a hundred fifty simoleons in my pocket. Is that bad? We can get to California if we're careful."

"California?"

"That's where we're going. Didn't you know?"

"I wasn't informed," she said, holding on to the leather strap over the door. She peered ahead, frowning. I had taken in partial trade a 1930 Chevrolet station wagon with wood-panel sides that shook and rattled, and floorboards that jumped in the air every time we hit a bump. It had a high polish on its tan-and-brown body and admitted to fifty thousand miles.

"I DIDN'T KNOW DEAD PEOPLE WERE THAT UN-usual. I saw them all the time. I wandered around holding my bottle and seeing these dead hunkies lying on tables. I dragged my blanket around behind me. I wasn't frightened. My father would smile at me.

"When I was older I began to understand things a little more. I thought, for instance, that anyone who was dead had to have a hole in them. I didn't know people died without holes in them. Then I figured it out one day. Some old guy was being dressed who died of natural causes. He'd made it all the way. So I knew then about natural death.

"But it was just the business, you know, it was nothing special, we lived in an apartment right over the business I played after school outside in front of the stoop and there was my father driving up with his hearse, they'd back up into the garage and he and my brother took the body into the back. And that was the way things were on West Twenty-ninth Street.

"And then my mother died but my father didn't handle it, someone else from another funeral parlor came and took her away. Just like doctors don't treat their own families. But maybe it was because she was religious. None of our church got buried with us. We

175

were Greek Orthodox but the business was nondenom-
inational. My father was not highly regarded in
church. I saw more Romans and Jewish rabbis at
Lukaćs' than I did priests. Anyway, my father moped
around a long time. He didn't know what to do with
me. He hired this black lady to take care of me. She
was okay but she drank. She stood at the window
whenever there was a funeral downstairs. She'd count
the numbers of cars to see how important the dead guy
was. She'd count the number of flower cars. Sometimes she called me to come look and I began to look
too. You'd see all these flowers in the flower cars,
sometimes in three, four cars of flowers, it was too
much, like huge mounds of popcorn, I didn't like it. I
hate cut flowers. All my life they made a stink coming
up through the floor below, there was always somebody downstairs you could smell flowers through the
dumbwaiter.

"But then if it was really a big affair it would be
worth watching. My father and brother all dressed up
in their shiny black suits. He'd hire on men on these
days. People coming to pay their respects, filling the
parlor, crowds standing out on the street. And then
outside all the cars in a line, double-parked with their
headlights on, all these black mourners' cars twice
around the block. And the cops would be there check-
ing on who showed up, standing across the street and
watching. And the photographers with their big flash
cameras taking pictures, and the next morning in the
News or the *Mirror* there was a picture of somebody
and in the background the canopy said Lukaćs' Funeral Parlor.

"But he didn't need the publicity and he didn't care.
He was just some dumb hunky, he didn't care about

anything, he didn't talk much, he just did this work. And he got this clientele over the years, he wasn't in the rackets himself, but he kept his mouth shut and didn't make judgments and he just got to be the one they used. He didn't care who he buried, why should he, the kind of work he did why get excited. After a while he had to expand. He bought the brownstone next door, and put a new streamlined face across both houses. And then there was a showroom and a reception desk.

"And I was pretty grown-up now. I wouldn't stay in school. I'd worked for a while at the five-and-ten just to have something to do. But he was getting fancy now and he needed someone for the reception desk and to answer the phone who could talk right. So he asked me. So I thought, Why not? I mean when I was a kid I used to get it at school. That's why I had no friends at St. Clare's. They came around at Halloween with sheets on and rang the front bell. Clara Cadaver, Clara Cadaver. Well, shit, I only had boyfriends, anyway. I mean as a kid my friends were boys. I played street hockey.

"But anyway, I didn't mind. I wore a black dress. I wore stockings and high-heeled shoes. I had an allowance for the beauty parlor. And that was my job. I got to meet some real people. It was an entrée, as they say. What's that sound? The engine doesn't sound right."

"No," I said, "it's okay. Maybe I need a little oil."

"It's getting dark, anyway—where do you suppose we are?"

"Are you hungry?"

"A little."

I had a terrible feeling, a chilled feeling because of

her lineage, her criminal lineage, I thought of it as a caste, some kind of contamination she had been born into through no fault of her own and I thought it was mine now too; if I wanted her, what she was was mine too, what she brought with her we both had now.

But I was also happy that she had told me, that in the dreamlife of the road the hours sitting next to each other and facing in the same direction brought things out we might not have otherwise said. We told each other about our lives, we gave each other our lives while we looked at the road backward into ourselves. Even though afterward we didn't remember what we said, or were too proud to admit we remembered.

"We lived across the river from each other, you realize that? We could have shouted at each other across the Hudson, two snot-nosed kids. Little did we know we were destined to meet! We saw the same Tom Mix movies. We ran along the sidewalks pointed to the sky at the same airships!"

"What?"

"No, really, playing hockey"—I wanted to make her smile—"don't you remember? Maybe our teams played each other. We made the puck from the end of the wooden cream-cheese box, right? We wrapped it in black tape, am I right?"

It seemed very important in this moment to make her smile.

"Don't you remember? Don't you remember the 'I cash clothes' man? On Twenty-ninth Street? The water wagon, running alongside it for the spray? Don't you remember how we went to the candy store for ice cream?"

"What are you talking about?"

"No, really, Clara. One hot afternoon we bought Dixie cups and stood on the sidewalk in the sun with our wooden spoons. You remember. Licking the ice cream off Joan Crawford's face?"

WHEN CLARA FELL ASLEEP I PUT ON MY COAT, closed the door quietly and went out to look around. In addition to everything else snow had hit this burg, a heavy wet fall that stuck to your eyelashes and got into your shoes.

The rooming house was highway robbery—twelve dollars a week, paid in advance. Restaurants came to another two, three dollars a day. If I took her to the movies, another forty, fifty cents.

I had even bought her a gold wedding band—for her protection, I said.

I hadn't told her there was no money to get the valves reground. She thought we were in Jacksontown another day or two at the most. I could manage two day-coach fares to Chicago. But what would we do in Chicago—freeze our ass there?

And so, hunched in his khaki coat from the Great War, the big spender wandered through downtown Jacksontown, Indiana—Heart of the Hoosier Nation, as the sign said. Everything built of red brick, the bank, the library, the city hall, the armory. Stores occupied, the black cars parked at angles against the curbs, he notices the traffic, a heavy traffic rolling quietly through the snow, the sky gray, heavy flakes like soundproofing tamping down the horns, muffling the engines, even the streetcars grinding along hushed in the flanges, sparks flaring in the dark afternoon, the dark turrets of the armory the dark green cannon on the lawn with the mantle of white snow.

I saw everywhere on every street jalopies of every description, valises and boxes strapped to their fenders, children and grandparents high in the rear seats, scarfs wrapped around their heads. I saw furniture covered with blankets tied with rope on the beds of broken-down trucks. I saw out-of-state license plates: Kentucky Tennessee Georgia Arkansas Michigan Missouri.

I boarded the Railroad Street trolley to see what would happen. It banged its way sharply around corners and picked up speed. Soon it was out of the downtown area barreling between two endless rows of semiattached bungalows, block after block. Eventually it veered into a dark street, a canyon of the sides of buildings, moving slowly now, many men walking in the street, the bell clanged, an unbroken chain-link fence blurred my eyes, if I opened the window I could touch it.

Last stop the doors hissed open at the main gate. Here a crowd of men stood waiting to get in, a quiet intense crowd not orderly but silent. The snow came down. Even as I watched, the crowd grew pulsing like something underwater.

Behind the locked gates uniformed men stood chatting as if nothing was going on.

I looked up at the block-long sign across the tops of two buildings. BENNETT AUTOBODY NUMBER SIX was what it said.

That evening I took Clara to dinner at the Jacksontown Inn, the best restaurant in town. It had tablecloths, candles, black busboys, and the roast beef au jus went for two dollars and a half.

"I see in the paper where every state is covered with snow from here to the Rockies," I said.

She eyed me warily. The true color of her hair beginning to come through, her hair was fluffier too, she had given up the beauty parlor she believed they would ruin her if she had her hair done in the Midwest.

"Anyway," I said, "I did a little exploring while you were having a nap. We could be in worse places. There are jobs here, people have money in their pockets, they're shopping in the stores and going to the movies. They have three movie houses downtown."

She cut her roast beef.

"And you want to hear something funny? The big employer and why everything is humming is your friend and mine Frankie W. Bennett. His Number Six plant."

She put down her knife and fork, dabbed at her mouth with her napkin and sat there.

"Oh, Clara," I said. "I'd be happy if I could just look at you across this table for the rest of my life."

"That would be a lot of roast beef," she said.

"You didn't wear your gold ring!"

"I forgot."

I ate and drank energetically. "Anyway," I said, "as long as we're stuck here—so long—as we're here awhile—I thought I'd tap into old Frank—build up our cash reserve for the run to California."

"What does that mean?"

"Well, they're hiring at the Number Six plant."

"So?"

A sip of water from my cut-glass goblet. "I caught on there this afternoon. Nothing to it. I just gave them my shining innocent face. I mean there were these guys standing around with their toolboxes and employment records all wanting the same dumb unskilled jobs I put in for. No contest."

"Why?"

"Because it was obvious I didn't have a union background. They don't want someone who's a wiseass. They want the ones who don't know any better."

"Why did you do it?" she said.

"I thought I explained," I said. "I thought I explained that."

She didn't say anything, we resumed dining. Occasionally she'd look up and smile sweetly at me, in the silence there at the Jacksontown Inn the unarguable terror of things was driven home to me.

"I don't see why you should get on your high horse," I said. "Is it any worse than sleeping in his bed? Is it any worse than stealing his car?"

"I think I've got to leave now." She stood.

"Do you mind if I pay the damn check?"

We walked through the snow back to the room. I grabbed her elbow, she shrugged me off. "Clara, for God's sake, what is it I've done, after all? I got a job! A Job! Is it a fucking crime to get a job? There's no money! We're here in the real world now, don't you understand? There's no money!"

In the room she started to pack. I willed myself to be calm, there were other roomers on the same floor, I didn't need landlady trouble on top of everything else. "Clara, please don't be like this. Please listen. All right, this is the worst shithole town in the frozenest fucking country there is. It's so fucking cold I can't believe how cold it is. And there's no reason to stay here. Except that it's Bennett's! That's why, Clara. That is the true reason why. Because I'm gonna work his line without his knowing and walk away from his machine with my wages in my pocket and he's going to get us to California! That's why."

She was still.

"You hear me, Clara? Because it's living right under his nose. That's why. Because it's the riskiest thing! It's the toughest and most dangerous and the classiest thing. That's why."

She sat on the side of the bed. "And what am I supposed to do here all day while you work his line and make your classy wages? Huh, big boy? What am I supposed to do?"

My God, it was laughable, it was heartbreaking but at least she asked the question. Neither of us was twenty! We were children—who were we, what chance did we have? In her question was one half of an instant's perceiving, dimly appreciated, of only the most obvious possibility of life comprising the history of mankind.

I sat on the side of the bed next to her, whispering in her ear, "You don't realize what you've done to me. Me, the carney kid! You're making an honest man of him, it's horrible. I have all these godawful longings to work to support you, to make a life with you, I want us to live together in one place, I don't care where, I don't care if it's the North Pole, I'll do any fucking thing to keep you in bonbons and French novels, Clara, and it's all your fault."

"Oh Jesus, he's crazy, this boy is crazy."

But I felt this weird tickle-behind-the-spine unprecedented truth of what I was saying. Before I said it I hadn't known I felt it: we could change, we could make our lives however we wanted! And the steps Clara had taken to molldom and to the high forest of Loon Lake were dainty steps, steps avoiding the muck of her reality and mine. And this was where we truly belonged, not on the road but stationary, in one place, working it all out in the hard life.

"You got anything better to do?" I said.

She sighed. "That's the crying shame of it."

Data comprising life F. W. Bennett undergoing review.
Shown in two instances twenty-five years apart of
    labor
relations lacking compassion or flexible policy under-
    standing
workers' needs. His dramatization suggests life de-
    voted almost

entirely to selfish accumulation of wealth and ritual
    use thereof
according to established patterns of utmost class. It is
alleged he patronizes unsavory elements of society for
    his
business gain. It is alleged that he is sexually exploit-
    ative.
It is suggested he is at least unmoved by the violent
    death
of another human attributable to his calculated negli-
    gence.

Countervailing data re his apparent generosity to
worthless poet scrounge and likely drunkard Warren
    Penfield.
A hint too of his pride in Lucinda Bailey Bennett's
    aviation
achievements. A heart too for spunky
derelict kids.
Your register respectfully advises the need for addi-
    tional
countervailing data. History suggests of the class of
    which Mr.
F. W. Bennett is a member no unalloyed spirit of evil
    the dimes
which John D. Rockefeller senior gave away compulsi-
    vely to
people in the street became the multimillions of his
    sons'
philanthropies. Andrew Carnegie's beneficence well
    attested,
as well as William Randolph Hearst's Milk Fund for
    Babies.
And examination of the general practice of families of

immeasurable wealth in US suggests their generosity cannot

be explained entirely as self-serving public relations
but

may be seen as manifesting anthropologically identi-
fied

principle of potlatch observed operating in primitive
social

systems throughout the world from northern forest
aboriginals

to unclad natives of tropical paradises. The principle

regardless of currency of benefaction breadfruit pigs
palm

fronds or dollars is that wealth is accumulated so that

it can be given away thus bringing honor to the giver.

I refer to an American landscape from every region of
which

rise hospitals universities libraries museums planetaria

parks think-tanks and other institutions for the public
weal

all of which are the benefactions of the utmost class.

I cite achievements F. W. Bennett in his lifetime the
original

endowments of the Western miners' Black Lung Re-
search Facility,

Denver, Colorado. The Gymnasium of Miss Morris'
School,

Briarcliff Manor NY, the Mexican Silver Workers'
Church of the

Holy St. Clare, Popxacetl Mexico, The Bennett Library on the

grounds of Jordan College, Rhinebeck NY, the Bennett

Engineering Institute, Albany NY, plus numerous on-
    going
benefactions of worthy charities and researches plus
    innumerable
acts of charity to individuals never publicized.

I attribute to F. W. Bennett in his death a last will and
testament of such public generosity as to receive ac-
    knowledgment
on the front page of the New York *Times* data avail-
    able
upon request.

Generally speaking a view of the available economic
    systems
that have been tested historically must acknowledge
    the immense
power of capitalism to generate living standards food
    housing
education the amenities to a degree unprecedented in
    human civilization. The benefits of such a system
    while occasionally
random and unpredictable with periods of undeniable
    stress
and misery depression starvation and degradation are
inevitably distributed to a greater and greater percent-
    age
of the population. The periods of economic stability
    also
ensure a greater degree of popular political freedom
and among the industrial Western democracies today
    despite

occasional suppression of free speech quashing of dis-
sent

corruption of public officials and despite the tendency
of

legislation to serve the interests of the ruling business

oligarchy the poisoning of the air water the chemical
adulteration

of food the obscene development of hideous weaponry
the

increased costs of simple survival the waste of human
resources

the ruin of cities the servitude of backward foreign
populations

the standards of life under capitalism by any criterion
are

far greater than under state socialism in whatever
forms

it is found British Swedish Cuban Soviet or Chinese.
Thus

the good that fierce advocacy of personal wealth ac-
complishes

in the historical run of things outweighs the bad. And
while

we may not admire always the personal motives of our
business

leaders we can appreciate the inevitable percolation of
the

good life as it comes down through our native American soil.

You cannot observe the bounteous beauty of our country nor take

pleasure in its most ordinary institutions in peace and
safety

without acknowledging the extraordinary achievement
  of
American civilization. There are no Japanese bandits
  lying
in wait on the Tokaidoways after all. Drive down the
turnpike past the pretty painted pipes of the oil refin-
  eries
and no one will hurt you.

No claim for the perfection of F. W. Bennett, only that
  like
all men he was of his generation and reflected his times
  in
his person. We know that by the nineteen-fifties at an
  advanced
age he had come finally to see unions as partners in
enterprise and to cooperate fully on a first-name basis
  with
major labor leaders playing golf of course at that age
  he
only drove a ball twenty or thirty yards but they called
  him
Mr. Frank and with humor admired his sportif outfits
  the
beige-yellow slacks the brown-and-white shoes with
  the tassels
the Hawaiian shirt with his breasts showing. Note is
  made here
too that this man had a boyhood, after all, woke
in the astonishment of a bedsheet of sap suffered acne
had feelings which frightened him and he tried to sup-
  press
was cruelly motivated by unthinking adults perhaps re-
  buffed

or humiliated by a teacher these experiences are not
the
sole prerogative of the poor poverty is not a moral
endowment and a man who has the strength to help
himself
can help others. I cite too the ordinary feats of
mortality the inspection of a fast-growing mole on the
side
of the nose blood in the stool a painful injury or the
mournful witness of the slow death of a parent all this
is
given to all men as well as the starting awake in the
nether hours of the night from such glutinous night-
mare
that one's self name relationships nationality place in
life
all data of specificity wipe out amnesiastically asiatic-
ally you
don't even know the idea human it is such a low hour
of the
night and he shares that with all of us. I therefore de-
clare
F. W. Bennett to embody the fullness of the perplexity
of
living, as they say.

I cite here his voice which people who knew him only
in his
later years believe to be ridden and cracked with his
age
but in fact his voice had always been rather high reedy
with a gravelly consistency around its edges and some
people
found this menacing but others thought it avuncular

especially after his operation for cataracts when they
wear

those goggle glasses. But it was one of those voices of
such

individual character that people who never heard it
can

imagine it just by the mention of his name and those
standing

in the great crush of honors at his funeral could believe

themselves likely to hear it for many years afterward as
if a

man of this strong presence could not release his hold
on

life except very very slowly and, buried or not, manifest

a half life, probably, of twenty-five thousand years.

I WAS ON HEADLIGHTS. FIRST I ATTACHED WITH
four screws two metal frames the screws lay in a bin
the frames met at the convergence of two small belts
the left frame from the left belt the right down the
line. Sometimes the pieces didn't match, sometimes
the wrong piece came down the wrong side and sometimes, the thread not being true, I had to hammer the
screws in, everybody did.

Next I affixed the crossed pieces to the inside of a curl of tin shaped like a flowerpot. I then inserted through a hole in the pot about four feet of insulated wire that came to hand dangling from a big spool overhead. I snipped the wire with a pair of shears, knotted the wire so it wouldn't slip and put the whole thing back on the line for the next man, who did the electrical connections, slapped on the chrome and sent it onto the main line for mounting on a fender.

That was the operation it's what I did.

High above my head the windows of the great shed hung open like bins and the sun came through the meshed glass already broken down, each element of light attached to its own atom of dust and there was no light except on the dust and between was black space, like the night around stars. Mr. Autobody Bennett was a big man who could do that to light, make the universe punch in like the rest of us.

And all around me the noise of running machines, conveyor belts, the creaking of pulleys, screeching of worked metal, shouts, the great gongs of autobodies on the line, the blast of acetylene riveting, the rattling of moving treads, the cries of mistakes and mysterious intentions.

And then continuously multiplied the same sounds repeated compounded by echoes. An interesting philosophical problem: I didn't know at any moment what I heard was what was happening or what had already happened.

It was enough to make me think of my father. The man was a fucking hero.

Then they speed things up and I'm going too slow I drop one of the tin pots on the wrong side of the belt the guy there is throwing tires on wheel rims and giving the tubes a pump or two of air he ignores my shouts he can't take the time. And then the foreman is coming down the line to pay me a call I can't hear him but I don't have to—a red bulging neck of rage.

And then they stop coddling us and throw the throttle to full and this is how I handle it: I am Fred Astaire in top hat and tails tossing up the screws into the holes, bouncing the frames on the floor and catching them in my top hat of tin. I twirl the headlight kick it on the belt with a backward flip of my heel. I never stop moving and when the belt is too slow for me I jump up and stomp it along faster, my arms outstretched. Soon everyone in the plant has picked up on my routine—everyone is dancing! The foreman comes pirouetting along, putting stars next to each name on his clipboard. And descending from the steel rafter by insulated wire to dance backward on the moving parade of car bodies, Mr. Bennett himself in white tie and tails. He's singing with a smile, he's flinging money from his hands like stardust.

Shit, how many more hours of this . . . I thought of Clara I thought of us driving to California in the spring. And then I thought. What if she just left, what if she met someone and said to him, *How do I get out of here*?

And then I resolved not to think at all, if I couldn't think well of Clara, I'd turn my mind from her knowing I was racked, knowing I couldn't physically feel hope in this hammering noise. But I didn't have to try not to think, by the middle of the afternoon my bones were vibrating like tuning forks. And so it had me, Bennett Autobody, just where it wanted me and I was screwed to the machines taking their form a mile away in the big shed, those black cars composed bit by bit from our life and the gift of opposition of thumb and forefinger, those precious vehicles, each one a hearse.

* * *

On the other hand everyone had the same problem I heard stories of people hauling off on a foreman, or pissing on the cars, or taking a sledge hammer to them, good stories, wonderful stories, probably not true. But the telling of them was important. I was the youngest on my line, jokes were made about that—what a woman could still hope for from someone my age. Jokes were important.

The line was a complex society with standards of conduct honor serious moral judgment. You did your work but didn't kiss ass, you stood up for yourself when you had to but didn't whine or complain, you kept your eyes open and your mouth shut, you didn't make outlandish claims brag threaten.

Yet none of this was visible when we pressed through the gates in the evening, a nameless faceless surge of men in soft caps in full flight.

Clara and I lived on Railroad, the street of the endless two-family bungalows. I had my choice—to take the streetcar, which was faster, or walk and save the carfare.

I ran.

I stopped only long enough to pick up a movie magazine or *True Confessions*, I liked to bring her small surprises keep her busy keep her occupied.

Sometimes I'd find her waiting at the window looking out the window—the dark industrial sky, the great bobbing crowd of men flowing down Railroad Street making a whispering sound on the cobblestones like some dry Midwestern sea—and she'd be holding her arms, the bleak mass life scared her as some elemental force she hadn't known, not even realized by the way she stood and watched that she gave it her deference.

We ate things heated from cans. We had two plates two cups two spoons two knives two forks. Our mansion was furnished army-camp fashion by the company. Behind the back porch was the outhouse.

We stayed in the kitchen till bedtime, I tossed pieces of coal in the stove, it never seemed to be enough. Clara sat reading, she wore her fur jacket she wore it all the time. She was fair and couldn't take the cold, the winter had done something to her face, coarsened it, rubbed the glamour from it. Five minutes out of doors her eyes watered, her cheeks flamed up. She didn't use make-up anymore.

All of it was all right with me. I still couldn't take my eyes off her. I tried to remember the insolent girl with the wineglass in her hand and the firelight in her eyes.

"I'm glad you're laughing," she said.

I had a scheme for getting us from kitchen to bed. I heated water in the black coffee pot and then ran the pot like a hot iron over the mattress. I undressed her under the covers.

I loved it cold, I loved the way she came to me when it was cold, as if she couldn't get close enough. But this particular evening I remember she stopped me in my lovemaking, she put her arm on my shoulder and said *Shhh*.

"You hear that?" she said.

"What?"

"Next door. They've got a radio."

I lay on my back and listened. I heard the wind blowing the snow in gusts along Railroad Street. Sometimes the snow came in through the cracks and in the morning you'd find it lying like dust inside the front door.

"I don't hear anything," I said.

"Listen."

And then I heard it, very softly through the wall, it was dance music, the swing band of a warmer world, it made me think of men and women on a terrace under a full moon.

THEIR PLACE—THE MIRROR OF OUR THREE ROOMS —astounds me. No trace of company domicile, it's all been washed from the walls and strained from the light coming in off the street. We sit on stuffed horsehair chairs, there is a matching sofa, behind the sofa a lamp with a square translucent shade of the deco design. A braided rug covers the parlor floor and glass curtains adorn the windows. Amazing. On the desk in the corner a private phone. Who would have thought people on Railroad Street had their own phones?

The subtle giving to the newcomers of their protection. Lyle James smiles sitting on the sofa with his hands on his overalled knees, he's one of those crackers, hair like steel wool, reddish going to gray, a face of freckles so that he appears to be behind them looking from his pink-lidded eyes through them as from some prison of his own innocence, buckteeth smiling.

What does he see? In Jacksontown, crossroads of the world, he thinks he'll see everything given enough time. These two are just getting their legs, the boy looking at her as if she's sick about to die, or have a fit, but it's his fit more likely, that's what's important to this boy, not how he feels but how she feels. And she, one spooked little old girl, she smokes her cigarettes, crosses her legs, stares at the floor, that's the way it is with folks from the East.

Mrs. James comes in from the kitchen holding a platter with chocolate cake and cups and saucers and napkins. Another freckle-face redhead, but a pretty one with light eyes, a plump mouth sullen in a child, provocative in a woman. Which is she? She is very shy, blushing when her husband boasts that she baked the cake herself. She wears an unbuttoned sweater over her dress, school shoes, ankle socks.

We're all Bennett people, neighbors, fellow workers, this is Clara, hello, this is Sandy, hi, Clara, this is Lyle, this is Joe.

They are Southerners, like so many of them here, but with my tenacity, I recognize it, they talk slower but feel the same. He must be thirty-five, a lot older than his wife, crow's-feet under the freckles, they act dumb but I don't believe it.

I detected the sly rube who liked to take city slickers.

Clara talks to the wife. Clara in this conversation is the older woman from New York, Mrs. James maybe sixteen years old stands in awe of that sophistication. And then a baby is brought out, the child wife has a baby!

The establishment of them sitting modestly for our admiration: people are strong, they prove themselves. You see, Clara? You can wrest life from a machine and walk away.

"'A course," he was saying, "all this work ain't just the season. You wouldn't know but they was a wildcat strike last summer. Quite a to-do at the main gate. The company brought in strikebreakers. A feller was killed. They closed the plant down, fired everone. Everone!"

I nod, this is man talk.

The baby began to cry, the young mother unbuttoned and gave her breast right in the parlor, neither of them made anything of it. I glanced at Clara. She was intent. She watched the infant suck, she watched the mother and child. Expressed in Sandy James' face just that absorption in the task as the doll mother's in her solemn game.

"I started out in trim," Lyle says. "Now I hang doors. You get a few more cents a hour. Hands don't cut up so bad. Lemme see your hands," he said. I held them out, swollen paws, a thousand cuts. "Yeah," he says, "that's it."

After a while he went over to the radio we had heard, obviously his pride and joy, a Philco console of burled wood big as a jukebox. A circular dial lit up green when he turned it on, it had regular and short-wave broadcasts, and a magic tuning eye like a cat's green eye with a white pupil that grew narrow when he brought in a station.

He had turned it on as casual as he could be and while it warmed up consulted a newspaper. "How 'bout *Mr. First Nighter*," he said, "seein as you folks're from New York," he said to Clara.

Yes, they had culture!

We sat in dutiful appreciation and listened. Mrs. James had put her baby back to bed and sat now, a child herself, cross-legged on the floor right in front of the speaker, she wanted to get in there behind the cloth with those people.

In the casual grant of their warmth and circumstances we are so installed in the life as to have neighbors, we have started to live in their assumptions. I look at Clara she is way ahead of me, she is wearing her gold band.

As the drama crackled through the night the husband displayed enlightenment as to how the sound effects were made.

Someone kicked down a door. "They don't really wreck a door," he said. "'At's just a ordinary vegetable crate they stomp on. Splinters real good."

A horse-drawn carriage. "Shucks, them's coconut shells rapped on the table."

"Hush, Loll," his wife said. "I cain't hear!"

After the program was over he lectured on how they made houses burn, typhoons blow, trees come down. He had us close our eyes and did these things up against our ears to get the effect of amplification. He was good, too, insane, I began to realize, once people got through their courtesy it was their madness they shared.

He had heard some *Arabian Nights* drama about a desert chieftain who skinned his victims alive.

"Ah don't wanna hear this, Loll," his wife said.

"Hold on, honey—see, Joe, I couldn't figger it out, Ah thought and thought, it was the damnedest thing! But I got it now, close your eyes a minute, this'll turn your hair white."

I hear a piteous wail, screams, sinister laughter and the unmistakable stripping off of human skin inch by inch. I have to look. Off my left ear he was tearing a piece of adhesive tape down the middle.

* * *

No, not exactly my type, I would not under ordinary circumstances choose to associate with Lyle Red James, but I knew when we walked off to work together in the morning Clara would have coffee with his wife, maybe during the day they'd go to the grocery store together I saw the child given from one pair of arms to the other—I would listen to a hundred nights of radio for that.

And at the front gates of the plant every morning a car or two of cops parked there, just happening to be there. Not that I thought they were looking for me but if they were I imagined Red James as my disguise. If the cops were looking at all, it was for a man walking by himself—that was my reasoning. And anyway, what they would have to accomplish to get to this point wasn't very likely. They would have first of all to locate Mrs. Lucinda Bennett's car in Dayton, the guy wasn't that stupid that he wouldn't paint it. But even if they did, they would know only that they were looking for a wooden station wagon registered to clever Joseph Bennett Jr. But even then, how did that get them to Jacksontown, Indiana? But supposing they were here, they wouldn't find it anyway, it was parked off the street behind a garage and under a ton of snow. I probably couldn't find it myself. But supposing they found it, they'd be on the lookout for a hobo boy, a loner walking by himself to work in the morning and not Mr. Joe Paterson loping along step after step with the world's biggest fucking hayseed.

It always proved out to my satisfaction if I thought about it but that didn't stop me from thinking about it again each morning going to the punch clocks under the thousand fists like rifle fire we are going into the trenches and over the top in the barrage of time clocks, I always checked my position before I went down there.

I sought disguise, every change in Clara and me a disguise, nobody who knew Clara Lukács and was in his right mind would look for her on Railroad Street. I liked us having neighbors, yes, and living to the life the same as everyone else, living married, looking like an automobile worker's family for life, appearing to these people next door as mirrors of themselves, shining in their eyes so they couldn't even describe us after we'd gone.

I remember the way Red James walked. He wasn't especially tall but he took long stiff-kneed strides, loping along there in the freezing morning while everyone else was hunched up, head bent in the wind, it was something you had to tear to get through, but here was Red, shoulders back, head up out of his collar, the long neck bobbing, and he chattered constantly, made jokes, told stories.

"A smart man'll put beans in his mule's feedbag. You know why?"

"Why?"

"Doubles the rate of progress."

"Come on."

"'Strue! The fartin moves 'em along. Clocked a mule once sixty miles a hour on a handful of dry beans. Fastern' 'ese here cars."

That was the kind of thing. He held out his arms; the snow driving thick like white sheets flapping in your eyes, yelling, "Toughen me up, God, usen me up to it!"

And he sang, too, always some damn hillbilly song in that adenoidal tenor of his kind as we went down toward the plant one point of raw color bobbing crowing.

Hear the mighty eng-ine
Hear the lonesome hobos squall
. . . A-goin through the jungle
On the Warbash Cannonball!

And at work I found myself hearing his voice in the
machines, in the rhythm of the racket, without even
knowing it, doing headlight after headlight, I would
sing to myself in Red James' tenor: keeping time to the
pounding racket, I would hear the mighty eng-ine,
hear the lonesome hobos squall, a-goin through the
jungle, on the Warbash Cannonball.

One evening I came out of the gate and somebody
tapped me on the shoulder. I turned around, no one
was there. When I turned back, Red James was grinning at me.

"You comin to the meetin, ain't ya?"

"What meeting?"

"Union meetin."

"Well, I'm not a member, Red."

"I know you ain't. This is a recruitin meetin, anyone's got the balls."

"Well, I don't know," I said. "I never told Clara I
wouldn't be home."

"Boy, the little woman sure has a holt a you. She's
with Sandy anyways, you come on with me, they'll figger it out."

So I went along with him to this meeting in some
decrepit fraternal lodge a few blocks from the plant. It
was up a couple of flights, fifty or so men sitting on
camp chairs in a badly lighted room. I recognized a
few faces from the line, we smiled, catching each

other out. I thought, Look, if you're doing the life, do it. I took a seat in the last row. Red had disappeared. The people running the meeting sat at a table in front of the room. I couldn't see all of them but they looked like Paterson toughs, they wore buttons or had their union cards stuck in the bands of their hats. I thought as Mr. Bennett was spread out and made into a corporation he may have enlarged, but so did the response, I couldn't see anyone in his personal service wearing his green putting a union button on their collar.

The meeting began with the pledge of allegiance and then the president rapped the gavel and called on the secretary to read the minutes.

Lyle Red James stood up and cleared his throat. "Herewith the o-fishul minutes at the last meetin'," he said in a most formal manner. "As taken by yo Sec'tary Loll Jimes, Bennett Local Seventeen, union card number three six six oh eight?"

This called up a cheer and a burst of applause from the audience.

"Just read the damn minutes, James," the president said.

I hadn't known he was a union official, he had sprung it on me, it was queer, the faintest misgiving, I had thought the deception in our friendship was mine. I tried to think that whole meeting why I was bothered, I knew he was a damn clown I hadn't understood I was his audience.

I wanted to talk to Clara about it when I got home. Anyway, she'd be interested to know why I was late— but something else was on her mind entirely.

"Did you know," she said to me, "Sandy James is all

of fifteen years old? Did you know that? She got married at thirteen. Can you beat that? And she does everything, she goes to the store she knows what's good and what isn't, she takes care of that kid like royalty, feeds that stupid hick better than he deserves, washes, shops, cleans, Jesus! The only thing I haven't seen her do is sew the American flag!"

WHAT KIND OF TIME WAS THIS, A MATTER OF A few weeks, a couple of days, minutes, and this other couple was in us, through us, I couldn't remember when we hadn't known them and lived next door.

In the second war we used to jam each other's radio signals, occupy the frequency, fill it with power.

Clara didn't think much of Red James but she never said no to one of their invitations, she had fixed on young Sandy, in that way she attached to people who interested her, locking on her with all her senses. I sometimes became jealous, actually jealous, I felt ashamed, stupid it was the diversion I had hoped for, it was just what I had counted on, I jammed myself when I saw the way Clara looked at Sandy, watched every move she made. Worrying about survival was something new to her and she was engaged by it, as by the little baby, the smell of milk and throwup, a bath in a galvanized-tin tub with water made hot on a coal stove, and all the ordinary outcomes of domestic life which presented themselves to her as adventure—how could I feel anything except gratitude! I thought every minute with Sandy James put Clara's old life further behind us, I felt each day working for my benefit I was a banker compounding his interest.

In the James kitchen Clara watches Sandy James dry the baby after her bath, the baby in towels on the kitchen table, two lovely heads together and laughing at the small outstretched arms, the gurgling infant, the women laughing with pleasure. I am noticed in the doorway, the heads conspire, the flushed faces, some not quite legible comment between them as they turn and look at me, smiling and giggling in what they know and what I don't.

I liked Sandy myself, I thought of her as my ally, the chaperone of my love, this child! I found her attractive especially in the occasional surprised look she gave me, as if she were an aspect of Clara and the current of attraction was stepped up by that.

"She was made to have babies," Clara said to me. "You can't see how strong she is because she doesn't know anything about clothes, all her things are too big for her, I don't know where she got them, but when she doesn't have anything on you can see how well built she is in the thighs and hips."

Clara's attentiveness to his wife did not go unnoticed by Red James, when we were all together he did what he could to affirm the universal order of things. One night he brought out his infant girl from their bedroom. Baby Sandy had no diaper or shirt. He held her up in his hand and said, "Looky here, Joe, you see this little darlin between her legs? You ever see them pitchers of gourami fish in the *National Geographical*? You know, them kissin fish? Ain't I right? Now I got two of em, two lovin women with poontangs just like that!"

This made Sandy James stare at the floor, her face reddening to the roots of her hair. "Lookit!" he said, laughing. "Colors up like the evenin sun!"

Clara sighed, stubbed out her cigarette and took Sandy and the baby into the other room.

He one night pours two shot glasses of Old Turkey I don't know what we're celebrating does he see Clara's hand touch Sandy's hair?

He says, "Hey, y'll see this here little girl, I kin make her do what I want, laugh, cry, anythang, watch." He begins to laugh, a silly high-pitched little laugh. Sandy ignores him, he jumps around to get in front of her puts his hand over his mouth, tries to keep from laughing, after a minute of his pyrotechnics she can't help herself, begins to laugh, protesting too of course, "*Shh, shh,* your gonna wake her Loll, *shhh,* you're wakin her up!,*" but he's really funny and she is laughing now, a child laughing, and in fact I'm laughing too at the mindlessness of the thing and suddenly he stops, face blank, staring at her puzzled his mouth turns down at the corners a sob comes out of him, he puts his arm up to his eyes, cries pitifully, we know what he is doing so does Sandy but she goes very quiet and asks him quietly to stop, he ignores her, keeps it up, crying to break your heart. "Oh Loll darlin'," she said, "you know I cain't tol'rate that," and then her eyes screw up, her lower lip protrudes, she is reduced, begins bawling, arm up, fist rubbing her eyes, she has a hole in the underarm of her dress, her red hair.

"What I tell you!" Red James says, laughing. "This li'l ole thang, look there she's a-just cryin her heart out!" and she is, she can't stop, he goes to her to comfort her maybe a bit sorry now that he's done this but she's furious. He tries to put his arms around her, she brings her leg up sharply, knees him in the groin, stalks off. Red James has to sit down, he takes a deep whistling breath.

And that's when Clara began to laugh.

IN A GREAT DRAMATIC SCRAWL, FULL OF FLOUR-ishes:

To Joe—
Herein all my papers, copies of chapbooks, letters, *pensées*, journals, night thoughts—all that is left of me. Dear Libby is to keep them for your return. And you will return, I have no doubt about it. I have thought a good deal about you. You are what I would want my son to be. More's the pity. But who can tell, perhaps we all reappear, perhaps all our lives are impositions one on another.

W.P.
Loon Lake
Oct 24 1937

THREE LITTLE WORDS. *SUREE RITTU WARUZ*. THE girls had voices like cheap violins and they kept their wavery pitch as the car careened around abrupt corners, horns blasting, peddlers and old monks falling out of the way. It was three o'clock in the morning and the shopkeepers were already unrolling their mats heaving the flimsy boxes of fresh wet seagreens from the beds of trucks pitch-black the Tokyo sky above, Warren looked up as if to pray like a seasick sailor keeping his eye on a fixed point a light in the Oriental heavens channeled by tile roofs the heavens flowing in an orderly manner unlike the progress of the Cord, its headlights flashing the startled faces of the poor Japanese street class taking their morning fish soup hunkering beside small fires in metal drums. White-gowned attendants at the Shinto shrines sprinkled the cobblestoned courts with handfuls of water. *Suree rittu waruz*.

The car braked to a halt and Warren and the ladies pitched forward over each other hysteric laughter they all climbed down where are we he said and they led him triumphantly to the next bistro of the infinite night this one a *mirikubawa*. A what? Warren kept saying as they were led in through the smoke up on the platform

three black musicians were playing *jazzu* and a waitress got to the little table almost before they sat down
and they all watched the expression on Warren's face
as the drinks were ordered and then the rollicking hys-
terico laughter as he tasted the white substance in the
sake cup *mirik* it was milk this was a milk bar and their
civilization had triumphed again in producing for the
American their friend the one substance they never
drank and were astonished that anyone could, cow's
milk, the very sort of thing that made the Westerners
smell that characteristic way from their consumption
from birth of the squirted churned curded and boiled
issue *issyouee* of the ridiculous cow. They did not like
the smell of course and only one *garu* from whom he
learned the *Chiara-stun* and what merriment that was
that they had to teach him his dance, a bold brown-
eyed bow-legged thing with her bobbed hair and low-
waisted dress pleated to flare out above the knees had
the nerve in the intimacy of his room one dawn to hold
her fingers squeezing her own nostrils while he fucked
her looking down over the upraised knees upon which
he rested his bulk she was lying there holding her nose
and squeezing her eyes shut but making the sounds of
pleasure too how odd and later he said do I smell so
bad do I need to bathe no no she said with *moga* merriment you can never washu away you it is *ura smerr*,
you *smerra butta* Penfield-san a *whore tubba butta*

They were his friends his introduction to the world
of flappers I had to come seven thousand miles from
home to meet a flapper he thought and all the things
he had read in the papers at home about the new people their jazz their late nights their haircuts and merry
step up from provincialism he found there in Japan
how odd they were relentless and because he was

American he was an authority they came to him for authenticity and all the protests he made were regarded with approval as ritual modesty the kind of social grace they thought only they had so he was an ideal teacher they thought he understood the Japanese way so humble he fit right in and he learned to make decisions simply because he was their authority. I'm from the working class he had announced when he first arrived with his introductions from his Seattle labor movement friends but something was misinterpreted here or there the upper class liberals the modern boys and girls rebels of the loins of the Meiji the *mobo* and the *moga* they took him up and he was forced to have cards printed in the Japanese way everywhere you went you presented your card or received someone's card on a salver a lacquered salver Mr. Warren Penfield Teacher of Western Customs ordinarily this consisted in not much more than appearing somewhere and allowing yourself to be observed your dark suit and rolled umbrella, one man to his embarrassment asked him to disrobe in front of the whole family to his boxer shorts so the women could see the undergarments and sock garters and make them on their own for the father and brother. Mr. Warren Penfield slowly learning the contact language by which he could communicate The Handshake lesson one The Tip of the Hat lesson two the Stroll with the Umbrella lesson three Helping Ladies Across the Street very *difficurr resson* four the deference shown to women the most genuinely unpleasant of the customs but they did it he looked at the *jazzu* pianist and the *jazzu* pianist looked at him and smiled and shook his head here they were together in service the smile said the frank and somewhat contemptuous self-awareness mirrored in the other doing the same thing what are we doing here man I mean I got an excuse what's yours that look of economically dependent expatriate we really down the ladder man to be stuck on this island making nigger faces for these little yellow men.

But one day Warren's reputation was made when a low-level official of the American embassy called and asked him to come by for a chat and it was to see if he would consent to offer his services to certain Japanese diplomats preparing themselves to sail to Washington, D.C., for an interesting naval conference cutaway striped coats gray trousers top hats I don't know anything Warren said my father mined coal I was a corporal in the Signal Corps what do I know but the embassy man said we have no choice you're up on the latest fashions everybody else has been here too long our faces are turning yellow yours is still pink and white like a cherry blossom he laughed and so Warren gave a lecture in recent cultural history in America about which he thought he knew nothing but which from having observed the Japanese he knew by refraction. There is a great liberalizing trend he said because of the Great War and internationalization to taste a sense the old ways must be overthrown and the old beliefs and restrictions are absurd. Young men and women marry because they fall in love and sometimes when they fall in love they don't even marry they live together in defiance of propriety half the point to the way they live is to insult propriety. People generally expect more, I think that is what you can say about us at this modern age of the 1920s, more love more money more freedom more dancing *Chiara-stun jazzu* men and women hold each other to dance in public and there is a music industry that produces their dance music for them and wickedness is a form of grace, transgression is seen as the liberation of the individual spirit but, he said, looking with alarm on the impassive frowns of his distinguished audience, you won't find any of that in Washington, D.C. Washington under Mr. Harding is the soul of propriety, he spoke slowly so the translators could keep up one word was equivalent to three or four sentences before the word, the word, after the word, the three little words blossomed like a bowl of chrysanthemums Mr. Harding himself is devoted to Bach and Boccherini especially the andantes, and the distinguished audience leaned back in its chairs and the look of impassive disapproval was replaced by the look of impassive approval. Afterward there was a reception and he found himself bowing it was easy quite easy and the embassy man said you missed your calling you should have come into State and he bowed to him too. A junior Japanese diplomat said he had studied at Harvard University. A blond young woman glanced at him. A Japanese publisher asked him if he did any writing. The same young woman glanced at him. She had a ring on her finger eventually they spoke she spoke of the entire Japanese nation as if they were all servants, making remarks about their character and reliability, she was married to one of the embassy staff. They became friends, Warren had now established within himself those women he was prone to love and those with whom he was most intimate in conversation two separate classes and always he recognized them when they appeared, this young woman was of the second class. Her husband was always busy but they were totally married in spirit in purpose in confidence so that all possibly naughty emanations from her were totally muffled in

marriagehood, that was more than all right with Warren they became devoted friends she was a Midwes-
terner not that smart but in some blind instinctive way
constantly putting him in touch with just the experiences that provoked his deepest response which then
expressed what she might have felt had she been that
articulate or generally sensitive to the meanings of
things. She knew he was a poet. She was a prim neat
young woman with a slender figure and the most ap-
palling provincial drawbacks she had even found herself a Methodist congregation for Sunday mornings but
she methodically introduced him to Japanese civilization. She knew the secret restaurants where you could
get the best raw sea bream or salted baby eggplant or
bean paste flavored with thrush liver or chrysanthe-
mum petals dipped in lemon vinegar, they went to the
shrines he sat in rooms perfectly furnished with no furniture slowly very slowly the authority on Western
manners customs and English speech began to see
things with a Japanese eye to cherish small things a
lovely comb a lacquered bowl a shallow pond with fat
orange carp the way some trees looked in their foliage
as if tormented by wind or a madwoman having just
extended her hair with the pads of her fingers. The
young Midwestern wife became the audience for the
drama of his life if she had not been there watching
and finding it important he might never have changed
but found his period with the irreverent flappers or
lapsed into the paternal delusions of the foreign diplo-
matic community enjoying with a smirk the Japanese
discovery of *besbol* the humor of Adolph Menjou Lil-
lian Gish speaking in ideograms. Instead he began his
withdrawal first from the Americans then from the
Japanese trying to be like the Americans then from the

wide streets of the city in which he shuddered to see men in derbies and rolled umbrellas riding bicycle cabs, he grew thin and ate no meat he turned sallow and began to look actively for a style of expiation he could manage without self-consciousness but he couldn't have been that brave unless someone like the young wife from Minneapolis was there to pay attention.

The afternoon before he left on his pilgrimage she took him to the Bunraku puppet theater. Each large puppet was manipulated by three figures in black hoods one for the right arm and spine and face including the lifting of the eyebrows one for the left arm one for the feet, the puppets moved dipped bowed gesticulated raised arms to heaven walked ran, each movement was accompanied by the three black shadows behind to the side and underneath and to further disintegrate the human idea the voices of the puppets their growling thrilling anguish was delivered from the side of the stage by a reader whose chants were punctuated by the plunks of the samisen like drops of water falling on a rock and Warren Penfield after several hours of this thought yes it's exactly true, when I speak I hear someone else saying the words when I decide to do something someone else is propelling me when I look up at the sky or down at the ground I feel the talons on my neck how true what genius to make a public theater out of this why don't we all stand up and tear the place apart what brazen art to tell us this about ourselves knowing we'll sit here and not do a thing.

The puppet play told the story of two lovers who, faced with adversity, decided to commit suicide together and so at the intimate crucial moment there were eight presences onstage.

A COLD BRIGHT SUN GLITTERING ON THE SNOW, dazzling the eyes, you couldn't tell where you were, in what desolate tundra of the world. But men got to work. The stamping of thousands of feet muffled by the deep snow.

Inside the Autobody the great clamoring noise seemed distant, a distant hum, as if the peculiar light reflecting the snow outside were a medium of shushing constraint.

It was an ominous day, I felt something was wrong, from down the line it came like a conveyed thing, going through my station like a hunk of shapeless metal with no definable function.

But I knew secrets, I was in on secrets.

At lunchtime the whistle blew, belts slowed down and stopped. I listened to one generator in particular, pitch whine dropping deeper and deeper to nothing. I went to my locker, men rubbed their hands on rags and looked at each other. Then someone came in who thought he knew where the trouble was, and holding our sandwiches and thermoses, we drifted toward it, we climbed over the car bodies and trod the motionless belts as if walking on tracks, and we came finally to an area flooded with bright daylight.

Two great corrugated sliding doors were open, I could see outside to the flatbed railroad car. Granulated snow gusting in. Sticking to spots of oil and grease. The cold sting of the day blowing in.

"Here, you men, you don't belong here!" A uniformed guard coming toward us with a scowl.

They were dismantling a whole section of machines, unbolting them from the floor and preparing to hoist them on pulleys. Someone said they were tool-and-die machines for the radiator grilles.

At quitting time I waited in front of the tavern across the street from the main gate. Red didn't show up. I walked quickly in the dark down Railroad Street.

"The train I ride on is a hundred coaches long, you can hear the whistle blow nine hundred miles. You see, Joe, when the New Year comes soon as everone's past the Xmas bonus, soon as everone begins to think a the spring layoffs as you cain't help but doin when the year swings round, that's when we're a-settin down. You understand the beauty o' that? The union's allotin considerable monies. You see what you don't know is that Number Six makes all the trim for the Bennett plants in three states. Do you take my meanin? Ever bumper. Ever hubcap. Ever runnin board. Ever light. When we set down come January, ever Bennett plant in Michigan, Ohio and Indiana is gonna feel it. 'Course I'm trustin you with this, you cain't tell no one, it's a powerful secret compris'n the fate of many. *Ohh-oh me, ohh-oh my, you can hear the whistle blow nine hundred miles."*

When I got home Clara wasn't there. I went next door. She was standing in the bedroom doorway holding Sandy's baby.

Two men were sitting in the parlor. They were

dressed in work clothes. Sandy introduced me, they
were members of the board of the local and I thought I
recognized one of them from the meeting. He was a
skinny little man and he didn't look at me as he talked.
"Yeah, Paterson," he said, "I seen you around." His
eyes darted to the phone on the desk.

The other man was younger, bulkier, he had a fixed
smile on his face as if he had trained himself to it.
"We're waitin for Red," he said.

They sat back down. Sandy James didn't know what
to do with them, she stood there rubbing her palms on
her hips. The parlor was awfully crowded, I thought,
with all of us and a Christmas tree too with the tip
touching the ceiling the star awry.

"You and James buddies, Paterson?" the little man
said.

"Yes."

He nodded, kept nodding as if unaware of the brev-
ity of my answer.

And then the phone rang and he jumped up as if he
had been waiting, and grabbed the receiver. "Yeah,"
he said, "yeah, that's it." He hung up.

"Well," he said looking at the other one, "I guess
we'll be on our way," indicating the door with his chin.
"Sorry to trouble you, Mrs. James."

"Red should be home right soon."

"No, no, that's okay," the little man said. "Just tell
him we were in the neighborhood. Nothin important."

They left, she locked the door after them.

"Oh, it gives me the jitters," she said, "strangers
comin round and askin questions."

"Like what?"

"Where we got our lovely furnishins? How long we
had the radio?"

I went over to the desk, for the first time I noticed the phone had no number written on it the little white circle was blank.

"Where is Red?"

Sandy looked at me and down at the floor.

"Come on, Sandy, for God's sake," I said.

"To a meetin," she said. "A secret union meetin."

"A board meeting?"

"I guess."

I didn't argue with her. I motioned to Clara and we went back to our side. The house, banked with snow, was without draught, sealed, like a tomb. I didn't know why but I felt bad, I felt desolate, I didn't care about anything.

"Hey, big boy," Clara said. "Let me see you smile."

Later in our bed I was so huge with love for her it was a kind of mourning sound I made, plunged into my companion. The ceiling light was on. Her head was turned from me, her eyes were closed, her knuckles were in her teeth, high color spread up from her throat suffusing her face, her ears, this was not my alley cat of gasping contempt raking her nails down my back this was my wife connected to me by the bones of being, oh this clear ecstasy ravage on the skin, reluctance it was happening, lady's grief of coming.

I SAID TO RED JAMES, "WILL YOU TELL ME WHAT'S going on?," my voice feeble and complaining. I already knew in this town of thirty thousand the crucial action was at my eyes, I was centered in it, it could not be less clear than something I would read in the newspaper. I was at the fulcrum where the smallest movement signified distant matters of great weight.

And he answered wonderfully not as if he had until this moment deceived me but as if I'd always known and admired him for what he was.

"See, Joe, I coulda stayed on, you know? Hell, I had it so finely made I mighta run for somethin someday in the national. But the client don't give a hoot fer that. He gets the intelligence and he spooks like a horse in a hurricane. I mean I'd laugh if I didn't feel like cryin."

We were walking home men everywhere talking in groups LAYOFFS! in the headlines flyers announcing a mass meeting trampled in the snow. Red suggested we stop in for a drink. We stood in front of a tavern I'd not been in before, the light in the window was gold and orange, it looked warm in there, I felt I'd better have something.

We sat in a booth in the back under a dip in the patterned ceiling. Behind us was the door to the toilet. We sat in this plywood booth drinking twenty-cent shots with water chasers I smelled the whiskey in my head odor of piss cigarette smoke the sweat of every man in the room.

"Course I ain't without choice, they's a little job at the Republic Steel in Chicago. Ain't no auto worker in Jacksontown gonna follow me to pull steel in Chicago. An' ifn there is, just in case, looky here."

He pulled a paper bag from his lunch pail, shook a small bottle uncapped it put a drop of liquid on his right index finger rubbed the liquid into the red hairs on the knuckles of his left hand. He spread the hand on the table: the red hairs were black.

"You like that?" he grinned, my stunned silence, he signaled the bartender for two more. "But hell, I'm thinkin to drop industrial work. You been to the city of Los Angeleez?"

I shook my head.

"Well, they's a need for operators there. They's so much messin around what with them movie stars and all, you see, ever good wife needs to make her case sooner or later, if you get my meanin. As does ever good husband. Yessir, they's opportunity in Los Angeleez."

He was nervous, talking with much careless confidence his glance kept flying up to the room behind me and coming back to me and flying off. It happened in the crowded bar that the lower register of his voice was lost in the babble of the room, so half of what he said I couldn't hear, I only saw the trouble he was in enacted on his face, in the animated appearance of him spiky unshaven red hair around the Adam's apple, the sud-

denly large teeth threatening to engulf his chin, pale
white eyelashes pink-lidded eyes staring through their
mask.

Joe was suspended, blasted. Gone was the wiseass
street kid, gone in love, gone in aspiration, gone in the
dazzlement of the whole man, the polished being.

"See, if the union was smart they wouldn't never let
on they knowed. Take their losses this hand, play for
the next, string me along without me knowin and use
me against the company and tell me one thing and do
another an trick Bennett right out of their shoes. An'
shit, everyone woulda made out all around, the union
'cause they knowed 'bout me, the company still thinkin they had their inside op, and me still drawin my
pay in good faith and doin my work."

He slumped against the back of the booth. "Hell,
it's all the same anyways, the boys'll get their wages
and grievance committees and such and it won't matter, the company'll just hike their prices, everthin'll be
the same. But you see, they let me know they know
and the company knows they know and I'm not good
to anyone anymore leastwise to myself and now I gotta
take that poor chile and move her out of her home."

"Red, it is so weird! You recruited me!"

"I surely did. I brought in numbers a good men an'
true."

"Let me ask you, does Sandy know?"

"What, about me bein a detective? Aw, Joe," he
said with a grin, "The poor chile has so much of a man
in me already did I tell her the whole truth she'd go
out of her natural mind with love!"

It now occurred to me to ask why I had been told. I
was at the point of perceiving his peculiar genius,
which was to make a lie even of the truth. He was

waving his hand, calling someone, I turned just as two men arrived at the table.

"Set yourself down!" Red greeted them.

One slid in beside me, the other beside Red. I had never seen them before. They were heavy middle-aged men, one wore a suit and tie and coat with the collar turned up, the other had on a lumber jacket and a blue knit cap.

"See," Red said to them without any preamble, "I ain't sayin I didn't make a mistake. I don't want you to think that, whatever happens."

"That's all right, Mr. James," the one in the overcoat said. He was sitting next to me. He pointed at me with his thumb. "And this is him?"

"My good friend and neighbor Mr. Paterson," Lyle Red James said.

"I see," the man in the overcoat said. He twisted in his seat and leaned back to look at me.

The fellow across from him pulled off his cap. He sat hunched over the table holding the cap in his fists. He was a white-haired man and his florid face was covered with gray stubble. He now spoke, his eyes lowered. "James," he said, "there is a particular place in hell, in fact its innermost heart, where reside for eternity the tormented souls of men of your sort. They freeze and burn at the same time, their skin is excoriated in sulfurous pools of their accumulated shit, the tentacles of foul slimy creatures drag them under to drink of it. This region is presided over by Judas Iscariot. You know the name, I trust."

Red began to laugh. "Aw, come on," he said, incredulous, "that ain't no kind of talk."

Then this man with the cap in his hands turned to Red and looked at him. I saw tears in his eyes. "On behalf of every workingman who has gone down under the club or been shot in the back, I consign you to that place. And may God have mercy on my soul, I will go to hell too, but it'll be a joyful thing if I can hear your screams and moans of useless contrition from now till the end of time."

"Hey, brother," Red James said, "Come on now, you ain't even tried to see if I'm tellin the truth. That ain't exactly fair!"

Both men had risen. The man with the blue knit cap leaned over and spit in Red's face. The two of them made their way into the crowd and went out the door.

Red was impassive. He splashed some water from his glass onto his handkerchief and washed himself. He glanced at me. "Catholic fellers," he said.

A few minutes later we left the bar. My blood was lit with two whiskeys, and with the imagery of sin and death in my brain I wanted to ask him more questions —questions!—as if I didn't already know, like some fucking rube I beg your pardon would you spell it out for me please! Clara, I still had time, there was still time for me to get her and throw our things in a bag and get us the hell out of there. Instead I walked with Red James down Railroad Street in this peculiar identification I made with him, as if only he could guard me from what I had to fear from him, and on Railroad Street where it made a sharp turn there was a shortcut across an empty lot the moon was out and going across this terrain Red glanced at me as I tried to phrase my questions he looked at me with genuine curiosity, as if, with all his figuring he had not figured me to be, in this outcome, that stupid. And we went across the snow moon of the frigid night making our way to our joined homes and fates as if nothing had happened and two ordinary workers had only stopped for a drink in the time-honored way. He was singing now in his nasal tenor the ritual that comes on the excommunicated

The train I ride on is a hundred coaches long
You can hear the whistle blow nine hundred miles
Ohh-oh me, ohh-oh my
You can hear the whistle blow nine hundred miles

A T ONE POINT THE POLICE ASKED ME IF I KNEW who it was. I shook my head. "I never even saw them," I said. This technically was true. But I thought I knew them anyway. I recognized the sentiment. I heard in the furious contention the curses of my own kind. Swaying and tumbling all together, we were one being in the snow, one self-reproaching self-punishing being.

The police wore their blue tunics over sweaters. Their hips were made ponderous by all the belts and holsters and cuffs and sticks hanging from them. They were tough and stupid, there were four of them in the hospital emergency room, four cops writing their reports on pads wound with rubber bands. Then the reporter arrived from the local paper, a thin small man in a Mackinaw and fedora, and he asked them if they had found anything in the lot. I could tell it had not occurred to them to look.

When Clara got there with Sandy I was lying on a table in one of the treatment rooms and on the table next to me was the body. I think I'd been given something before they set my arm because I saw Sandy's stunned very white face but I didn't hear the sound she made. The attendant pulled away the sheet the lips were curled back from the teeth like he was grinning and Sandy passed out. Clara, who was holding the baby, grabbed Sandy's arm and kept her from falling while the attendant ran for the smelling salts. I thought it was still Red making her do whatever he wanted.

Sometime later I had a chance to talk to Clara for a minute.

"He was a company op," I said.

She shook her head. "The poor dumb galoot."

"None of this had anything to do with us," I said, "and I danced us right into it." I didn't want to talk this way. I looked in her eyes for the judgment and not finding it tried to put it here by talking this way.

She touched her fingers to my lips.

"He couldn't have been placed better," I said. "It was a secret strike plan, nobody knew except the officers. And then the company took out half the machines."

"Some men came to their house this afternoon," she said.

"What?"

"Just when it was getting dark. We happened to be

on our side. At first Sandy thought it was the radio, that she left it on."

"Did you get a look at them?"

"I didn't want to. I heard what they were doing. They tore the place apart."

"Jesus."

"It's lousy that she got hit with all this," she said.

"Well, now I know why they didn't believe him."

"What? I don't think you should try to talk."

"No, it's all right, I'm doped up. I'm saying he was trying to pin it on me. I guess he couldn't think of anything better."

"What?"

"But they weren't buying it because they must have got into his files." I found myself panting in the effort to speak. I was having trouble catching my breath.

At this moment I saw in Clara's calm regard the disinterested understanding of a beat-up face—as if nothing I had to say was as expressive as the condition I was in.

"He tried to make me the fink," I said. I realized I was crying. "The son of a bitch. The goddamn hillbilly son of a bitch!"

She turned away.

I stayed that night in the hospital and once or twice I realized the moans on the ward were my own.

In the morning I caught a glimpse of myself in the metal mirror of the bathroom—arm in a sling, a swollen one-sided face, a beauty of a shiner. I found myself pissing blood.

I was released—I supposed on the ground that I was still breathing. I walked a couple of blocks to the car line. A clear cold morning. I sat in the streetcar as it gradually was engulfed in the tide of men walking to work. I thought of trying to work the line with a broken arm. I was out of a job.

Men stepped aside to let the streetcar through. Faces looked up at me. I had pretended to be one of them. That was the detective's sin.

When I got home I found Clara and Sandy James and the baby asleep in my bed. The house was cold and there was a fetid smell, faintly redolent of throw-up or death, it was a very personal smell of mourning or despair. I got the fire going in the coal stove—I was learning with each passing moment the surprises of a one-armed life.

I went next door. The place was a shambles. Red's desk had been jimmied open, the sofa cushions and chair cushions were piled up, the braided rug was thrown back, his collection of pulp magazines was tossed everywhere. His secretarial ledgers were on the floor, one with the names and addresses of the membership, another with his meeting minutes. I found boxes of mimeographed form letters, a loose-leaf folder with directives of the National Labor Relations Board, a scattered pack of blank union cards.

Inside the splintered front door, stuck in a crack, was the carbon copy of a handwritten memo dated some months before. It had been stepped on. It was addressed to someone with the initials C.I.S. It was signed not with a name but with a number. But I could tell who the writer was, Red wrote a very chatty espionage report, very folksy. He spelled grievance *gree-vins*.

The bedroom was no less worked over. I straightened the mattress and lay down and pulled a blanket over me. I knew that I should be thinking but I couldn't seem to make the effort. Eventually I fell asleep. A wind came along and worked at the broken front door, banging it open, banging it closed, and I kept waking or coming to with the intention of seeing who it was, who it was at the door who wanted to come into this pain and taste of blood.

In the parlor a man was picking up papers and tapping them into alignment on the floor. It was the tapping that woke me.

"Hey, pal," he said.

He wore a topcoat that was open and followed him like a train as he duckwalked from one item to another. His hat was pushed back on his head.

He stood up with an effort. "Oh boy," he said, "these old bones ain't what they used to be."

A lean face, pitted and scarred, very thick black eyebrows, and carbon-black eyes with deep grainy circles of black under them. A heavy five o'clock shadow. But the skin under all was pale and unhealthy-looking. He had collected Red's union records and was stuffing them now in a briefcase. He righted the armchairs and looked under the cushions. He felt around the desk drawers. He stacked Red's pulps, flipping through each one to see if there was anything in it. He was very thorough. And all the while he talked.

"Whatsamatter, the lady's husband come home early? Well, you tell me: was it worth it? I'll tell you: no. I know about ginch. It is seldom worth it. It is seldom worth what you have to go through to get it. I been married twice myself. I was happy in love for maybe five minutes each of those women."

It was speech intending to divert, patronizing speech, his eyes and hands busy all the while.

"Put that stuff back," I said. "It doesn't belong to you."

He smiled and shook his head. He came toward me. "Where's the widow?" he said.

"What?"

"His bereaved."

"I don't know."

He came over to me. "Hey, kid, look at you. Look at how they worked you over. How much can you take? What's the matter with you?"

I immediately recognized the professionalism of the threat.

"Listen," he said, "Don't be a wiseass. I'm here with the money, her death benefit." He waved an envelope in front of my eyes. I could feel the breeze on my hot face.

"She's at my place. I'll get her."

"I would be grateful," he said.

The women were up, they were in the kitchen, Clara was drinking coffee, she was wearing the clothes she had slept in, she looked gaunt, grim.

Sandy James' eyes were large and glistening with the unassuageable hurt of someone betrayed. The corners of her mouth were turned down. She was trying to feed her baby and the baby was enraged, it was twisting and turning, and making dry smacking sounds. It pulled on her breast and waved its tiny arms.

I explained, but even as I did he appeared in the doorway behind me. Sandy stood and thrust the baby at me and pulled her dress closed and buttoned the buttons while I held the crying baby, wriggling and twisting against my cast.

Now we all stood there frozen in that way of those overtaken by ceremony. Even the baby quieted down.

"I'm sorry for your trouble, Mrs. James," the man said. He held a legal-looking paper in one hand, an uncapped fountain pen in the other. "Your husband, Mr. James, was a brave man. The company knows it has a responsibility to his family. It ain't something we have to do, you understand, but in these cases we like to. If you will sign this receipt and waiver, both copies, I have a death-benefit sum of two hundred and fifty dollars cash on the barrelhead."

Sandy James looked at Clara. Clara sat with her head lowered, the fall of her hair hiding her face.

Sandy James looked at me. I knew what the waiver meant. Two hundred and fifty dollars seemed to be the going rate. Sandy James age fifteen was in no position to sue anybody. I nodded and she signed the waiver.

The fellow tucked one copy in his pocket and put the other on the table. He glanced at Clara. He took out his wallet and counted the money and put it in Sandy's hand. He came over to me and stuck his finger in the baby's cheek. "Hey, beauty," he said. He looked at me and laughed. "Beauty and the beast," he said.

When he was gone Clara found a cigarette and lit it.

"Two one-hundred-dollar beels," Sandy James said. "And a fifty-dollar beel."

I sat on the kitchen table and read the waiver. The party of the first part was Mrs. Lyle James and all her heirs and assignees.

The party of the second part was Bennett Autobody Corporation and its agents, C.I.S., Inc.

I said to Sandy, "You know what C.I.S. stands for?"

She shook her head.

Clara cleared her throat. "It means Crapo Industrial Services," she said. She took the baby from me. She hugged her and began to pace the room, hugging the baby and saying soft things to her.

"Mah milk's dried up,." Sandy said. "She'll have to get on that Carnation?"

"Red worked for Crapo Industrial Services," I said to Sandy. "Did you know that?"

"Nossir."

"Neither did I. Why should it surprise me?" I said. "Clara? Does it surprise you?"

Clara didn't answer.

"No? Then why should it surprise me?" I said. "After all, a corporation like Bennett Autobody needs its industrial services. Spying is an industrial service, isn't it? I suppose strikebreaking is an industrial service. Paying off cops, bringing in scabs. Let's see, have I left anything out?"

"Why don't you take it easy," Clara said.

"I'm trying to," I said. "I'm just one poor hobo boy. What else can I do?" I went out to the privy. The sky was clear but a wind was blowing dry snow in gusts along the ground. I was still pissing blood. When I spit, I spit blood. Someone who had business connections with F. W. Bennett was big-time. Tommy Crapo was big-time. Surely he did not even know the name Lyle Red James. It was a coincidence that the fucking hillbilly who lived next door to me was an operative of Crapo Industrial Services. That was all it was. It was not a plot against me. It was not the whole world ganging up on one poor hobo boy.

But in my mind I saw the death-benefit man stepping into a phone booth and placing a call.

I went back inside.

"Can you eat anything?" Clara said. She spoke in a hushed voice that irritated me. "Do you want some coffee?"

"Sit down," I said. I faced her across the kitchen table. "You knew that joker."

She folded her hands in her lap. She sighed.

"Well, who is he?"

"Just some guy. I used to see him around."

"A friend of yours?"

"Oh Christ, no. I don't think I ever spoke five words to him."

"What's his name?"

She shrugged.

"What's his name, Clara?"

"I don't remember. Buster. Yeah, I think they called him that."

"Buster. Well, did Buster say anything? Did he recognize you?"

She didn't answer.

"Clara, for Christ's sake—do you think he recognized you!"

Clara bowed her head. "He may have."

"Okay," I said. I stood up. "Fine. That's what I wanted to know. See, if we know what we're dealing with we know what to do. Am I right? We need to know what the situation is in order to know what to do. Now. Is Tommy Crapo in Jacksontown? You tell me."

"How should I know? I don't think so."

"Well, where would he be?"

She shrugged. "He could be anywhere. Chicago. He lives in Chicago."

"Good, fine. When Buster calls Mr. Tommy Crapo

in Chicago to tell him he's found Miss Clara Luckaćs, what is Mr. Tommy Crapo likely to do?"

"I don't like this. I don't want to talk about this anymore."

I leaned over the table. "Hey, Clara? You want to talk about us? You want to tell me how you love me? What is Mr. Tommy Crapo likely to do?"

"I don't know."

"Is he going to hang up the phone and laugh and call in his manicurist? Or is he going to come get you?"

She wouldn't answer.

"I mean what happened at Loon Lake? Why did he leave you there? Did you do something to make him mad? Or was it just a business thing?"

She slumped against the back of the chair. Her mouth opened. But she didn't say anything.

"Well?"

"You fuckin' bastard," she said.

"Oh, swell," I said. "Let's hear it. Step a little closer folks. Sandy!" I shouted. "Come in here and listen to this. Hear the lady Clara speak!"

We heard the front door close.

"You're terrific, you know?" Clara said, her eyes brimming. "That kid has just lost her husband."

"Don't I know it. And what a terrific guy he was. They're coming at me right and left, all these terrific guys. They run in packs, all your terrific friends and colleagues."

I ran next door.

Sandy James had put the baby in her carriage and was standing in the middle of the room pushing the carriage to and fro very fast.

"Sandy," I said, "I'm very sorry for all this and

when we have the time we'll talk about it if you want to. I'll tell you everything I can. Did Red ever give you instructions who to call or what to do in case something happened to him?"

"Nossir."

"Does he have family in Tennessee, anyone who should be notified? Anyone who could come help you?"

She shook her head.

"How about your family?"

Her lower lip was protruding. "They cain't do nothin."

"Well, did Red carry life insurance?"

She shook her head.

"Do you know what that is?"

She shook her head.

"Well, where does he keep the family papers? I mean like the kid's birth certificate. He must keep that somewhere."

That's when Sandy James began to cry. She tried not to. She kept rubbing her eyes with the heels of her hands as if she could press the tears back in.

I looked around the room. With Buster's tidying, the parlor was not too badly messed now. I began to go through it myself, opening the desk drawers, tossing things around. What was in my mind? I thought if Red James had not told his wife of an insurance policy, he would be likely to have one. I was looking with absolute conviction in the clarity of my thought for an insurance policy but why it seemed to me the first order of business I couldn't have said. I supposed it would lead to something. Different pieces of Lyle Red James had been lifted—his espionage self by the union avengers, his union self by the industrial-service hoods, surely there must be something left for me, something of value to me, something he owed me. Maybe there was a strongbox and maybe along with a birth certificate and an insurance policy there would be cash. He owed me something. He owed me a broken arm and a battered face and a considerable portion of my pride. He owed me my abused girl, he owed me the care and protection of his own wife and child. He owed me a lot. I ran into the bedroom and began to go through the closet. Every move I made was painful, but the more I searched—for what? where was it?— the more frenzied I became. My body had thought it out: I needed to get us all off Railroad Street. I needed to save Clara. I needed to get Sandy James and her baby home to Tennessee. I needed the money for all of this. I think I must have whimpered or moaned as I searched. I was in a cold sweat. At one point from the corner of my eyes I saw the two women standing in the door watching me. I took the sling off my arm so that I could move around more easily. Without the sling I felt the true weight of my cast. I thought of the weight as everything that had to be done before I could get out of Jacksontown. I wanted to shake this cement cast from my bones as I wanted to shake free of this weight of local life and disaster. None of it was mine, I thought, none of it was justly mine. I had stopped over. That was all. I wanted to be going again. I wanted to be back at my best, out of everyone's reach, in flight. But I had all this weight and I felt there was no time for condolence or ceremony or grief or shock or tears, there was hardly time for what I had to do in order to lift it from me so that we could get free.

EVENTUALLY IT DAWNED ON HIM, THE FUCKING radio of course, he pushed it away from the wall.

It was a small radio in a big cabinet. Under the tubes and behind the black paper speaker was a cigar box. In the box a .32-caliber pistol. He had never handled a gun before. It was heavy, felt loaded smelled oiled and sufficient. He put it back closed the box.

Wedged in the space between the tube chassis and the cabinet one of those cardboard accordion files with a string tie. This he lifted out. He pushed the radio back against the wall.

"Sandy!"

He sat on the floor. She knelt next to him. He watched her hands, she withdrew a marriage license a white paper scroll, she unrolled it holding it with both hands to her face as if she were near-sighted. She withdrew newspaper cutout coupons, a pack of them, the kind people saved for premiums, she withdrew the baby's birth certificate, she withdrew a wedding photo of Mr. and Mrs. Lyle James all dressed up smiling on the steps of a clapboard church. He had to let her cry over that one in her silent way palming the tears as they flowed. She withdrew a leather drawstring purse, he thought the deliberation of her movements would drive him out of his mind, she untied the string widened the mouth of the purse and shook out several shiny bright medals with ribbons.

"Was Red in the war?"

"Nossir."

"Stupid of me to ask."

She withdrew a printed policy of the Tennessee Mutual Life Insurance Policy. Its face value was a thousand dollars. That would have to do.

"Aren't there people who cash these things right away? Wills, IOUs, stuff like that?"

"Factors," Clara said.

"Yeah, factors. I bet I could get sixty, seventy cents on the dollar. This is as good as cash."

"It's not yours," Clara said.

"I didn't say it was. Would you mind coming into the other room a minute?"

Clara followed him into the Jameses' bedroom. He closed the door.

"I don't know," he said, "maybe you want to see your old sweetheart again. Have a few laughs."

"Is this what you think?"

"I don't know what I think. But if we don't move our ass out of here we're finished."

"Maybe so, but that's our problem, not hers."

"If we are all tending to our own problems," he said, "we can walk out this minute. We'll let the fifteen-year-old widow shift for herself. Is that what you want?"

"You're hurting my arm!"

"Why do I have to explain these things!"

"Let go of me. It was your idea, big boy. I didn't tell you to move to this shithole."

He went back to the parlor.

"Sandy, I'm prepared to take you back to Tennessee. I mean we're all finished in Jacksontown, I assume you understand that. You will spend Christmas with your family at your ancestral home. I am proposing we join forces, you and Clara and me, pool what we have and help each other. And I give you my word I will make good on every penny of the whole thousand."

The kid was silent. He waited. He realized this meant yes. "Okay," he said, "it's settled. We have a lot to do. He has to be buried. What are we going to do about that?" He looked at Clara. "Hey, Sandy, I bet you didn't know we had an expert among us."

The briefest bewilderment on Clara's face, what had she done wrong, did he blame his broken arm on her, his stitches? His mind was functioning now, he had calmed down, he was the old Joe of Paterson working things out. But one nick of this gem of a mind flashed the spectral light of treachery.

She smiled appreciatively almost shyly, with a dip of her head, a curl at the corner of her lips, her eyes sparkled, she had it, she knew it before he did, the secret wish, the resolution.

"Ah want the best," Sandy James said.

"Why not?" said Clara. She knelt down next to Sandy and put her arm around her. She tilted her head till their heads touched. "You'll have the best," Clara murmured. She looked up at him. "In Jacksontown it won't cost that much."

WHILE CLARA WAS ON THE PHONE I ASKED SANDY James how she felt about her furniture.

"It's all paid," she said.

"So much the better. I could get it appraised and you'd make a clear profit."

She clutched her baby and looked around the parlor. Her eyes were large. "Wherever I live I'm gonna need a chair and table. I'm gonna need a bed to sleep in."

"Okay, okay, I'm just asking, is all. I'll figure something out."

An hour and a half later I had everyone packed. I called a Yellow Cab and by the time it pulled up I had both women and the baby and the bags out on the sidewalk.

Nobody was watching. No car followed us. I took us back to the rooming house Clara and I had stayed in when we first hit town. I rented two rooms adjoining. I got everyone settled.

"Do you mind telling me what you're doing?" Clara said.

"Not at all. I'm going to the factor. Then I'm going to pick up my back pay. Then I'm going to see what I can do about a truck for all that shit of theirs."

"You better slow down. You don't look so good."

"I can imagine."

"You can't leave town before the funeral."

"I understand that. But we'll get a good night's

sleep. You don't object to a good night's sleep, do you?"

"She doesn't know what hit her yet. You're not giving her the chance."

"I'll leave that to you."

WE STAND ON EITHER SIDE OF SANDY JAMES, who holds her baby. I hunch into my khaki greatcoat. It is buttoned over my cast and I have pinned the sleeve. The grave has been dug through the snow and through the ice and, with scalloped shovel marks, into the frozen earth. I study the crystal formations of the grave walls. I imagine lying there forever, as he is about to do.

The stones around us lean at all angles as if bent to the weight of the snow banked against them. The graveyard is in a desolate outlying section of town. It is on a rise that commands a view of the adjoining streets, one filled with the blank wall of a warehouse, the other fronting a lumberyard. A traffic light at the intersection. Over the racks and open sheds of the lumberyard I can see to the tracks and the signals and swing gates of the Indiana Central.

The Baptist preacher is garrulous, Southern, like the fellow in the coffin. He speaks of God's peppers.

An image comes into my mind of a green field of pepper plants and I wonder at the eccentricity of all the glories of God's fecund earth to speak of peppers.

I look from the corner of my eye at Sandy James. She stares into the grave. I see the tracks of her tears on her cheeks. I see the corneal profile of her green eyes. The baby comes into view, leaning forward in curiosity, her arms wave over the grave, cheeks puffing their steam of baby breath.

I cannot see Clara, the mother and baby block my view of Clara.

I shift my weight from one leg to the other. A dozen or so union men are standing behind us. They hold their caps. There are others too. The reporter who questioned me in the hospital, his ferret face under a brim hat, his plaid Mackinaw.

Two green-and-white police sedans and police motorcycle and sidecar are parked in front of the warehouse across the street from the entrance to the graveyard. The cops sit on their fenders and smoke cigarettes.

A cream-colored La Salle with whitewall tires turns the corner and slowly cruises past the cops and out of my line of vision. I hear a motor cut off, the wrench of a handbrake.

"Do not question God's peppers," says the preacher.

I'm trying to think. What are all these people doing here? All night I sat in a chair by the door with a heavy pistol in my lap and I tried to think. I tried to lift my head and open my eyes, shake off the exhaustion of my bones to think.

Now I do have a thought. It is really very foolish. It is that these people—the union men, the cops, the reporter—they're all staying. I mean this is where they live, Jacksontown, Hoosier Heart of the Nation, it's their home, it's where they make their lives. The reason this preacher twangs on and on is because he too lives here. He's in no hurry, why should he be?

All of them, it's a big thing this funeral, an event. I look at the landscape, nothing is moving, even the sky looks fixed, residential.

I shiver, a chill ripples through me. I feel their entirety of interest and attention as some kind of muscling force. Some large proprietary claim in the presence of these people displaces me.

I am dispossessed.

I square my shoulders and stare straight ahead. It seems important not to reveal from my expression or my posture that I understand this. I know what it is now. It is the whispering return to my body of my derelict soul. Oh, my derelict soul of the great depression! What's happening to me—I feel guilty! Guilty of what? I don't know, I can't even imagine!

Finally the twanging ends and with great satisfaction in the holiness of his calling, he closes his Bible, turns his face upon me and I nod and shake his hand. The ten-dollar bill folded in my palm passes to his. He murmurs something to the widow and for no additional charge grazes the baby's cheek with the tips of his theistic fingers. Then he's gone. Clara moves around in front of Sandy and hugs her and turns her away from the gravedigger, who with his shovel propped against his hip is spitting on his hands getting ready to go to work.

We walk slowly to the gate, a hand taps me on the shoulder. "Paterson?"

I turn. The heavy-set man with the blue knit cap the

expert on hell. Behind him three or four others.

"We don't want to disturb Mrs. James at this time. We have made up a pot." He puts a folded wad of bills into my hand. "The boys from the local."

I must have looked shocked. He moves close to me.

"Do you think, Paterson," he says in my ear, "that we would be so stupid as to permit ourselves to be overheard threatening a man in public not ten minutes before we meant to jump him in a dark alley?"

"What?"

"Use your brains, lad. I'm sorry for the beating you took, but if it was us you'd be in the grave beside him."

He moves off, I find Sandy and Clara, I hold Sandy's arm, I feel her bewilderment of sorrow. Faces appear, condolences drift in the cold air flutter for a moment fall.

They knew my name.

They thought it matters to me who killed him.

Clara catches sight of the cream-colored La Salle. She frowns and turns away with an involuntary glance back uphill to the grave. The color in her cheeks, the thin skin she has for the cold, the blue translucence of the eyelids, the tears in the corners of her eyes.

We are through the gate, walking on pavement. I'm between the two women. I hold their arms. It is becoming more difficult to move forward. Several bulky policemen, awkward, they don't seem to know what to do with themselves.

"Pardon me." A man tips his hat to Sandy. "Mr. Paterson, I wonder if you'd mind." I can't hear him.

"What?" There seems to be some problem. It is some misunderstanding, it's becoming difficult to move forward, we're in a crowd, it banks higher and higher against our progress.

"What?" I hear my own voice. "What questions? I already answered questions."

"We just want to talk to you a few minutes, clear up some things."

I look behind me—we're completely hemmed in now, cops in front, the working stiffs behind us, the reporter at the edge of things his chin upraised. Everyone is terribly interested.

"I'm sorry," I say truthfully, "there's no time."

I hear laughter.

"I'm responsible for these ladies, I can't leave them alone here."

It is explained that they will come down to the station house with me. They can wait for me where it's warm. I am reasoned with. Just a few minutes. Sorry for the inconvenience. Clara and Sandy are being led to one police car, I to another. Just as the door opens for me I balk. "Clara!" I try to turn around, call her. I have changed my mind. I want to put her and Sandy in a cab. I want them to wait at the rooming house.

"Don't make it hard," a cop says.

My good arm is twisted behind my back I am bent forward at the waist the muffling of blue bulk a stick is brought up smartly between my legs I'm pushed into the car. I have the terrible sickness. I'm aware of people scattering as the police car makes a careening U-turn and picks up speed. A siren. I'm thrown against the back seat against the door we veer around the corner the cop next to me pushes me away with the tips of his fingers. "Relax, sonny," he says. "Enjoy the ride."

A T A CERTAIN POINT RAILROAD STREET MADE A ninety-degree curve and you could leave it, cut across an empty lot, and reach it again a block closer to home. The lot was filled with rubble, bricks, rusted sled runners, pieces of baby carriage, garbage a feast for Saint Garbage remnants of chimneys and basement foundations and all of it covered with snow. I was thinking it was the place to be, the place to be, I stumbled along drunk, to tell the truth, drunk on two glasses of rye through this moonscape of white shit. I heard the distant bell of the trolley and saw over a tenement roof the flash of its power line like the explosion of a star. I fell and fell again, cutting my knee on something sharp, getting a sockful of snow, but Red James jaunted along smoothly he even sang one of his songs the funeral dirge of the Southern mountains, hearing the whistle blow nine hundred miles, the condemned man in prison the betrayed lover the orphaned child everyone across the night suffering loss and failed love and time run out raising his head to hear the whistle blow through the valleys of the cold mountains. And then I was down again, hard this time and I shook my head to find myself on all fours I hadn't fallen. I heard something terrible, a grunt of punched-out breath, snapped bone, a man retching. I tried to stand I was flattened by a great weight, a violent steam-rolling weight pressing my face in the snow my forehead slashes on something sharp at my eye the snow turning wet and black the weight is gone, I scramble to my knees, breathing that is tearful, a desperate exertion, a mass of bodies tumbled past me I heard Red scream and hurtled myself against this mass of black movement butting it with my head taking purchase like a wrestler grabbing a leg a sleeve a back. Everything fell on me and I felt going down my arm twisted the wrong way I heard it break. This seemed to me worth a moment's contemplation. I lay still and even found a small space in the snow to spit out blood. I lay there under the murder. The intimacy of the shifting weights, the texture of their coats on my face, sobbing rages, one vehement crunch and I heard, we all heard, the unmistakable wail of a dead man. Then a hissing gurgling sound. Then no sound. After which, silence from us all and the night coming back in this silence, the weight lifted from me by degrees I look up portions of the night sky reappear suffused in the milk light of the moon I hear something sibilant, hoarse, it is my own breath, the wind brushing past my ears, I hear hitting hitting but it is the heart pounding in my chest.

He was heavier than he looked, I dragged him one-handed by the collar he kept snagging on things at the edge of the lot I found the right terrain, pulled him to the top of a flat rock and then sitting on the incline below it and easing him over my shoulder and sliding down in a sitting position to the sidewalk and standing up with the full heft of him in a fireman's carry on my good side, I took us to the curb under the streetlight to wait for someone passing by.

The police chief nods. It's cold in this room. I sit shivering in my coat. There's a clock on the wall, like the clocks in grade school. The minute hand leaps forward from one line to the next.

The chief is not cold. He sits at his desk in a short-sleeved shirt. Arms like trees. His wrist watch appears to be imbedded in the flesh. His badge, pinned to his shirt pocket, pulls the material to a point. He's enormous but with an oddly handsome unlined face prominent jawline straight nose. He is a freak who has managed to make himself a full life out of being born and raised in Jacksontown. I try to look as if this is not my opinion. He goes back to reading his file.

I have been very cooperative. Even though they did that to me I have told my story as completely and accurately as I can.

I hear the minute hand move on the clock.

We're in some room on the ground floor that looks into the courtyard. A couple of cops are standing around out there. The window has bars.

I don't even ask to smoke. I show no impatience. I don't want to give them anything to work on, if I don't seem to be in a hurry they'll be quicker to let me go.

A cream-white La Salle with whitewall tires pulls up in the courtyard just outside the window. The driver holds open the rear door and the man who gets out immediately has the attention of the cops. He wears a dark overcoat with a fur collar. A pearl-gray fedora. They seem to know him, they come over, they seem eager to shake his hand. He says something and one of the cops moves out of my view.

"Are you deaf, son?"

"What?"

"I said where are you from?"

"I'm from Paterson. Paterson, New Jersey."

"Like your name."

"Yeah."

He nods. "I see. What was your last job?"

"What? I rousted for a carnival."

"Whereabouts."

"Uh, upstate New York. New England."

"What carnival?"

"What?"

"What was the name of it?"

"I don't remember."

"You don't remember the name?"

"No."

"Well, how long did you work for them?"

"I don't know. Listen, is this going to take much longer?"

"It's up to you. You worked at this carnival?"

"Yeah. A couple of months. It was a summer job. Some lousy carnival."

"And before that?"

The man in the courtyard sees something. He removes one gray kidskin glove, takes off his hat. He's a short man, dark-complected, his black hair shines, shows the tracks of the comb. He is shaking his head, he seems genuinely relieved, he raises his arm, lets it fall. His eyes are large, dark, glistening, with long black lashes, they are shockingly feminine eyes.

There is Clara.

They look at each other, a wave of emotion overcomes them both and they hug. He holds her at arm's length and he laughs. He is charmed by her. He shakes his head as if to say, Oh what am I going to do with you!

"Sit down, son."

Side by side they lean against the cream-colored car and they talk. Clara's wearing her fur jacket. He says something to her, he smiles and holds her arm, whispers in her ear, it is as if he is in some night club somewhere at a dark table, and the intimate things he has to say are covered by the music of the swing band.

I am at the window.

"Son of a bitch, what does he see out there?"

"Clara!"

She has pulled her arm away, I hear something, I hear the high wordless whine of impatience with which she sometimes fends off the male approach.

"Clara!" I pound the window. He seems undismayed by her response, as if he knows too well it is a ritual, that it is in fact a form of encouragement.

"CLARA!" My arm, I am jerked back, a cop is pulling down the dark shade, is this my last sight of her head half turned as if she's heard something hair blowing back from her face eyes shining the winter courtyard as if she's heard something in her past, someone, just losing hold in her consciousness?

"Boy, don't you know you're being interrogated? Don't you understand that?"

I am slammed back in the chair.

"I gotta talk to Clara Lukács. She's out there."

"All in good time."

"It's important! Look, I'll answer anything any goddamn questions you can think of just let me talk to her a minute."

The cop is still behind me I have risen from my chair he presses me back down.

Another cop has come in and places Red James' gun on the desk. He takes up position with his back to the door, his arms folded.

The chief examines the gun. "A very serious piece of equipment. This is what the department should be carrying," he says to the cop. "Not the shit we got."

"Never been fired," the cop says.

Do I hear a car door slam? If I am to remain sane I must believe she is not leaving. I must believe she is handling things in her own way. I must believe that she is capable of dealing with Tommy Crapo as she knows he must be dealt with to get him off our backs. I will believe these things, and take heart and deal for my part with the situation in this room. An hour from now we'll be on our way. We'll make a slight detour down to Tennessee and then head for California. We'll be laughing about all of this. We'll be talking about the adventure we had.

"Where'd you get this, son?"

"It's his. Red James'."

He shakes his head and smiles. "Didn't do him much good, did it? You take it off him?"

"No, it was in his house. It was hidden behind the radio."

"Yesterday you went down to Mallory the pawn-broker's. You collected six hundred dollars on the de-ceased's insurance policy."

"That's right. The money belongs to Mrs. James. I'm holding it for her. She's fifteen years old and we're taking her home to her folks."

He nods, not to indicate he believes me, but as if to maintain the rhythm of the questioning. I look at the clear-eyed, steadfast face of the police chief, the lean face carved from his mountainous self. I've underestimated him.

"You expect them to give you trouble?" he says.

"Who?"

"Her folks you're taking her home to. That you were packing this thing."

"It wasn't for that."

"What was it for, then?"

"I was glad to find it. I sat up all night guarding the door with it."

"Why?"

"Until we got out of town, in case someone came after me."

He gives me his full attention. "Who?"

"I don't know who. Whoever killed Red."

"Why would they do that?"

"I don't know. If they thought I saw them? If they thought I could pin it on them?"

"Could you?"

"I told you. I didn't see anything. I got hit from behind and went down and it all fell on top of me. Could I see my girl, please?"

"Well, if you were afraid, why didn't you call the police? You think this is the Wild West?"

The policemen guffaw.

"Why would anyone want to kill him, anyway?" the chief says.

"I don't know."

"You're in the union, ain't you?"

"You have my billfold!"

"Maybe you killed him," he says.

"What? Jesus H. Christ!"

"Sit down, son. And watch your language."

"Oh, this is swell. This is really swell. No, I didn't

kill him, he was my friend, we lived next door to each other!"

"Did you fool with his wife?"

I hear the ticking of the school clock. From far away comes the metallic screech and thunder of the car couplings as they make up the trains at the freight yards.

"Answer, please. Did you fool with his wife?"

The way is open for my full perception of official state-empowered rectitude. I am suddenly so terrified I cannot talk.

"Did you?"

I shake my head. A weakness, a palpable sense of my insufficiency drifts through my blood and bones.

"Okay," he says, "we could hold you for possession. But I think we have enough to hold you as material witness. You know what that is?"

I shake my head.

"You're all we have to go on. You were there when it happened. It means we hold you while we work up the case. I make it you diddled the wife and decided you liked it too much. The insurance didn't hurt neither."

And now I find my voice. I'm swallowing on tears, I'm producing tears and swallowing them so that they don't appear in my eyes. "Hey, mister," I say, "look at me, I don't look like much, do I? My arm's been broke, one side of my face is stitched up, I've been pissing blood...Jesus, since I came to this town I've been short-paid, tricked, threatened, double-crossed, and your Jacksontown finest felt they had to work me over to get me here. I probably don't smell so good either. But I tell you something. You wouldn't hear from my mouth the filth that has just come from yours. I mean that is so rotten and filthy, I'd get down on my knees and beg that little girl's forgiveness if I was you."

"You oughtn't to tell me to do anything, son."

"Or else you're being funny. Is that it, are you being funny? I mean what's the idea—that I killed him before he broke my arm or did I kill him after he broke my arm? After? Oh yes. It makes great sense, it really does: with my one arm I was able to get him to hold still so as I could bash his head in. And then just to make sure everyone would know it I lifted him on my back and took him out to the street to get a ride to the hospital. Smart!"

"He's pretty stupid," the police chief says to the cop, "if he thinks we have to be smart."

The policeman laughs. The chief looks at me with the barest hint of a smile on his face. "You don't like my story, maybe you have a better one."

You don't like my story, maybe you have a better one.

Do you think, Paterson, we'd threaten a man in public a few minutes before we meant to jump him in a dark alley use your brains lad.

My brains.

Clara asked me about my work one day I told her she was furious. What's the matter? Don't move, look at how you're standing: it was so, my hands were in the air as if I were tying the cable, my feet were spread as if I were standing on the vibrating cement floor, I had not only told her, I had acted it out and I hadn't known I was doing that. I understood then the abhorrence of men on the line for bravado. The failure of perception is what did you in.

A murder is valuable property it gives dividends how much and to whom depends on how it's adjudicated.

I thought this was about Clara it is not it is about my life.

Tommy Crapo didn't think this up, he didn't do this to me, he didn't have to. You don't have to buy the police chief in a company town—he's in place! This dolmen stone skull has been here since the beginning of time.

I held up my hands. "Look," I say softly, new tone of voice, "you're making it wrong, it wasn't like that. We were family friends, Red and me. My fiancée Clara and his wife Sandy. We took care of their baby for them when they went to the movies."

"Your fiancée!"

"Yes, sir," I say, "that's what I'm trying to tell you. Clara and I are engaged to be married. You don't know my Clara or you wouldn't think I had an eye for another woman."

"She's something, eh?"

"Well"—I sit back in my chair and smile in reflection—"only the best, most beautiful girl in the world!"

The chief folds his arms. One of the cops leans over, whispers something to him. He listens while he stares at me. "Maybe we ought to see the little lady," he says.

The cop leaves, closing the door behind him. We all sit there waiting. It might be night the dark shade a globe light hangs from the middle of the ceiling the wood floor the oak furniture my chair creaks. The walls are painted dark green from the floor to halfway up, light green to the ceiling. I hear footsteps. I stand. The door opens the cop holds it open for Sandy James with her baby. From the empty hall behind her a cold wind sweeps into the room.

"Sandy, where's Clara?"

She stares at me unable to speak. But from her eyes

gleams a sorrow not her own and a small light of courage or hope of possession. I see the decisive functioning matriarchy I have not before seen in her. It comes to them regardless of their age or intelligence when they have settled their claims.

IN THE WINTER OF 1919 PENFIELD IS IN SEATTLE, walking the streets down by the docks, the rain green-gray, the escalloped seascape etched by rain. Life is a mist shining on his young face soothing his eyes, what his eyes have seen. He is wet and cold but not uncomfortable, there seems in this section of the world at this moment of his life a letting up of insistent death, no one he loves had died lately, he is all out, no mother father lover or signalman the bombs are still, the machine guns silent, the awful murderous insolence of mankind for the moment distracted. But the peace is killing him. Why is he here? He knows no one in Seattle, he knows no one in the whole country, he is one hundred percent bereft, he has come across the continent because it made the longest journey, there had been in his mind some expectation, the importance given to the being from the presumption of travel, but he has a room in a boarding house in West Seattle like the room they gave him in Nutley, New Jersey, in return for his medal and he walks down the hills to the docks. Why? He stands on pilings and looks at the water sloshing into itself infinitely accommodating to all blows objects hammers rainpocks taking it all, pour beaches in drop mountains in break off continental shelves the water gulps the water caresses it is the nature of the water to leave nothing untouched unloved even me thinks Warren Penfield. It is not that he has the urge to jump in but only that he lacks arguments why he should not. It is a rather thoughtful unemotional contemplation. This dark drizzly afternoon he throws his book in, one of the precious copies of his volume of verse, *Sangre de Cristo*, it blots, spreads, wafts, and solemnly raising its binding like wings dives into the great Sound. He leaves the pier and goes down a cobblestone alley and finds a bar a space for his own broad back collar up between the other broad-backed collars up a whiskey the bar dark wood honorably scarred a whiskey the damp air hung with smoke making the smoke of cigarettes a cloudmist he notices how crowded the bar is on a working afternoon he leaves the mist now inside the brain drifting over the lobes of the brain like clouds over the stone mountains the city is still. A block or two from the waterfront it looks better to him at the end of streets the bows of steamships loom over the clapboard buildings, he finds the conjunction of the sea and the street exciting, bowsprits and lines of the old coal-fired riggers gently bobbing over the cobblestones, the creak in the green-gray rain the gulls in glistening drift through the rain there is another country, of course! the sea is to connect waterfront streets at the far ends of the earth. Such moments of elation keep him gliding over his despair he goes now for the solace that never fails up the hill toward the center of town to the public library. What goes on here the library is packed with men reading the newspapers riffling the card boxes roaming the stacks making the shapes of the words with their lips the librarians flustered by the sudden accession to learning of the working world flushfaced, glasses slipping down their noses they are reduced to whispering among themselves and feeling hurt. But Warren likes this! He unbuttons his jacket pulls off his cap sits at an oak table and feels the strength of these men reading the papers on sticks quiet respectful as can be of this repository of words he starts to ask a question quailed by the frown of the man next to him who *knows* you're not supposed to talk in a library Warren goes to the granite front steps the men clustered here smoking hunched in their collars in the sweet rain he is too shy as usual but something is happening that is very strange his landlady said nothing he will get a newspaper but block after block no newsboys on the corners alarmed now it is February getting dark in the afternoon the green is leaving the sky the street lamps beginning to glow weakly the rained emptiness of the city he hears something missing, no streetcars! the overhead wires gather the last light in silver lines an inadequately populated city in the bakery window there is no bread in the grocery no milk everyone knows something he does not know he waves at a passing car black ignoring him he begins to run stores closed where has he been follows men walking following other men walking stays close stays in step hears now a human sound of population turns a corner a suddenly illuminated warehouse great golden light pouring through the doors they are all going here and suddenly he is inside the clatter of plates and flatware, the steam of soup and the skyline of sliced bread he knows what to do it is twenty-five cents, a bowl of soup two slices of bread gobs of tub butter stew mashed potatoes an apple coffee in a tin cup twenty-five cents rows of saw-horse tables in endless lines refectory benches under the warehouse lights animation conversation all men thousands of men eating dinner and down at the end of one table at the far end in front of his tray in wonder Warren Penfield poet coat open the sound is of raucous life chopped fine in silver flutes and strings and drumfeet and shimmering lifesong the men eat hot food drink strong coffee it is not Ludlow it is not billets it is not distant thunder it is not the whingwhir of machine guns it is the General Strike of Seattle February 6, 1919, the first of its kind in the whole history of the United States of America.

Everyone is out the printers and milk-wagon drivers butchers and laundry workers hotel porters store clerks and seamstresses newsboys and electricians and bakers and cooks steam fitters and barbers all under the management of the central labor council and it is a very well-organized show Warren stands in the streets some trucks are running with signs under the authority of the strike committee and the milk gets to the babies and the lights stay on in the hospitals and the linen is picked up the food cold storage continues to hum and the water from the waterworks and the garbage trucks exempt by the strike committee continue to pick up the wet garbage but not the ashes and the watchmen continue to guard the fences and the mayor confers with the strike committee and not a shot is fired not a fist flies not a harsh word they even have their own cops war veterans big men standing with armbands the Labor War Veteran Guard to keep the strike out of the

streets, to break up crowds, keep the soldiers and cops
from finding excuses to make trouble they can't ma-
chine-gun air they tell Warren move on brother keep
your temper enjoy your vacation and by the third day
the provision trades are feeding thirty thousand men in
their neighborhood kitchen and the nonprofit stores
are springing up everywhere not even the union newspaper is allowed to print for fear of unfair competition
to the struck big papers Warren is thrilled the city is
being run by workingpeople it is that simple they are
learning the management techniques it started with the
shipyard strike and now it is Revolution pure and simple says Warren's landlady big woman large jaw blue
eyes taller than he wiping red hands on her apron the
Bolsheviks are in Seattle they're here just like in Rus-
sia, they are a plague like the flu it spreads like the flu
they ought to be taken out and shot I've worked hard
all my life and never asked favors nor expected them
and that's why I'm free and beholden to no one Warren tries to explain that's the same thing he's seen the
feeling beholden to no one independent men of their
own fate and also the incredible tangible emotion of
solidarity key word no abstract idealization but an ac-
tual feeling I had it too in the signal battalion the way
we looked after each other and were in it together an
outfit many men one outfit and I swear Mrs. Farmer
that has got to be a good thing when you feel it not
necessarily the woman said the Huns felt the same
feelings I'll bet and took care of each other in their
trenches and that don't make me love them anymore
they sank ships with babies in them she is in her way a
well-entrenched opponent and as always Warren thinks
about this point of view to which he is opposed to find
the merit in it and test it against his deepest supposi-

tions they are having a good time at the kitchen table
she likes him he talks well and is a gentleman and a
veteran and pays in advance every two weeks look Mr.
Penfield supposing they came in here and told me how
to run my house and when to clean the stairs and when
to change the sheets and what church to go to and how
to teach my children at this moment one of them runs
in a remarkable five-year-old little girl broad smooth
brow wideset huge light eyes thick hair natural grace
dirty knees little socks drooping wild little thing stands
between the great-legged mother stares at the boarder
with head tilted light in eye clear recognition of his
total flawed being what's that Mr. Penfield the great
granite mother how could she produce this wisp this
unmistakable deity she is scratching the inside of her
thigh now with the heel of her shoe a ballet dirty white
underdrawers he says inspired well Mrs. Farmer I'll
tell you now not hesitant confident fearless of oppos-
ing opinion nobody knows what human nature is in the
raw it's never been seen on this earth even Robinson
Crusoe came from something even Friday and so it
seems to me the Huns like us shoot if you give them
guns and enemies but love if you will give them friendship and a common goal come down with me and walk
among these men and see their spirits change because
they're not under someone's heel you take away men's
fear and be surprised how decent they can be you
don't make them climb over each other for their suste-
nance give them their dignity and the right to run their
lives you release the genius of the race in the forms of
art and love and Christian brotherhood. Oh Mr. Penfield you're a good gentle man I'm afraid you don't
know the ways of the world very well I have some
leftover pie here let me make a pot of tea go along and

play honey the child doesn't move she is cleaning her
lips with her tongue like a cat arms resting indolently
on her mother's skirted thighs outside the kitchen curtain the green rain makes its soft hiss it is Warren who
runs along in a flurry of stumbling knocking over the
kitchen chair proving his lack of ease in the ways of the
world she looks after him shaking her great jawed
head sweet dupe he goes to his room grabs books passport razor the child runs upstairs to the hall-landing
window looks out at Warren Penfield hurrying downhill he sees turns his head back sees her the power of
her eyes like a jolt to his heart his face is wet the rain
like her tonguelicks it is this more than anything which
sends him back to the docks in torment in scorn the
woman is right I am a fool if this strike goes on the
committee who runs things will be as bad as dictators
everything'll be the same only with different names do
these men on strike absolve themselves of personal
private insensitivity in bed in kitchen do they know
how to deal with their own children or parents refrain
from gossip and all the heavy baggage of personal private evils vanity lust self-abuse the things in Latin the
dreams it was she God what are you doing she is come
back in impossible form God what are you doing I am
haunted hounded you torment me with the little I have
to live for God what are you doing a basso horn from
the sound another from the harbor white smoke like
Morse code from the stacks of the ships berthed along
the streets what is going on pardon me a small Japanese turns what is all the horn-blowing he scintillating
merry-unsmiling we go now he says *stoorock ober*
What? Impatient Japanese shouts to clarify to this
white fool *stoorock ober*! *stoorock ober*! runs off from
the hills of the city church bells car toots the distant

shouts of men who have been men sounding like the gentle rain the Japanese runs up a gangplank one bulb hung from the prow throwing a dazzling green halo of rain over Warren's eyes the *stoorock* is *ober* Warren goes aboard the *Yokahama Trader* books passage God what are you doing

"YOU'VE GOT THE WRONG MAN," I SAID. THE chief smiled. He wore his hexagonal blue cap now with the raised gold embroidery on the peak. He wore his tunic. He was sitting here for revelation, he had brought in a stenographer, more cops, and an older man in plain clothes.

I said, "The F. W. Bennett Company employs an industrial espionage agency to find out what's going on in their plants. The name of the agency is Crapo Industrial Services. Maybe you don't know this but I think you do. They put spies on the line and if possible in the unions themselves."

"Let's not waste time," the chief said.

"Red James was one of these spies. He came here two, three years ago just as the union began to organize the men. He got to be an officer of the local. He was secretary, he took minutes, he kept records, he made reports to his employer Crapo Industrial Services."

The chief turned to the stenographer, a gray-haired woman with a mole on her chin. She closed her book. I might be setting up to finger the union but I was talking funny. True! I had found a voice to give authority to the claim I was making—without knowing what that claim would be, I had found the voice for it, I listened myself to the performance as it went on. These fucking rubes!

"The union scheduled a strike just after the new year," I said. "The idea, see, was that if the trim line was shut down, eventually every other Bennett plant would have to shut down too because Number Six makes all the trim. So it was a big strategy of theirs and Red reported this. Right away there are layoffs, half the machines are dismantled and shipped to another plant, and the strike is up the creek."

"And that's why the union goons killed him," the chief said, looking at the plain-clothes man.

"But it wasn't them," I said. "It *looked* like it should be, I myself thought for a moment it was, let me tell you, Chief, you don't look for complications when your head's getting beat in. Does anyone have a Lucky?"

Where was this coming from? I had learned the basics from my dead friend Lyle James. But the art of it from Mr. Penfield, yes, the hero of his own narration with life and sun and stars and universe concentrically disposed on the locus of his tongue—pure Penfield.

"I'll try to make this as clear as I can," I said, taking a deep drag on my cigarette and nodding thanks to the cop with a match. "I know by sight every officeholder in the local, and every national big shot who's been in town since October. I know by sight most of the members—and this will surprise you but there aren't that many, considering the size of the work force at Number Six. But there are people who wear the same clothes and talk the same talk who don't work on the line and never will. And they are the ones who jumped us."

The police chief had risen. "You better know what you're doing, son."

"I made them for a traveling band, one of Crapo's industrial services," I said. "And that's who they were. If you really want Red James's killers, it's very simple. Speak to Mr. Thomas Crapo, president. You can reach him in the phone book—unless he's on his honeymoon."

The man in plain clothes stepped forward. It was clear to me now he was not in the department at all. He was dressed in a pin-stripe suit with a vest and a high collar and a stickpin in his tie. He had thin graying hair, and had the prim mouth of a town elder or business executive. To this day I don't know who he was—a manager of Number Six, a town councilman, but anyway, not a cop. I knew I could work him.

"What is it you're trying to say, young man?"

"I'll spell it out for you, sir. The agency murdered its own operative."

"That's a most serious charge."

"Yes, sir," I said. "It certainly is. But we're in a war, we're talking about a war here, and anything's possible. Once the company moved the machines, Red's days were numbered. The union found him out. That made him no longer of any use to Crapo, in fact he was worse than no use, he was a real danger."

"What?"

"He was an angry man. They'd left him to the dogs. He knew probably as much about Crapo as he knew about the local. He wasn't just your average fink who's been hooked for a few dollars and doesn't even know what he'd doing. Red was a professional, an industrial detective, and he worked for Crapo in steel, he worked in coal, he'd done a lot of jobs and this particular assignment was very crucial and only the most experienced man could be trusted with it."

The police chief shook his head. He motioned to the stenographer to leave the room. He stood quite still and watched her close the door behind her. He turned to me he understood the reckless suicidal thing I was doing.

"But as I say, if you read your history of the trenches, the front lines at Belleau Wood, the Argonne, and so on, you find more than once the practice of sending out the patrol either to rescue or to kill their own man who has been captured—so that he doesn't give them away. War is war, other lives are at stake and war is war."

"I was with the Marines at Belleau Wood," the man in the business suit said. "I know of no such story."

"It was the British who did it," I said quickly. "I disremember the place and time, but it wasn't the Americans, it was the British and the French, and of course the Huns they did that all the time. But you don't have to believe it. Look at the chief here. First thing he thinks, a Crapo man is killed, it's the union who killed him. Why not, who would think different! And if he can make that case, if Crapo can trick him into making it, look what he's accomplished. He's set the union back twenty years. They're no union anymore, they're hoods and killers, nobody wants them, no working stiff wants comrades like that, not even Roosevelt wants that. Why, that in itself is enough to make it worthwhile—just to get the union defending itself from charges, just putting suspicion in people's minds—that's worth one op's life, I can tell you."

"All right, son," the chief said, coming around to the front of the desk.

"I know my rights," I said. "You are all witnesses. I'm telling you the truth as I know it, it's out now, it's out in this room and will be on every wire service in the country if you got any ideas of changing my testimony."

"I don't understand what's going on here," said the man in the business suit.

"This boy lies," the chief said. "He lied before and he's lying now. He's a punk from New Jersey who we found with a gun and the widow's insurance money in his kick. He's making this all up."

"That's right," I said. "I made up Tommy Crapo and I made up Crapo Industrial Services, didn't I? Or did I get it from the newspaper? That must be it, they must advertise in the newspaper. I can give you Red James' op number, the one he put on his reports, but that'll be made up too. I can give you the Illinois plate number of a cream-colored La Salle coupe with white sidewalls, but that's made up too. It's all made up. Buster is made up too, he doesn't exist."

"Who is Buster?"

"Buster who got Mrs. James to waive her rights for two hundred and fifty Industrial Services' dollars. Oh listen, mister, why doesn't anyone ask the right questions around here? Look at this, a roomful of ace detectives and not one of them thinks to ask how I know so much, how I knew Lyle James, how I got to be his friend, what I'm doing in this lousy town. Is it an accident? Do you think I like going around getting my arm broken and stitches taken in my face? Do you think I do this for laughs?"

An amazing current, a manic surge, I couldn't stop talking, listen Clara, listen! "I wonder at the human IQ when professionals cannot see through disguises. But if I was wearing a regular suit like this gentleman, if I was wearing my own suit and tie and my face was washed and my hair combed, then you would listen, oh yes. And if I told you Lyle Red James was not just an operative for Crapo but a double operative, that he really worked for the union, that they made him not two weeks after he came to this town, because you know, don't you, he was not much good, he was a fool, a hillbilly, a rube, I mean they saw him coming! And they made him, and showed him how if he kept working and nobody the wiser, he'd get not only his pay envelope from Bennett and not only his salary from Crapo but his payoff from the union's cash box! Why this strike at Number Six was a decoy! They never intended to strike Jacksontown, that was to send the company on a wild-goose chase shipping its damn machines every which way. Oh yes, gentlemen, when that strike comes, and it is coming, the birds will be singing in Jacksontown, it will be a peaceful day at Number Six and you won't know a thing till you hear it on the radio."

"What's this?" the businessman said. "What strike? Where?"

"Or maybe that isn't a good enough reason for taking care of Lyle Red James, that he was a dirty double-crossing Benedict Arnold."

It was an amazing discovery, the uses of my ignorance, a kind of industrial manufacture of my own. And the more it went on, the more I believed it, taking this fact and that possibility and assembling them, then sending the results down the line a bit and adding another fact and dropping an idea on the whole thing and sending it on a bit for another operation, another bolt to the construction, my own factory of lies, driven by rage, Paterson Autobody doing its day's work. I was going to make it! This was survival at its secret source, and no amount of time on the road or sentimental education could have brought me to it if the suicidal boom of my stunned heart didn't threaten my extinction.

"What strike, how do you know these things!" The businessman was beside himself. "Who is this fellow?" he said. "Damn it all, I want the truth. I want it now."

The police chief went back behind his desk and sat down. He looked at me, fingered the corners of his mouth. He lifted his hat and ran his fingers through his hair and put his hat back on.

"You don't like Crapo very much, do you?"

"We fancy the same girl," I said.

"And that's why you're fingering him—or trying to?"

"No more than he's done to me, Chief," I said. "But I got a better reason: I don't condone killing and neither does Mr. Bennett."

"Mr. who Bennett?" he said, frowning terribly.

"Mr. F. W. Bennett of Bennett Autobody. Is there any other?"

Here the man in the suit found a chair near the wall and sat down and glared at me.

"I'm a special confidential operative," I said. "I was sent here by Mr. F. W. Bennett personally to check on the Crapo organization Their work has been falling off lately. Mr. Bennett takes nothing for granted, especially not the loyalty of gangsters. I worked into the confidence of Crapo's chief man in Number Six, Lyle James. Mr. Bennett himself arranged for the next door to be available. He thought I had a better disguise to be married and so I brought with me a lady"—here I faltered—"I happened to be serious about. This is the unofficial part, Chief, and I expect every man in this room to keep quiet about this part. I met this lady when she was with Mr. Crapo and we took to each other. We couldn't help it. And, well, he is not a man to forgive, as you can see by my condition and the circumstance of my being here before you."

And now there was silence in the room.

"You are awful young to be what you say," said the police chief. He turned to the others. "It's too crazy. Jacksontown don't need stuff like this. There are so many holes in this story it's like a punchboard. Why should Mr. Bennett need to do these things, you tell me? And if he did them, why would he find some kid like this not old enough to wipe the snot from his nose? No, I'm sorry, Mr. Paterson," he said, "you're smart enough to throw the names around, but you were a punk when we pulled you in and as far as I'm concerned you're still a punk."

"My name isn't Paterson," I said. I smiled and looked at the man in the suit and vest. "It's easy enough to check," I said. "In my billfold on a piece of paper is the phone number of Mr. Bennett's residence at Loon Lake in the Adirondack Mountains of New York. You may not know about that place, it's his hideaway. Call him for me. I get a phone call of my choosing anyway, isn't that the law? That's who I choose to call. Tell him also I'm sorry about the Mercedes. It may be on the lot of Buckeye State Used Cars in Dayton, Ohio. But it may not. Tell him I'm very sorry."

I thought in the silence that ensued they could hear my heart beating its way back to survival.

"Yes, sir," the chief said, "and who should we say is calling?"

One of the men laughed. I was livid with rage. Oh Penfield. Oh my soul. I could barely get the words out. "You stupid son of a bitch," I said to the chief. "Tell Mr. Bennett it's his son calling. Tell him it's his son, Joe."

I DON'T REMEMBER THE NAMES OF TOWNS I REmember the route, southwest through Kentucky and Arkansas, across northern Oklahoma and the top of the Texas Panhandle and then into New Mexico, a spooncurve that I thought would drop us gently into the great honeypot of lower California.

We drove through small boarded-up towns, we drove down dirt rut roads and through hollows where shacks were terraced on the hill beside the coal tipple. We drove through canyons of slag and stopped to pick up chunks of coal to burn in the stoves of our rented cabins. The road went along railroad tracks, alongside endlessly linked coalcars loaded and still.

We drove over wood-paved iron bridges I remember rivers frozen with swirls of yellow scum I remember whole forests of evergreen glazed in clear ice, shattered sunlight, I had to strap a slitted piece of cardboard over my eyes to see the road.

In January the thaw and false spring in the Southwestern air and when we were stopped at a roadside picnic grove for our lunch we could hear the thunderous cracks and groans of rivers we couldn't see. But then it froze again, cold and snowless and I remember stretches of brown land treeless swells of hardscrabble imbedded with rotted-out car frames and broken farm tools.

We had problems with the truck blown tires batteries fan belts oilsmoking flipping up the vented hood hot to the touch it was a journey fraught with peril. But you didn't have to think. It was simple, life was staying warm keeping on the move finding food beds being thrifty. We met people in trucks loaded like ours with furniture and we talked with them and gave the appraising looks of peers, the few chilled humans in motion. But most of the time we had the road to ourselves.

I bought the newspaper wherever we were. In Arkansas and Oklahoma lots of people were robbing banks, it seemed to me important to come into a town looking respectable. People on the go did not have social standing. The eyes of the waitresses in the cafés or the grudging grim men and women who rented rooms. I held the baby like a badge. Cleanliness, propriety, the cheerful honest face, mediation in a cold suspicious land. I made a point of tipping well and flashing my roll, I didn't like that moment of hesitation before the man cranked up the gas tank or the landlady took the key off the board.

In every state Sandy noticed the Justice of the Peace signs in front of clapboard houses. I told her they were legalized highway robbers who lifted travelers of five- and ten-dollar bills I said they handed out jail sentences to hobos but she knew them from the movies as kindly old men who would open their doors late at night to marry people they had wives in hair curlers and ratty bathrobes who smiled and clasped their hands Sandy and I were not mental intimates.

I don't mean she was stupid she was not, only that she asked no questions, she was already persuaded, like Libby at Loon Lake. She took instruction from the newspapers and radio she marveled at the Dionne quintuplets. But I was very kind to her and patient. We had shared sorrows, we knew something together, and this made me tender toward her. I liked the smell of her after a night in bed, the heat of her under the covers. I took a sweet pleasure in our lovemaking even though she was shockingly ignorant of what she could get from it. The first time as I sat on the edge of the bed she hiked up her flannel nightgown lay herself across my lap. "Not too hard?" she said over her shoulder and buried her face in a pillow. I caressed her ample buttocks and backs of the thighs I felt a film of clammy sweat in the small of her back I thought I had learned more of her late husband's tastes than I needed to know. She seemed relieved that I wanted no preliminaries and arranged herself on all fours on the bed presenting herself to me dog fashion here I did not demur. One had limits. She braced her arms and set her haunches and even gave them a little twirl now and then. I came quickly for which she afterward rewarded me with a quick kiss on the mouth before she went off to the bathroom.

She thought of it like cooking or changing the baby, a responsibility of domestic life. I wanted to awaken her surprise her but I was in no hurry. I enjoyed her the way she was. One morning with the light showing the streaks in the window shade I studied her face as she lay in my arms and suddenly her eyes flew open and she stared at me fearfully but not moving in that second or two before she remembered where she was who she was who I was. She drew a sharp breath and her green eyes swam with life. I hugged her and decided I loved her. I put her on her back and made love to her and took my time about it and detected a degree of thought or contemplation in her before the thing was done and she jumped out of bed to see to her baby.

Ahead of us on the road each morning a lowering sky, I felt under it as under a billowing tent as far as the eye could see. The roads became straighter, the land flattened out. No snow now, what blew across the land was gritty red dust that shimmered on the road in the sun in rainbows of iridescence. Also accreting spindly balls of desert rubbish bouncing over the rocks and blowing up against the fences like creatures watching us go by. We went through one-street towns with red brick feed stores and tractors parked in the unpaved streets. We passed foreclosed farms with notices slapped on the fenceposts like circus bills. The towns were less frequent. There were no rivers creeks mountains trees, just this rocky flatland. But one day Sandy yelled to stop the truck. I pulled over. She thrust the baby in my hands and jumped down from the cab and ran back along the ditch. I watched her in the mirror. She came back with a sprig of tiny blue flowers, she was so happy, she tied them with a string and hung them from the sun visor.

The desert didn't alarm her. She had grown up in the mountains but country was country and she knew its rules and regulations. She knew the names of snakes and birds and pointed out the dry beds of creeks. One day the truck broke down in the middle of nowhere and she turned all around with her hand shading her eyes wise Indian maid and figured where to get help by the way the land was fenced. I remember that. We found a ranch about three miles down a dirt road intersecting the road we were on, just as she predicted.

But it was slow going, I began to think we were strung between outposts of civilization, the shadow range of mountains that cheered me when I first saw it one late afternoon seemed each new day as far away on the windshield. I didn't know what we would do in California but I knew it would take as much money as we could save to do it with. I came awake at night and wondered what I had in mind. The truth was I had no ambition, no ideas, no true desire or hope for anything. I was aware in the darkness of the forced character of my affections. I'd find myself angry at Sandy. I liked to surprise her in her sleep and be in her before her body could respond to make it easier. She would come awake gasping but throw her arms around me and hold on for dear life.

One evening, trying to do something about the way I felt, I found a reasonably good roadside café and we had steaks and beans and red wine. There were candles in little red glasses on the table.

"Clara told me about you," Sandy said.

"What?"

"Oh, long before I dreamed anything like this."

"What did she say?"

"Just that she was sweet on you. You know. The way girls talk."

"Yeah, well, I was sweet on her too."

"I thought you was married. I thought she was your wife!"

"Yeah, well, she'd be anything you wanted if you wanted it badly enough."

A particularly cold day, with the enormous blue sky turned almost white, we saw a man and a woman and a boy at the side of the road beside their old Packard touring car. I pulled up. Their gears were locked. A decision was made that the man would remain with the car and its heavy freight of steamer trunks and crates. He wrapped a scarf around his head and folded his arms and sat down on his running board and his family got up in the truck with us to ride to the next town. The woman must have been in her forties. She wore a dusty black coat with a fur collar half rubbed away and a tired felt hat that was nevertheless set off at a smart angle. She said her husband was a pharmacist. He had had his own store back in Wilmington, Delaware. Now they were on their way to San Diego, where they hoped to make a new start. "A new start!" Sandy said. "Why, that's what *we're* doing!"

When we had dropped them I said, "What do you mean we're making a new start?"

"What?"

"All they want is to open another drugstore. They want to do what they've always done. That's what a new start means."

"Well, I was just chattin with that lady."

"You think I want a job in an automobile factory? Or is it *your* new start you're talking about? I mean this furniture of yours we're dragging three thousand miles: Is *that* your new start? So you can find some rooms and put the furniture in them just the way you had it in Jacksontown? That kind of new start?"

"I don't know why you're so put out with me."

"Because if that's what you mean, say so. Let's settle it here and now. I'm not your husband and even if I was I wouldn't make my living as a stoolpigeon."

She looked at me now in bewilderment, and holding her baby to her, sat as far from me as she could get. She stared out the windshield with her chin on the baby's head. God knows her remark was innocent enough. But the confidence behind it I found irritating —as if living and traveling with her I must fit her pre-conceptions. I suppose what really bothered me was the strength of character behind this. I felt if she didn't even know what she was doing as she did it, I couldn't hope to change her.

Then of course in a few miles Joe was sorry, he apologized, which encouraged her to sulk and afterward to regain her good cheer.

Sandy could have said he was traveling on her money. But it never occurred to her. It occurred to him, however—he was not unaware of his talent for using other people's money, he was not unaware of his attraction to other men's wives, he was not unmindful that his life since leaving Paterson had been a picaresque of other men's money and other men's women, who in hell was he to get righteously independent with anyone? This kid was giving him her life everything she owned and all he could do was kick her in the ass for it.

He wondered seriously if love wasn't a feeling at all but a simple characterless state of shared isolation. If you were alone with a woman your feelings might change from moment to moment but the circumstance of your shared fate did not change. Maybe that's where the love was, in the combined circumstance. This was not the Penfield view but it could be argued. Joe looked at other couples old and young and wondered what they saw in each other, working their little businesses, or pushing their jalopies west, or eating their meals together or holding the hands of a child between them. Maybe all the world's pairs, dreary and toothless and stumbling drunk, or picking at garbage pails or waiting on the street for a flop knew about love as, say, he and Clara Lukács never had. They knew it could incorporate passion or prim distaste, it might be joyous or full of rage, it might carry extreme concern of any kind, or unconcern, but it was presumed to survive challenge. All it was, was a kind of neutral constancy. Sandy knew it! You just made the decision, all you needed to do was decide to have it and love was yours. Nothing grand, nothing monumental, and not a prison either, but a sort of sturdy structure of outlook, one that wouldn't break under the weight of ideas and longing feelings terrors visions and the world's awful mordant surprises.

"Sandy," he said, "let's get married."

She hugged him until he thought the truck would go off the road.

"We don't want a new start, Sandy, we want a new life. A whole new life. When we get to California. Okay? That's the place."

She was more than amenable. "Oh my, oh my," she said, hugging the baby. "You hear that, darlin? We're gonna have a proper daddy. Yes we are! Oh my!"

There followed a period of solemn discussion. I explained that to make a true marriage we both had to shuck the ways of our old lives, its attitudes, its assumptions. "I know I won't be able to live a road life anymore," I said. "I know I have to plan to make something of myself. And I have ideas, Sandy, a man can do a lot starting from a small investment. More than one fortune has been made that way, I can tell you."

She nodded.

"So I know I've got to give up my past life and I want you to think about giving up yours. Do you ask in what way?"

"Yes sir."

"In the way of style, Sandy honey. In the way of more ambition of style. Now, take this truck for instance. They stop trucks like this by the hundreds at the California state line. They don't want people coming in looking like Okies, you know? In fact I've read if you can't prove you have a job waiting they won't even let you in."

"This truck is bad?"

"Very bad."

"But how else we gonna move the furniture and all?"

"Ah, well, the furniture, that's the next thing I want to talk to you about."

An hour later we were in a fair-sized town east of Albuquerque, New Mexico. There was a big junk store at the edge of town. Sandy and I stood with our luggage in the dusty street while the furniture was unloaded. A man scrawled a big number in chalk on each piece or tied a tag to its leg. Sandy watched her chair and sofa, her big Philco radio disappear into the darkness of the store. I patted her shoulder.

It was cold and very sunny. The man counted out sixty dollars into my hand.

"Where's there a used-car lot?" I said to him. He walked around the truck, looking it up and down. He leaned his weight on the lowered tailgate. "I'll take it off your hands," he said. "Not worth much, though."

I got seventy-five dollars for the truck, for which I had paid a hundred in Jacksontown. Twenty-five dollars to transport us across six states didn't seem at all bad.

I tied two of Sandy's bags with rope and slung them over my good shoulder. I held another valise under my good arm and a fourth in my good hand. Sandy carried the baby and the remaining bag and, slowly, and with many halts, we shuffled several blocks to the railroad depot. It was a small station on the Santa Fe line and in a couple of hours a train was coming through to Los Angeles.

I checked the bags and took my wife-and-baby-to-be across the street to a diner and left them there. I found a barbershop a few blocks away. The barber removed my bandages and pulled out the stitches. He shaved me and gave me a haircut. He gave me a hot towel.

Then I had an idea. I stopped in a drugstore. My cast was supposed to be on for six weeks, but it was a torment. The druggist did the job as several customers looked on.

I was shocked by my pale thin arm. The break had been down toward the wrist. My fingers ached when I tried to move them. But it was good to be rid of the weight of all that plaster and to sport instead a couple of splints and adhesive tape.

To celebrate I stopped in a haberdasher's and bought a dark suit with a vest and two pairs of pants. Eighteen dollars. The tailor did up the cuffs for me on the spot. I bought a white shirt and a blue tie for three-fifty. Even my old khaki greatcoat looked good after the man brushed it and put the collar down. "Wear it open," he said, "so the suit shows."

Sandy didn't recognize me when I walked back into the diner.

"Is that you?"

"It's either me or George Raft," I said.

The idea was coming clear to her. We still had an hour before the train arrived. She took one of her bags from the check-in and repaired to the ladies' room.

I remember that depot: it had wooden strip wainscoting and a stove and arched windows caked with chalk dust. I sat on the bench with Baby Sandy and held her on my lap. I felt her life as she squirmed to look at this or that. She wore a wool cap from which hair of the lightest color peek through. I untied the string under her chin and pushed back the hat and it seemed to me now the hair was more red than I remembered. It seemed to me too as we regarded each other that her facial structure was changing and the father was beginning to show. "Oh, that would be a shame," I said aloud. She grabbed my tie in her fist.

And then I looked up and standing there Sandy James in a dress of Clara's and hose and Clara's high-heeled shoes. She was looking at the floor and holding her arms out as if she were on a high wire. Her face was flushed, she dropped her bag and grabbed hold of the bench.

"I'm fallin!" she said with a shriek.

"You're not falling," I said.

She had combed her hair back and put on lipstick a little bit crooked. She wore a coat open over the dress I hadn't seen it before it was creased but it was fine a dark creased coat not originally hers any more than the dress or the shoes, but it looked fine, it all looked fine.

She was awaiting judgment with mouth slightly open eyes wide.

"Aw, Sandy," I said, "you look swell. Oh honey, oh my, yes." And she broke into smiles, glowing through her freckles, her pale eyes crescented behind her cheekbones in a great face of pleasure, and there was our life to come in the sun of California—all in the beaming presence she made.

And so we sat waiting for our train, this young family, who would know what we had come from and through what struggle? We were an establishment with not a little pride in ourselves and the effect we made in the world. I thought of a bungalow under palm trees, something made of stucco with a red tile roof. I thought of the warm sun. I imagined myself driving up to my bungalow in the palm trees, driving up in an open roadster and tooting the horn as I pulled up to the curb.

A while later an interesting thing happened. The stationmaster told us through the gate that the famous Super Chief was coming through from Los Angeles. We went out on the platform to watch it go by on the far track. And after a minute it thundered by, two streamlined diesel engines back to back, and cars of ridged shiny silver with big windows. It shook the station windows with its basso horn, and a great swirl of dirt flew into our eyes. It was going fast but we could see flashes of people in their compartments.

Sandy grabbed my arm: "You see her! It's her, omigod, oh, she looked right at me!"

A moment later the train was gone and I stood watching it get smaller and smaller down the track. "Didn't you see her?" Sandy asked. "Oh, what's her name! Oh, you know that movie star, you know who I mean! Oh, she's so beautiful?"

It was true, the stationmaster said a few minutes later, you could get a glimpse of Hollywood stars every day, east and west, as the Super Chief and the Chief went by. But he wouldn't know in particular which one we had seen. "Oh, you know," Sandy kept saying to me. "You know who it is!" She stamped her foot trying to remember.

I had thought it was Clara. I laughed at myself and lit a cigarette, but long afterward something remained of the moment and located itself in my chest, some widening sense of loss, some heartsunk awareness of the value I once placed on myself.

The cars were crowded, valises and trunks piled near the doors at each end, bags and bundles stuffed in the overhead racks. We found a place toward the rear of one overheated car and we settled ourselves. We sat stiffly in recognition of the established residence of the other passengers. The car gave off the smell of orange peel and egg salad. People wore slippers instead of shoes, they slept covered with their own blankets and they chatted with each other like neighbors. Children ran up and down the aisle.

Passers-by stopped to admire the baby. We could not resist the social demands of the situation. Sandy was soon talking away, introducing us in our prematurely married state. Everyone else in the car, and in the car ahead of it and the car behind, was from the same town in Illinois. They were members of a Pentecostal church. A man told us they were moving to California to set up a new community on donated land south of Los Angeles. "Yes, thank Jesus Christ our Lord," he said. "We shall take ourselves into the Pacific and be baptized in the waters of His ocean." The idea so overwhelmed him that he broke into song. Soon everyone in the car was singing and clapping hands. Sandy smiled at me in the excitement of the moment, she was thrilled.

By evening I believed I had heard every number in the repertoire. They were good generous people if you didn't mind their conviction. After Sandy fell asleep across our seat they covered her with their blankets. An older woman happily shushed Baby Sandy to sleep in her arms.

I stood between the cars and smoked my cigarettes. This train was no Chief, it made frequent stops, and each time I got off to look around. As the night wore on, the train lingered at each stop although no one got on or off and only a sack or two was flung aboard the mail car. At one station, small town in the desert, I thought I smelled something different in the air, like a warmer breeze or another land. It was very late. All the pilgrims on the train were asleep. Steam drifted back from the engine. I felt strange, as if coming out of shock. I felt as if I knew no one on earth.

I wondered if this wasn't really the last stop, if California was like heaven, unproven. In this flatland of grit and rubble, you might sense the barest whiff of it in the air or intimation in the light of the sky—but this was as far as you got.

I wandered to the rear to the end of the platform. I picked up a folded newspaper from a Railway Express baggage cart—the rotogravure section of a Sunday paper a week or two old. I looked at the pictures. I was looking at Lucinda Bailey Bennett the famous aviatrix, two whole pages of her at various times of her life. She stood beside different airplanes or sat in their cockpits. A separate ruled column listed her speed and endurance records by date. At the bottom right-hand page of the story she was shown under the wing of a big two-engine seaplane. She was waving at the camera. The caption said: HER LAST FLIGHT. Behind her, climbing into the cabin, was a large man, broad of beam, unidentified.

I turned back and found the beginning of the feature: Lucinda Bennett's plane *The Loon* had been given up for lost over the Pacific somewhere between Hawaii and Japan. F.W. Bennett was quoted as saying that if his wife had to die, surely this was the way she would prefer, at the controls of her machine, flying toward some great personal ideal.

Images of falling through space through sky through
    dreams
through floor downstairs down well down hole
    downpour.
Birds that fall into the sea as a matter of lifestyle
    include
kingfishers canvasbacks gulls heron osprey pipers
    tweaks.
Birds that fall most prominently into fresh water are
    loons
a type of grebe. Sixteen lakes in the Adirondack
    Mountains
named Loon Lake. The cry of loons once heard is
    not forgotten.
Clara has time to think, the space to realize her
thinking mind. Never in her life has her life been so
uncrowded, something she never before realized con-
sciously how crowded her life was how people from
her infancy had always been in her eyes, how the
sounds of them had always been in her ears, how their
presence moved in her their wills directed her even
insofar as she created opposition she had been
crowded by them their wills their voices their appear-

ance directing her their cars and trucks the rumble of
the elated horns horses pulling wagons splatting dung
in the street, peddlers pushing their carts the stone
blasting out of the rock of Manhattan tying in the
girders with rivets, slapping in the stone, every manner
of machine whining growling rumbling roaring in its
own pitch, and all the gangsters of menace all the pain,
others and her own, and the sound of fear in her, her
own fear which she hated most of all because it was the
loudest noise in the universe, the nuns at their prayers,
kids shouting down the street, the muttering of murderous intention, and every square inch of space in her
eyes blocked out by stone and tar and moving metal,
by dark stairs and painted apartment walls, by over-
stuffed furniture by cots and pots and sinks and
roaches and tin plates and later by phony butlers and
the pretensions of the earth's scum, there was nothing
left in her eyes for a bee gravid with being bending a
flower to the earth, or for simple blue skycolor unpen-
etrated by the spires of skyscrapers, or for something
small and lovely to be contemplated for its own seriousness, like a comb or a hand mirror or a goldfish in a
bowl, there was no chance, nothing reflected, nothing
gave back from the contemplation of it, even her
dreams were pure shit they did nothing for her, they
were her days all over again, filled with the same people the same things in different arrangements or pro-
portions but the same the same. So she stands quietly
after some days molecularly reassembled widely
spaced in her own density and watches through some
branches and some leaves which have interest in themselves and pay her for the most marginal attention as
she watches between them the lake water flung like a
cast of silver grain in the gray day, two wakes widening

behind the pontoons of the airplane finally losing the chase like porpoises turning back underwater as the green-and-white plane exchanges one environment for another and rising slowly turns, twists in the air rising turning its wings concentrating to a point then flaring out the plane falling swiftly away into the sky losing its color finally its shape and becoming possibly a speck of dust in her eye and when she blinks it is gone altogether, made of cloud made of sky gone even the sound of it gone, and she stares at the silver-scattered lake, the green leaves at her eyes, the branches and the big important journey of the ant along the twig.

So she's alone with him at Loon Lake and finds that still there is no intimacy and the mysteriousness of this fact begins to interest her. This is the way the rich do things. Getting herself dressed, she marches downstairs defiantly accepting it all and sits down for breakfast on the terrace overlooking the lake and waiting till they come out to see what she wants and eating a half grapefruit sitting in its silver shell in ice and daring anyone Bennett included to look at her the wrong way.

But nothing has happened, the schedule is unaltered, the drinks at certain hours, the meals at certain hours, the morning a certain time in a certain place, the afternoon and evenings all timed, the past between them unacknowledged, the past ignored, personal reactions forsworn, you-naughty-girl forborne, every breath in its good time and Bennett keeps his distance with the utmost courtesy and only sees her at the times planned for seeing, at table, or on the tennis court her lesson or riding on the trail and she is left alone at her wish and settled into the timed ordered planned encounters of the rich in their family life who dole out time in carefully measured amounts to each other, they even sleep in separate rooms so as not to wear out their lives on each other, so as to avoid anything like the fluid mess of most people's lives, and those who are closest to each other are as timed to be apart as anyone else. So at last she understands what wealth is, the desire for isolation, its greatest achievement is isolation, its godliness is in its isolation and that's why never in her life before, her days and nights of time, has she enlarged this way, has her mind enlarged to the space this way, and has this voice been heard this way in reflection of herself. And the point is that she is growing to the environment, beginning to match it, and it is all beginning to make proportional sense, the timed encounters, the ceremony of courteous meetings, the space between people sharing space, the great distance to be traveled even in an obvious situation like this, so crudely obvious as to outcome, the aloneness of the two of them now, not the ironic wife not the fat poet sharing the fifty thousand acres, even now the isolated distance will have to be traveled before he can allow himself to put his hands on her. And that makes her smile. Because now she will know when that time is too, it will match her awareness and nothing will shock her or surprise her because the distance he must travel is the function of his wealth, as separative as it is powerful, and she waits in grim amusement knowing that by the time something happens he will have become recognizable to her, her familiar, and their intimacy will be all that's possible for her, so natural she will wonder what it ever was that enraged her when her gangster left her sleeping and took the private train.

But it was all in my mind, it was the furthest thing from everyone's mind except mine. She had not come

back, he had not thought of bringing her back, the
world had gone on and only I, like Warren Penfield,
mourned its going. The ant on the twig was at my eye
and I saw no plane and in fact knew I wouldn't, in fact
felt the wolfish smile of secret satisfaction on my face,
a simple mindless excitement just being back at this
place, redballed home in comprehensive correction of
my life, more comprehensive than the wild hope of
seeing Clara again or the desire to take revenge. No
simple motive could fill the totality of my return.

> Following job description fall into sea: fighter pilot
> > naval
> bomber pilot naval, navigator bombardier gunner
> > naval
> carrier-based Pacific Fleet World War Two
> with or without parachute drowned strafed dead of
> > exposure
> or rescued one thousand and eight six.
> This is apart from individuals going down in their
> > aircraft
> shot down or deprived of carrier landing
> from attack of Divine Wind or heavy seas
> collapsing their landing gear or snapping constraint
> > cable
> or sailing into lower deck amidships or
> otherwise stippling the sea like rain like the
> > hammers of sculptors.

I thought oddly of eviction, a city street miniatur-
ized in one cell of the remembering brain, a cityscape
of old cheap furniture piled on the sidewalk and an old
woman sitting on one of the chairs looking at old photographs of Paterson in an album. The chair arm had a
doily. She showed me the picture she was looking at,
herself as a girl, and she smiled. She smelled of urine,

her hands were frighteningly swollen and twisted, she was totally unashamedly in residence on the sidewalk with her furniture, in some state of dreamy peace, careless of the cold, the first snowflakes came down toward evening and there was no derision from the tough kids on the street because she didn't weep or bow her head or display grief or fear in her misfortune and so not misfortune itself, but sat and thought her chin in her hand, her elbow propped on the armchair doily, while the snow turned her hair white. What frightened them off was the triumph of her senescence, only a stickler for custom would demand that such a lady of property be required to have four walls around her a ceiling above her a light in the lamp and tea in her cup.

I had this same mind, unhoused but triumphant coming off the streets through the dogs up the mountain to Loon Lake. And I greeted him like a complicitor while he stared at me quite astonished and then turned nodding as if he understood and continued to make his lunch in the spring sun. I was given Penfield's old room. That night I heard the sound of surging power, some transformed connection, an electric pungency and pop, and everywhere around all the houses of the compound great floodlights came on, over every bit of space, the courts, the boathouse, the staff house, the stables. And a while later I heard the dogs but they came this time on leashes pulling three men with shotguns broken in one hand and leash straps in the other woven like reins, a dozen yelping matched hounds and uniformed guards with Sam Browne belts and boots.

I read the Penfield papers at his window from this outside light a peculiar bright amber night, and I heard the Poet's voice and saw his large debauched pleading eyes and tried to understand his death, what it was, what was terminated, if the voice and the face remained, if the presence lay in the rooms, and the faint winy redolence of his being was sniffed on my every breath. A wineglass still sat on the mantel, the dregs evaporated to a glazed scab in the bottom of the petal.

I mourn all change even for the better and in the days of my return I measured what I had known as the injured intruder against what I saw now as the sole guest. I mourned the absence of terror, the absence of hopeless desire, the absence of betrayals still to come.

I thought of Sandy James asleep in the train coach, curled on the seat and from the wrist under her cheek the trembling droop of her five-and-ten charm bracelet, a tiny tarnished lady's shoe, a tiny tarnished bottle, a tiny tarnished steam engine.

Bennett had changed too, he was in an interesting derelict state of mourning. A gray stubble grew on his face and he wore the same plaid flannel shirt day after day. The white hair of the careful shining pompadour was uncombed, shocked forward over his forehead and suggesting from a flash of boyishness what he might have been had he not been a Bennett—a farmer perhaps, a logger, or heavy-chested stevedore of some honest life. We took our meals together, the two of us alone, with a manservant serving heated canned food. All the women of the light green were gone, as if having lost Lucinda Bailey Bennett he wanted the race expunged. A couple of the outside men were now doing the household work and the cooking. In the kitchen the dishes were piled unwashed. I saw roaches going along the floor. It was as if the establishment was in some accelerating state of decrepitude, beginning with Bennett's heart and working outward. The grounds were immaculate as ever, Loon Lake was groomed for its spring. The stables were clean and horses shining and fit. But if he went on like this, the men of dark green too would be sent away and the boats would sink in their berths, the earth around the dolmen would grow back and the fence around the tennis court would fall and the clay court would crack like the surface of a blasted planet. Mourning had illuminated the natural drift of his life to isolation, and if it was not corrected it would go on, outward in all directions, spreading out over the universe in some infinite looming reclusiveness.

But his eyes were curious when they lit on me for a moment or two at each measured meal. And the days were, after all, timed just as they had been, the hours appointed for drinking and eating, and naps, and exercise. He looked at me as if he were waiting. I met him each day in a renewed wonder of my own. I had seen his kingdom and I appreciated him almost more for the distracted humanity he displayed, broken as easily as anyone by simple events. For men all over the country he was, finally, a condition of their life. Yet he wandered about here in his grief, caring for nothing, barely raising his head when the phone rang. He moved slowly, almost listlessly, which brought out the natural lurch of the short-legged top-heaviness of him.

In the mornings I heard the horses stomping in the stable, and looking out the window, saw Bennett come out galloping, having spurred his horse from the very portal.

At noon we took lunch on the terrace if the day was fair and he'd glance at the sky over the lake as if expecting a plane to appear.

At night while the guards in their belted uniforms

walked the floodlit grounds with their dogs I heard him playing his phonograph records, his favorites, I heard the song of the night of my arrival.

> I know why I've waited
> Know why I've been blue
> Prayed each night for someone
> Exactly like you.

He began to talk of Lucinda Bennett, imparting confidences that at first excited me inasmuch as I was there on the terrace in the sun at Loon Lake, in all the world the only one privileged to receive them. His voice lacked regret, his delivery was thoughtful, he chose his words as someone does who wants in as orderly a way as possible to impart information. So I hoped he was giving these thoughts to *me*, as instruction, and I trusted that his reasons would be forthcoming, that he had some plan, and that by being patient and attentive I would eventually learn what it was. Then I wondered if the confession itself was the gracious means by which I would pass through some subtle imperceptible moment of assumption from being something to being something else. But he went on, and the obsession of the subject became so apparent to me, and the confidences so intimate, I couldn't believe he was aware that I listened or that he would seriously divulge them if I did not lack all importance to him. Day after day I listened. I watched the white clouds disembowel themselves in the high pines across the lake. His man served canned soup, canned spaghetti, canned peaches. Bennett grew shaggier and smellier, looking more like a troll every day. I watched his beard grow. While I waited for a place in his mind I tested my status with the staff. I rode a horse one day with the stableman beside me showing me the elementals. I went upstairs to the storerooms that the maid Libby had shown me so long ago and took several outfits for myself, white ducks already cuffed, argyle sweaters, saddle shoes, shirts, ties, a pair of boots. I had the man in the boathouse bring out the mahogany speedboat and hold the line while I boarded her. I got the hang of it soon enough. I cruised around looking at the beaver lodges, the islands where the loons made their nests, and saw from the water the concrete ramp and hangar where Mr. Penfield and Mrs. Bennett began their round-the-world flight.

"She was a student when I met her. She was then, and remained, the most handsome woman I had ever seen. I secured a divorce to marry Lucinda. And in the years as they went by, no matter what passed between us, whenever she saw fit to spend time with me I was pleased to see her, I mean that no matter what the state of our affections I was always pleased when she came into a room. If she came into a room I had to look at her. I could not not look at her.

"I respect character in a man but I revere it in a woman. I am done in when I find it in a woman. That little doxie had it in a cheap sort of way. But in Lucinda it tested like the best ore, through and through, in the bones and in the beam of the eye.

"Long ago she lost the pleasure of—what?—the engagement. And I was able to appreciate her character in the depth of her withdrawal from me. And then how I wished she had less of it! Less pride, less distaste for—surprises. Less neatness of soul. I told her she liked the sky because it was clean. She liked to go up in rain. I never flew with her because I sensed that it was her realm. But everyone told me what a wonderful pilot she was. How cool. How capable. And then she began to pull down the prizes and I knew it was so.

"I was very proud of her. I bought her whatever she needed. She may have fallen in love with a fellow, some mail-service pilot, one of those adventurer types, and I was going to have it looked into. But when I thought about it I knew Lucinda would never permit herself an affair. It was not something to which she would give rein. And gradually she ceased to mention him. If it were possible for Lucinda to exist without a body she would have chosen to. Her body was of no interest to her. She did not like it . . . handled. She was a very orderly woman, Lucinda. If you look upstairs in her apartment you will see the order of her mind. She did everything with precision, and so was she affectionate with precision.

"She flew planes but her tastes were very delicate and refined. She knew art, she knew music. She had small bones as befitting a fine mugwump family. They none of them liked me. I took great relish in that. It was one of those things. I have no taste of my own but I could recognize the quality of hers. She could look at something for a long time, a painting, a piece of porcelain. Then I knew it was fine. I envied her vulnerability—that she could be transfixed by something that was beautiful. She became pregnant just once and immediately took measures to have it rescinded. We had no children. I have one child by my first marriage but he is an incompetent, I mean legally, a macrocephalic, he has water in the head, and he lives in a home in Sweden. They take good care of him. By all rights he should have been dead years ago.

"Lucinda went once to see him. Thereafter she sent

him thoughtfully chosen gifts, toys, tins of cookies, picture books appropriate to his mental age. She always sent him things. She liked helpless beings. I don't mean that the way it sounds. I mean she had a heart for people. It was she who saved Penfield a jail sentence. Penfield was from the working class and he decided to come here in the late twenties to assassinate me. You knew that of course. Well, the fellow was pathetic but she kept him on as a sort of a cause in personal rehabilitation. A sort of one-woman Salvation Army, except without the prayer. Lucinda was not religious except perhaps in some vague pantheistic way. She decided the poor man was a poet. I got to like him myself. He read aloud very well, he probably should have been an actor. He read Wordsworth and Keats, all that kind of thing. He was a sort of house pet she kept on and I indulged her. But then of course I did something I shouldn't have. I took Penfield's own verses to the president of the New York Public Library and asked him his opinion. In turn he called on a professor who was an expert in the field of literature. Oh my. And I showed Lucinda this fellow's letter. She perceived, accurately, that the opinion didn't matter so much as my malice in having asked for it. She threw the letter in the fire. She was a wonderful woman. She was not a prey to fashion, didn't give a damn for it. She always looked smart by looking herself. She always wore her hair the same way, cut short and brushed back from her temples. I thought it was most seemly. She had a thin, fit body. Thin waist. Ribs showed. She had good hands, small and squarish, nails trim, cut close. She would not paint her nails or wear make-up. I liked her mouth, a generous mouth. Sweet smile. A light came into her eyes when she smiled. She had almost no bosom. Just a slight rise there with good thick nipples. She told me once if I liked her body I must really like boys."

He paused. "You've come here to kill me too, I suppose."

"What?"

"But you don't have the guts for it—anymore than he."

"What?"

"See? I'm not even carrying my gun."

He pushed his chair back form the table and held out his arms.

The room empties. They have gone to make the call. I walk back and forth shaking a fist in the air. The fuckers! By my wits I have done this thing and the stupid sons of bitches have gone for it. But why not? They will hear him laugh, they'll hear him say, *Yes, let him go.* My heart fills with a passionate conviction. He and I are complicitors. We're both against them. As if, having made this up, I cannot make it work unless I believe it myself.

And I am released. And I strut out of that room bone-cracked, skin-stitched and betrayed and I glare at them all as I lead her by the arm out the door. I take my time. I think the illusion will endure only if I do not break and run. I sleep in Sandy James' parlor. I sleep eighteen hours. I take her money, buy a truck. I hire two men to load it. In the rear-view mirror I see only a black industrial cloud where Jacksontown was. I press the accelerator. Cars turn on their lights, the red lights of moving cars ahead of me. The furniture shifts and bangs against the tailgate. The heavy furniture rises in the air on the bumps. I am in transit on the road, the child bride beside me, bracing herself with her knee against the dashboard and holding her baby tightly. I open the window for the cold air. I want the wind to blow these feelings out of my eyes, blow them away, leave me without memory or love, leave me to myself.

"If you thought I would want to kill you," I said, "why did you tell them to let me go?"

"What?"

"When the police called from Jacksontown," I said to him. "With that message." I was smiling like a fatuous idiot.

"What message? I don't know what you're talking about. From whom?"

I choked on the answer. Bennett got up and stood at the parapet. He stood looking over the lake with his hands in his pockets.

That night we steal upon a station of the Tokaido and purchase disguises. We are a country lord and his serving boy. She wears bloused trousers. We travel in this humble manner because my mission is clandestine. Soldiers of the daimyo eye us warily. We book rooms in a modest inn where, to avoid suspicion, I call for a woman. She is a tired fat *artiste* who responds to the humor of the situation. The two of us climb all over her, I with ordinary lasciviousness, my young ward with the affection of a child for her mother. Of course the old whore is terribly moved. She reaches into the child's pantaloons, and my hand, like a band of steel, clamps around her wrist. If she discovers my serving boy is a girl, all is lost. Even so the situation is difficult. I use all the sexual arts of which I am capable to divert the old bag. But in the midst of passion I intuit that the more undone she becomes, the more shrewd. It is actually interesting. At the moment of her release she is totally withdrawn and quietly aware that we are not what we appear to be. But her tongue is extended. I grab the tongue and impale it to the polished floor with an awl. I shout and stamp about and raise an uproar. The innkeeper comes to the door. Other travelers come running. I berate the innkeeper for the poor quality of his house. He is abject. The woman moans, rump up, head on the floor, eyes glazed like a pig to be served. I put my foot on her back and behead her. The innkeeper begs my pardon.

At dawn we continue our journey. The sky is pink. We climb the trail alongside an amazing stream, so rock-strewn that the water, broken into millions of drops, falls like the sound of hail and bounces like steel pellets. I scrape the bark from a small pine tree tortured by the wind to grow like sunrays toward the earth. This lime-green powdery moss I allow to dry for four minutes in the palm of my hand. I then lick this powder from my palm and immediately my young love becomes a giantess looking down at me with amazement. I trip her and she falls backward, quaking the earth, I run into her vulva and by that means continue my lifelong search for the godhead. It is some sort of gland somewhere. The way becomes slippery. In this viscous darkness I use my knees and my hands like a water spider. The way becomes narrower. Soon I am flattened, drawn like a mote toward some powerful brilliantly lit eye. I feel myself enlarging. The light is blinding. I become my own size and break her open like an egg.

You are thinking it is a dream. It is no dream. It is the account in helpless linear translation of the unending love of our simultaneous but disynchrous lives.

Data linkage escape this is not emergency
Come with me compute with me
Coupling with me she becomes a couplet
Lovers leap in the sea
A drop of sunlit pee between two lips
Substitute a priapic navigator
I see inappropriate behavior
I recall Father Damien seeing his own pale blue
    eyes
Regarding him from a face resembling his own
    enlarged redblue heart
It is a woman, a leperess, expressing his sentiments.
I refer to the paired animals going up the ramp of
    the ark
Leopard leopard aardvark aardvark porpoise
    porpoise inchworm inchworm
The story of Noah is the religious vision of cloning.
Scientists tweeze pollen eyedrop spermatozoa
Dispatch flights of sexy sterile white moths to
    eliminate specie
They notice human lovers commonly resemble each
    other
Test it at home looking at their wives friends friends
    wives
Or if not each other then each other's brother or
    sister
But in any event that love conducts a shock of
    recognition
Question haven't I seen you somewhere before
    answer yes in the mirror
Given wars before wars after wars genocides
and competition for markets cloning will eliminate
    all chance
and love will be one hundred percent efficient

No *Sturm und Drang* German phrase no
    disynchronicity
but everyone having seen everyone else somewhere
    before
we will have realized serenity of perfect universal
    love
univerself love uniself love unilove
until the race withers and blows away like the dried
    husks
of moths but who's complaining

They had either believed me or not believed me. If they had believed me I had been so effective, so frighteningly effective that they did not want to confirm what I told them, they were afraid to. If they called, he would want their names. So they had let me go.

If they had not believed me, then my desperation was so patent or my cravenness so truly loathsome that they didn't have the heart to go on with it. Perhaps there were moral operations in this world that transcended the individual responsible for them and threatened to ruin everyone. Was that it? Was I perceived as a leper who threatened to ruin everyone. Was this it? Was I perceived as a leper who threatened to contaminate them?

In either case the result was the same, wasn't that so? I had been released thinking I'd made contact with Bennett and I had not.

That night I lay in Penfield's bed and stared at the amber windowpanes and listened to the watchdogs baying. I tried to compose my terrible shame into something I could deal with, I tried to comprehend the weird sick brokenness I felt, the sense of irreparable damage I had done to myself the catastrophic discomposure of everything but the small light in my mind. It was most difficult.

Sandy James asleep forever on the coach seat amid the pilgrims: I take a few dollars out of my wallet and tuck the fat wallet with her death benefits under her chin she does not wake the train begins to move the small flaked tarnished charms of her charm bracelet swing in their arc the train picks up speed I jump hit the embankment the cinders imbedding themselves in my knees.

Compare the private railroad car of the Meiji emperor the imperial beloved, as it makes its way through the sunlit valley of the Bunraku province. It moves slowly and from the populated fields no closer than a mile thousands of little children wave paper flags in time to the small white puffs of smoke rising from the engine. The children are well behaved. Their parents kneel beside them and hold their shoulders. Their grandparents lie prostrate on the ground not even daring to glance toward the distant train where the line of mounted imperial guardsmen cantering at the base of the embankment alongside the dark green imperial car give it the look of a lampshade with a rippling fringe.

The man resisted all approaches he was stone he was steel I hated his grief his luxurious dereliction I hated his thoughts the quality of his voice his walk the way he spent his life proving his importance ritualizing his superiority his exercises of freedom his arrogant knowledge of the human heart I hated the back of his neck he was a killer of poets and explorers, a killer of boys and girls and he killed with as little thought as he gave to breathing, he killed by breathing killed by existing he was an emperor, a maniac force in pantaloons and silk slippers and lacquered headdress dispensing like treasure pieces of his stool, making us throw ourselves on our faces to be beheaded one by one with gratitude, the outrageous absurdity of him was his power, his clucking crowing mewing shouting whistling ridiculousness is what stunned us into submission but not this boy, I know what to do about this pompous little self-idolator, I'm going to put the fucker where he belongs I swear oh my Clara I swear Mr. Penfield I swear by the memory of the Fat Lady I know how to do it, I know how to do it and I have the courage to do it and it will be a beautiful monumental thing I do I will testify to God that he is a human being, that is how, I will save him from wasting away, I will save him from crumbling into a piece of dried shit, into a foul eccentric, you see, I will give him hope, I will extend his reign, I will raise him and do it all so well with such style that he will thank me, thank me for growing in his heart his heart bursting his son.

And in the morning the whole spring of the earth has come forth and Loon Lake is a bowl of light. A sweet blue haze hangs in the trees. The sun is shining, a filigree of pale green leaf laces through the evergreens across the water. I run down the hill to the lake side pulling off my clothes as I go. I stop to remove my shoes. My feet thump along the boathouse deck. I stand poised on the edge and dive into the water. With powerful strokes learned in the filth of industrial rivers Joe swims a great circle crawl in the sweet clear cold mountain lake. He pulls himself up on the float and stands panting in the sun, his glistening white young body inhaling the light, the sun healing my scars my cracked bones my lacerated soul, the sun powering my loins warming them to a stir. I toss my hair back, smooth it back, shake the water from my arms, open

my eyes. Up on the hill Bennett stands on his terrace,
a tiny man totally attentive. He has seen the whole
thing, as I knew he would. He waves at me. I smile my
white teeth. I wave back.

Herewith bio Joseph Korzeniowski.
Born to a working-class family Paterson New Jersey
    August 2 1918.
Graduated Paterson Latin Grade School 1930.
Graduated Paterson Latin High School 1936. Voted
    by classmates
Best Shape of the Head. Hobbies: Street hockey,
    petit larceny.
Roustabout Hearn Bros. Carnival, summer 1936.
Aka Joe of Paterson, Loon Lake NY autumn 1936.
Employed Bennett Autobody Number Six, head-
    light man, winter 1936.
Enrolled Williams College September 1937. Letters
    in Lacrosse,
Swimming. Graduated *cum laude*, honors in Politi-
    cal Science, 1941.
Voted by classmates Captain ROTC and Most
    Likely to Succeed.
Commissioned Second Lieutenant U.S. Air Corps.
Legal name change Joseph Paterson Bennett, June
    1941.
Assigned newly formed Office of Strategic Services
    1942
parachuting into France in black sweater flight
    jacket trousers
black boots false passport black wool cap black par-
    achute
pockets of francs four thousand feet into windy void

face blackened teeth blackened, heart blackened
dropping into blackness.

Awarded Bronze Star with oak leaf cluster 1943.

Awarded Silver Star with oak leaf cluster 1944.

Decommissioned 1945 rank of Major, Office of
Strategic Services.

Appointed organization staff Central Intelligence
Agency 1947.

Married Dru Channing Smith 1947, divorced 1950;
no issue.

Married Kimberly Andrea Kennedy 1951, divorced
1954; no issue.

Continuous service Central Intelligence Agency to
resignation

1974. Retiring rank Deputy Assistant Director.

Retired US State Department rank of Ambassador
1975.

Chairman and Chief Operating Officer Bennett
Foundation.

Board of Directors James-Pennsylvania Steel Corporation.

Board of Directors Chilean-American Copper Corporation.

Trustee Jordan and Naismith colleges, Rhinebeck
NY.

Trustee Miss Morris' School for Young Women,
Briarcliff Manor NY.

Member Knickerbocker, Acropolis, New York;
Silks, Saratoga Springs;

Rhode Island Keel, Newport.

Master of Loon Lake.

ABOUT THE AUTHOR

E. L. Doctorow's first novel, WELCOME TO HARD TIMES, was published in 1960, followed by BIG AS LIFE (1966); THE BOOK OF DANIEL (1971), a National Book Award nominee; RAGTIME (1975), winner of the National Book Critics Circle Award; LOON LAKE (1980); LIVES OF THE POETS (1984) (called by *The New York Times* one of the best books of the year); and WORLD'S FAIR (1985), winner of the American Book Award. A play, DRINKS BEFORE DINNER, was produced at the New York Shakespeare Festival Theatre in 1978 and has since seen production in regional and university theaters all over the United States. Mr. Doctorow's work is published in over twenty languages. He lives in New York.

AWARD-WINNING FICTION FROM

E. L.
DOCTOROW